SPIRITS
IN THE
GRASS

Other Books by Bill Meissner

Learning to Breathe Underwater [poetry]

The Sleepwalker's Son [poetry]

Twin Sons of Different Mirrors [poetry]

American Compass [poetry]

Hitting into the Wind [short stories]

The Road to Cosmos: The Faces of an American Town
[short stories]

SPIRITS

IN THE

GRASS

BILL MEISSNER

University of Notre Dame Press
Notre Dame, Indiana

Published by the University of Notre Dame Press
Notre Dame, Indiana 46556
www.undpress.nd.edu

Library of Congress Cataloging-in-Publication Data
Meissner, William, 1948-
Spirits in the grass / Bill Meissner.
p. cm.
ISBN-13: 978-0-268-03513-6 (cloth : alk. paper)
ISBN-10: 0-268-03513-x (cloth : alk. paper)
1. City and town life—Wisconsin—Fiction.   2. Baseball stories.
3. Indians of North America—Wisconsin—Fiction.   I. Title.
PS3563.E38S65   2008
813'.54   dc22

2008026868

For Nate, the original archeo-boy

For Christine, soul mate and spirit mate

ACKNOWLEDGMENTS

I have many people and organizations to thank for their assistance, advice, and encouragement during the writing of this book. Thanks to Nakoma, Anishinabe (Chippewa-Cree), a teacher, for sharing his knowledge—both spiritual and practical—about Native American culture; to Pastor Dave Uhrich, Christ Community Church, Nisswa, Minnesota, for relating his experience with a Native American repatriation ceremony; to St. Cloud State University for an Alumni Foundation grant to study Native American mound-building history and tribal culture in Minnesota, Wisconsin, and South Dakota; and to the SCSU American Indian Center for its helpful information.

I am indebted to the following organizations for awards that supported my writing:

> The Loft-McKnight Foundation, for a Loft-McKnight Award of Distinction in Fiction, a Loft-McKnight Fellowship, and a Loft Career Initiative grant
> National Endowment for the Arts for a Creative Writing Fellowship
> Minnesota State Arts Board for an Individual Artist's Grant
> St. Cloud State University Alumni Foundation

The Loft, Minneapolis, for support of my teaching and writing
The Jerome Foundation for a travel/study grant

I want to thank my son, Nate, the first family archeologist, for his love and helpful advice during the writing of this book (and for agreeing to hit a few baseballs at all hours).

Thanks to my mother, Julia Meissner, the original storyteller, for her encouragement of my writing.

To Jack Driscoll, writer extraordinaire, for his long-time friendship.

I am grateful to the University of Wisconsin-Stevens Point for organizing Native American Student Tutoring as part of Student Youth Volunteers, a group I joined as an undergraduate.

I would like to thank those members of the St. Cloud State University creative writing staff and members of the English Department who have supported me over the years.

This book is written in memory of my father, Leonard Meissner, who nurtured me as we searched the fields of Iowa and Wisconsin for arrowheads.

And, most of all, to Christine, who kept my feet anchored to the ground and my spirits soaring during the writing of this book.

A portion of "Skip Remembers: The Tug of War," from *The Road to Cosmos: The Faces of an American Town* by Bill Meissner (Notre Dame, Ind.: University of Notre Dame Press, 2006) appears in a revised form in chapter 10.

Sections of "The Outfielder" and "Freight Trains, Flights of Geese, Shoes, and Homers: The Whole Truth about the Journey of an American Baseball" from *Hitting into the Wind* by Bill Meissner (New York: Random House, 1994; reprint: Dallas: Southern Methodist University Press, 1997) appear in revised form in chapter 39 and are used by permission.

PART

1

CHAPTER

1

IT'S NOT THE KIND of thing you'd ever expect to find on the in-field of a baseball field. After years of playing ball, Luke Tanner knows the usual things you find: cigarette butts, tarnished pop tops, frayed strips of cloth tape, the husk of a leather cover torn from a ball, or even a darkened Lincoln penny with the date worn off. But this object, partially buried beneath the dirt, looks thin and yellowish.

He drops his paint-chipped rake, kneels down on the dirt, and leans close to the infield. He pulls the object out of its socket in the earth, lifts it, turns it over and over. It's a small section of a bone, about four inches long; its surface is hardened, as if the sun had dried it for a thousand years. He wonders why it feels heavy and gives him a kind of tingling in his palm as he holds it. He thinks about dropping it, letting it go, kicking the soil with the toe of his worn leather cleats and burying it again. Instead, he just holds onto it, wrapping his fingers around it a little tighter, then stuffs it into the pocket of his T-shirt.

Luke turns and jogs to the middle of the ball field he loves already. It's a field he's dreamed of all winter, even though it's half-finished, just an expanse of bare soil surrounded by mounds of musty dirt, spirals of sod, and a flagpole balanced sideways on concrete blocks, its chain clanking insistently in the wind. It's a field he loves not for what it is now, but for what it *will be* when it's finished. He can't wait for that day in June when he'll sprint from the dugout in his Lakers uniform for the first time, the earth buoying him up on its taut green sea.

As the wind gusts hard, blowing grit into his face, he closes his eyes. When he opens them, he sees a whirlwind begin to spin just behind second base. It lifts ten, then twenty feet. Candy wrappers, sticks and leaves—caught in its skin of brown dust—rotate around its vortex. Impulsively, he dashes toward it from the outfield, wanting to run into it, reach out with his bare arms, and stand inside it for a few seconds, to know what it's like to be inside a wild, whirling dirt devil. The moment he reaches it, it stops spinning and disappears, paper and flecks of leaves falling around him like confetti. Luke stands there, disappointed that he couldn't have been faster. *If my father had been here watching*, Luke thinks, *I might have run faster. If he were sitting there behind home plate, watching me, I might have pushed myself a little harder.*

But his father's not there. The only person watching is a small boy of about ten pausing on his bicycle in the parking lot; Luke doesn't recognize the black-haired boy, who looks Native American.

Back at the infield, Luke picks up his rake again, drags it forward and back, leveling the dirt. It occurs to him that the boy on the bike wasn't even born when Luke was starting center fielder for the high school team seventeen years ago. He's probably never heard of Luke's game-winning homer in the conference championship, or the way Luke could break a brown Hamms beer bottle on the bench with a snap throw from two hundred feet in the outfield. Those days, everything seemed to be ahead of him, the calendar's outlined white squares stretching to the horizon, a clear, definable grid he could follow. Luke figures his records are forgotten and—for all he knows—probably broken by now. To this boy, he's just some grounds crew person, some everyday guy working on a field, and that bothers Luke.

When the boy gets bored and pedals away, Luke lifts his old Louisville Slugger with its worn-off trademark, its half-moons of scuff marks. The bat feels almost too big for him. The handle's tape is torn off, and the dried glue feels rough on the heel of his palm. Still, he wants to hit a couple of fly balls toward left center, toward the place where, once this field is finished, the outfield fence will stand. He takes a couple of warm-up swings, stretching the tendons in his arms and legs, and finally he's ready. He pauses a moment with a baseball in his palm, flips the ball into the air, then whips the bat around. He misses the ball completely, hears it fall to the ground with a dull thud. The pull of the bat twists his arms and legs around themselves so tightly he wonders how he can untie them. "Damn," he says, and then lets out a short laugh. *What kind of swing was that?* Maybe what he fears is true: his muscles and tendons and sinew have lost all memory of what it was once like to be a finely tuned ballplayer.

He picks up the ball, brushes his wavy brown hair back from his eyes, takes a long, slow breath. He swings again, this time hitting the ball too far up the bat's barrel. With a *clunk,* the short pop-up carries no farther than second base. He lifts another ball and stands there a few seconds, closing his eyes, focusing. As the breeze falls to its knees, the calmness becomes a sensation in itself, caressing the bare skin of his arms. He opens his eyes, tosses the ball in front of his face, sees its slow rotation, like the earth in space, then swings hard. He brings the bat around to the ball instinctively—not a planned or practiced swing, but powerful and quick, smooth and seamless, as the bat parts the air suddenly. This time his muscles wake from their sleep, and the bat finds the ball in its center, its heart, that exact spot where wood falls in love with leather. A solid vibration resonates through the grains of the bat, into Luke's hands, up through his wrists and arms to the center of his chest. In that instant, the old feeling comes back to him: a feeling rising from deep inside, a feeling that's been lost for a long time. The ball climbs high, tracing a towering arc. It lands deep in left center, takes two quick bounces into the pine trees, rolls, and finally comes to rest. He's a little surprised by how far the ball carries.

Then Luke hears the sound of his father's gravelly voice calling, as if it's coming from somewhere across the field. Or is it just the scrape of the freight train on the south side of town as the flat-nosed diesel engine begins to drag the rusted cars forward?

Luke pulls the bone fragment from his T-shirt pocket, studies it again, scrapes the caked dirt off its surface. *What kind of bone?* he wonders as he peers at it more closely. *Dog?* Or maybe something wild, like a badger, or a bobcat that wandered from the bluffs down to this broad Clearwater valley. He draws his arm back to toss it into the deep weeds at the edge of the field, back into forgetfulness.

Then he pauses. Maybe later, during a lull at dinner with his girlfriend, Louise, he'll lower it onto an empty china plate with a clink. Maybe it'll be a topic of conversation, something besides Louise's subtle questions about where their relationship is headed lately. He pictures Louise, tucking her long blonde hair behind one ear, leaning her slim frame forward, and, with a voice that sounds intrigued, asking, "So where'd that come from?" Then again, he might not even

6

mention it to her. Maybe there'll be enough to say tonight, enough to talk about over macaroni and cheese while, in the background, the TV newscasters murmur about war and real estate, about world hunger and the jagged rising and falling lines of the stock market.

He places the bone in the bottom of his blue canvas duffle, among the sunflower seed wrappers and his curled high school batting gloves, then leans into a run across the field. There's no grass in center yet, and the soil, wet from a recent spring shower, has soft spots that pull his cleats down an inch or two with each step. But he keeps his stride, crossing at an angle through the row of pine trees and into the clearing at the far end of the park. There the rolling wave of green grass is cut off by a city street.

He jogs down Fifth, where the asphalt crumbles into a dead end, sees his yellow bungalow with the white trim. When he reaches the uneven sidewalk chalked with hopscotch games, Luke slows to a walk, hands on hips, trying to catch his breath. Before bounding up the wooden steps to the porch, he pauses in the front yard, seeing the bare dirt spots where he tossed some grass seed the other day. He shakes his head at the cluster of sparrows, pecking and pecking at the last of the seeds.

CHAPTER 1

All heads turn in unison as Luke Tanner swings open the door of the Rainbow Café. Lined up at the counter on red vinyl stools, the customers are like dummies, their heads on mechanical swivels, turning to look at him and then turning back to their coffee or morning special. It's the same way they had rotated each time, thirty years ago, when he and his father walked in the door every Saturday morning. It was just a local custom, the patrons' way of checking on the comings and goings in the café. Luke makes his way toward the counter amid the low murmur of voices, the clatter of silverware on plates, and the steady voice of the livestock report crackling from the portable AM radio perched on the stainless steel milk dispenser. "Wheat futures down," the bored nasal voice announces. "Hogs and cattle up slightly." The clock on the wall, circled by a pink neon tube,

8

reads 8:21, and Luke knows he's still got time for breakfast before his nine to five shift at the sod company.

"Hey there, Luke," Cyrus says.

Luke nods to him. Cyrus, a retired railroad worker who used to lay track for the Burlington Northern, is an old friend of Luke's father. He has an odd twitch that makes his head wag side to side slightly, like a man forever saying no. Luke often wonders if that's why he retired, finally—because when he bent his knees and peered at the track, he couldn't quite tell whether it was straight or not.

"Workin' on the field this morning?"

"Yeah. For a while." Luke slides onto a sighing vinyl stool at the far end and plants his elbows on the Formica countertop.

Ruth sidles up to him. "What'll it be, Tanner boy?" she says, smiling at him with a spunkiness in her voice, strange for a woman in her early seventies. Luke orders a bowl of Ruth's chicken dumpling soup, which is on special today, though it seems to be on special no matter what day you stop in.

"Coffee?" she asks. Some days Luke can hear the flirtation, even when she says that one word.

"Just give me a root beer."

She wrinkles her pug nose. "Root beer? Isn't that a kid's drink?"

"Well, that's what I want." The boy in Luke climbs up and grins.

"You're too cute." She writes his order down on a small notepad, as if she might forget, even though it's the only order she's taken lately. She attaches the slip on a stainless steel clip above the kitchen window, where the rest of the orders hang like yellowed laundry.

Through the layer of haze from the grill that sizzles with eggs and sausage, Luke spots the regulars—several tables of retired farmers, their broad foreheads anchored by faded red, green, or blue feed caps. Puffing on Camels or Luckys, the men are surrounded by an island of smoke. In a booth, one man wears a green and tan camouflage outfit, suitable for duck hunting, while his buddy, dressed in blaze orange overalls, looks as if he's ready to grab a deer rifle, though it's the middle of March.

Hans cracks two eggs and tosses a frozen, centipede-shaped slab of hash browns on the griddle. Behind the counter, bicentennial plates adorn the dark wood paneling, along with a cheaply framed photo of Eisenhower and a small rack of antlers poised over a bronze plaque from the Clearwater Businessmen's Club commemorating *40 Years of Service*. Below is a row of parfait glasses, sharing the glass shelf with Hans's three skeet-shooting trophies, a tarnished hunter taking aim atop each one. The reflection in the mirror behind the shelf makes the three trophies appear as six. A few of Jeannie's Daylite Bakery cinnamon buns that will—as everyone proudly claims—be gone by nine A.M., sit on the shelf next to a white box filled with orderly rows of powder crème donuts, a close second to the cinnamon buns. Luke feels a sudden aching nostalgia come over him as he looks around at this place; it's as if he's six years old again. For a fleeting moment, he looks for his father's reflection in the big wall mirror, expecting to see the man he never understood sitting next to him on the red stool.

"So how's Louise these days?" Cyrus asks. Cyrus is friends with Louise's dad, so he takes it on himself to check up on her. "You know, I used to live next door to her when she was just a little shit." By now, everyone in the café knows the story of how Luke moved into a rental house with Louise last year. It seemed like a big step, but Luke talked her into it, and one spring day her El Camino backed over the curb, and Luke hauled in boxes of her things while Louise, rocking slightly on the porch swing in her faded jeans, smiled at him.

"She's good." Luke nods. He thinks about last night, when he and Louise parked in his pickup on a back road below the bluffs. She wore a gray T-shirt with the red letters *Wisconsin* on it, the letters *o* and *n* dipping gracefully with the curve of her breasts as she leaned against the passenger's side door. When he slid over to kiss her, it seemed that all the stars from the night sky had fallen and landed in her eyes.

Not getting enough of an answer, Cyrus prods, "What's good?"

"Good's *good*," Luke says, avoiding his question. He notices Ruth's prying stare; she's waiting, along with the rest of them, for the details Luke doesn't want to give. He knows this crew at the Rainbow can take one sentence of gossip and spin it on its end like a china plate, then watch as it drops to the hard tile floor and breaks into a thousand pieces.

Seeing Luke's tight-lipped expression, Cyrus eases up on the subject. "So, how's things going with the ball field?" Cyrus smells faintly of booze, and Luke can't tell if the guy has been drinking in the morning or if it's just hangover breath from last night. After the railroad job, Cyrus had worked for a few years on city planning with the mayor. Now that he's retired, his main jobs seem to be reading railroad history books at the Carnegie library by day and hanging out at the Water-in Hole with his whiskey in the evenings.

"It's little by little. We're getting there."

Ruth brings his order over and slides the bowl of soup in front of him on the Formica with oval worn spots where patrons, over the years, have anchored their coffee.

"Think she'll be ready by the time the season starts?" Cyrus's International Harvester cap is tilted slightly, exposing a purplish birthmark on his forehead that looks like the state of North Dakota.

"Hope so."

"I hear this year's team can beat the tar out of the rest of the league," Cyrus says. "Just about everybody in town's talking about it."

"So," Ruth pries, "Is Louise working somewhere these days?"

"Casino," Luke replies.

"She working up at Spirit Island?" Ruth looks surprised and folds her arms beneath her bosom, which sags under her pale blue blouse. "Since when?"

"Since a few weeks ago. She's getting better pay than at the gift shop." Then he adds, just to show this isn't her dream job, "She's still thinking about going back to grad school, though."

"So since when are them Indians up at Spirit Island hiring whites?" Cyrus asks.

"Since they got a big goddamn business going," Walter's high voice pipes in from down the counter. Walter, a small, spidery man in blue overalls, is retired but still tough and wiry. He used to work in the grain elevator on the north end of Clearwater, the big gray corrugated tin building with the sign *Farmer's Co-op of Clwtr. Wisc.* He slides a couple stools down so he's next to Luke.

"Yeah?" Cyrus says, eyes darting to Walter.

"You bet. No taxes," Walter says with a knowing nod. "Heap big profit." He chuckles at his own comment.

Luke just spoons the steaming soup to his mouth, irritated by the tone of this talk but still opting to stay out of the conversation. The broth tastes a little like beef instead of chicken.

"I hear they're going to do a new addition up there, remodel the place," Cyrus says, shaking his head ruefully.

"That so? I can't imagine them getting all that done. Them Indians are lazy, you know."

"They're not *all* lazy, though," Cyrus concedes. "Not the ones who are part American."

"Oh come on, fellas," interjects Ruth. "Tone it down. I know some decent people from up on the reservation."

"By the way," Bob Sewell says, trying to sound knowledgeable, "they've applied for a couple of building permits." He hasn't contributed to the conversation yet, but as city attorney with Mayor Butch Sobieski, he feels it's his civic obligation to jump in now.

"So I hear," says Cyrus. He shifts his weight on the stool, his high-waisted polyester slacks sticking to the vinyl. "There's even a plan to put in a big hotel across the road, so people can stay all night and gamble their brains out."

"That ain't all the hotel room's for," Walter smirks. "It's not *just* for *gambling* your brains out. You know what I mean?"

Ruth whacks him with a towel she'd been using to wipe the tables. "Let's keep it clean here, boys."

"Okay, okay." Walter sniffs the air and raises his index finger, his red shirt pulling loose. "My point is, they got too damn much money, that casino. And that's a fact."

"But it gives the Indians jobs," Cyrus muses. "That ain't a bad thing. Whites, too, I guess, judging by Louise."

"Yeah," Walter shakes his head. "But it takes away from our downtown, is what it does. I mean, people go for the buffet at that Papoose Restaurant up there. Instead of goin' over to Elmer's, like they used to, they head over for drinks at the casino bar. Plus, them Indians live rent-free on that land. No taxes or nothing."

"You know," says Sewell, who grew up in Clearwater and then went to Milwaukee for law school, "the city's looking into that whole operation, Walter." He anchors the elbow of his gray polyester suit jacket.

Both men look up at Sewell. "Oh?" Cyrus grunts. "That so?"

"Yeah. Nobody's really clear about property lines between the casino's land and Clearwater Township." He gives the men an authoritative nod, then punctuates his sentence by poking a toothpick in the middle of his teeth. "The city's thinking of filing a lawsuit."

"A lawsuit?" Luke asks.

"Sure. The county would get a lot more revenue if the disputed land was turned over to them again."

"How much disputed land?" Luke asks.

Sewell wiggles his nose, takes a sip of his black coffee, then sips it like he's swallowing a fine wine. "Quite a few acres on the northern tip. That's all I can say. *Quite* a few. Some of it's real good farmland. And besides, Rock Lake is up there," he says knowingly, "and right now, the tribe has spear fishing rights."

"Damn well *should* be a lawsuit." Walter leans toward Sewell, slapping his palm down. "Try fishing on a lake where the Indians netted every goddamn fish out of it. Hate to say it, but they're suckin' the life out of this town. They're all getting rich, while Clearwater's dying out. Pisses me off, is what it does."

Cyrus nods with a wheezy laugh, his voice always a little hoarse from too many cigars.

"Hey," Luke finally interjects, having heard enough, "They have a right. It *is* their land, isn't it? The government gave it to them."

"Yeah, but that don't mean shit," barks Walter. His voice is loud for such a small, wiry man. "The government can just as well take land away. Happens all the time with farm foreclosures, don't it, Bob?"

"It does. And," Bob Sewell says, pausing for emphasis and gnawing on the toothpick a few seconds, "nobody's really sure whose land is *whose.* That's the thing."

Luke takes a few sips of soup, still so hot it scalds his tongue. He sets his soupspoon on the edge of the saucer, and it teeters off, tumbling to the black-and-white tile floor below. When he leans over to pick up the spoon, the bone he found on the field slides out of his shirt pocket and onto the floor.

"What the hell's that?" asks Cyrus as he watches Luke pick it up.

"Don't know," says Luke. "Found it on the field."

"No kidding. Lemme see." Cyrus reaches for the bone, studies it with a wagging head.

"Pass it down here, will you, Cyrus?" Walter squints at the bone. "Yep, must be turkey."

"Not turkey, deer," Cyrus's guttural voice counters with authority. The high court is in session this morning, and Cyrus is the self-appointed presiding judge. "They come into town at dusk, you know. Right through the churchyard, I heard Rollie say."

"Turkey," Walter repeats, straightening up on his seat and pinching his small mouth shut. Years ago, he used to bowl against Cyrus on the Co-op bowling team. It seemed like his team was always competing with Cyrus's railroad squad, the De-Railers, for the city championship. From what everybody remembers, the wins were about even. "I seen turkey bones like this on my farmland. They come out of the brush, get killed by badgers."

"Deer," Cyrus insists.

"Turkey," Walter says, his voice raised above the twanging Dwight Yoakam song on the radio.

Cyrus stands and faces Walter as though this is a prelude to a WWF wrestling match.

"Okay boys, settle down," Ruth says, making the peace. She waves both arms as if she's treading water in a swimming pool. "It's a turkey-deer then. Or a deer-turkey. Whatever the hell. Walter, why don't you just hand that thing back to Luke?"

Walter studies the bone a few seconds, giving it his best scientific gaze, then passes it down the row to Bob Sewell and toward Luke. When it reaches Luke, Cyrus reaches out to intercept it with his thick fingers. The bone drops, with a yellow splash, into Luke's soup.

There's a long pause while Ruth glares at the spilled soup, then at Cyrus, then back at the soup again. "For cryin' out loud," she sighs, wiping her hands on her stained Rainbow apron. Luke fishes out the bone with his spoon and dries it on a napkin.

"Not the first time someone's found a bone in their soup," Cyrus chuckles. Then, pleased at his own joke, he repeats it, chuckles again, louder. "That's bone soup now," Cyrus muses. "Yup, bone soup."

Ruth shoots him a dirty look.

"Could I get another bowl?" Luke asks.

"Who's buying?" asks Ruth, her scowl showing that she's more than a little tired of the jokes. "Cyrus?"

"Don't worry, I'm buying," Luke assures her. He knows Ruth scrimps to keep up with the new Happy Chef that opened up along the highway a few miles from town.

Ruth dumps Luke's soup in the aluminum sink, sets his bowl in the dishwasher, ladles another bowl from the bin. She slides it toward Luke, the steam rising in wisps. "On the house," she says, her voice lowered so Hans doesn't hear.

"Appreciate it," Luke says.

After he finishes his soup, he stands and glances at the clock, which hasn't shifted from 8:21. Luke realizes that time stops here—it never moves forward, no matter when you walk in or out. The same smoke that circled the clock in a halo a half hour ago still circles it now. But no matter how much time stops in this café, it never brings back what's gone.

"Hey," Ruth calls out as Luke reaches the door. "Forgot something." She lifts the bone from the napkin, waves it in the air. "Want me to dump it?"

Luke pauses, then steps back and takes the bone from Ruth.

"Put that in your front pants pocket and give Louise a hug for me, will you?" Cyrus says, then bursts into guffaws.

Luke pushes through the warped screen door and lets it clack shut behind him as he heads to his pickup truck. He passes Walter's low-slung '78 Bonneville with rust spots the size of fists and a bumper sticker that reads *Gun control is being able to hit your target.* He glances up and notices that his meter is expired. "Shit," he mutters, wincing at the bright yellow ticket placed securely beneath his windshield wiper. Then he shakes his head as he sees scrawny, self-important Sheriff Rollie down the block. He's making his morning rounds, pulling his spotlight-adorned squad car up behind the next lethal offender. Luke yanks the ticket from the windshield, lets the wiper snap back with a *thwap*.

CHAPTER

3

Louise Stiller closes the door of her Chevy El Camino and drives to the casino for her shift. As she passes the city limits sign, she sees the fields on both sides of the county highway, the gray scaffolding of the irrigation pipes ready for spring.

The two-story brick buildings and white wood-frame houses of Clearwater seem to be closing in on her, day by day, ever since her messy divorce three years ago from Denny Wilkenson, son of Andy Wilkenson, the assistant to the mayor who owns half the town, including Grand Irrigation Systems. As manager of the business, Denny knew everything about irrigating topsoil. He knew about water pipes, nozzles, and water pressure, but nothing about women.

"Hey, let's go out in the field and get rained on," he said on one of their first dates, a couple years after high school. When Louise hesitated on that hot, humid August night, he opened the car door, held out his hand, and pulled her out there, carrying a quart of Colt 45 in his other hand. As they sat on a stadium blanket, the water was cool and refreshing on their skin, a steady sprinkling from those big water jets a hundred feet away that tossed the water, like translucent wings, high into the night sky. Before she started dating Denny, she remembered being awed by those large sprinklers, their aluminum scaffolds disappearing into the morning fog of the field. That night, her pink T-shirt got soaked, and so did Denny's green and gold Packers jersey; he smiled at her romantically, his hair wet and matted. When her lips began to feel chilled, he leaned into her for a long, warming kiss. That night, in that field, she learned what it meant to be rained on gently.

Two years later they were married, and stayed married for what became three long years. Denny would go out drinking with his buddies—sometimes three nights a week—to the Wildlife Tap, and he'd come home late, turn up the stereo, playing his Metallica or AC/DC or Pink Floyd albums way too loud. He'd lean against the dark doorway at three A.M., and once Louise, still awake, whispered, "Where were you?" and he just slurred, "Told you. Over at Curran's. With the guys." Curran Schaff was one of Denny's buddies from high school, an all-state quarterback who now worked with him at Grand. Denny and Louise had just turned thirty, but Denny and his friends started hanging out with a burnout crowd in their early twenties.

"So, the guys stay up 'til three on a work night?" she asked, lifting herself from the double bed and standing. Her silky nightgown felt too thin on her skin.

"Yeah. So what?" She took a step closer to him, slid her arms around his neck languidly, her long blonde hair grazing his shoulder. The back of his short-cropped hair felt damp.

"I missed you," she said, and that's when she smelled it: the stale odor of smoke mingled with the faint scent of perfume. The scent stung her nose; it surprised her, and hurt her, too. She'd heard from her friend Andrea weeks ago that Denny was at a bar making out with a woman, but when she confronted Denny, he denied it, said he and the woman were only talking.

"Missed you too," Denny replied, but his words were emotionless, flat as paper.

"I don't think you did." She felt the pressure of the tears beneath her cheeks. "I don't think you were thinking of me at all."

Denny pushed away from her. "What the hell?" he said, backing away. "What are you accusing me of?"

"I just want to know where you've been."

"So I stopped for a few beers. So what? So freakin' what?"

She brushed a few strands of hair away from one eye. "So freakin' what? I want the truth, that's freakin' what."

"I told you," Denny said through clenched teeth, as he turned and started down the hallway. She followed close behind him, insisting on an answer. "Just leave me alone!" Denny's shouting voice echoed against the sheetrock walls.

She reached out and grabbed the back of his T-shirt.

"Goddamn! Let go of me!" Denny growled, and before she knew it, his hand was rising up in the air and swinging back down, the same way he used to swing bales of hay at his uncle's farm. When the slap stung the side of her face, she felt it—not just the icy needles stinging her cheek, but that other pain deep inside her, that wouldn't stop aching.

That was just the first time he hit her. For months, she endured the arguments, the mental and physical pain. Then, in mid-January, she filed for divorce. The bitter proceedings dragged on for months, with Denny protecting his earnings and investments in the irrigation company, even hiding some of his assets under his father's name. Bob Sewell represented him, and the county judge was duped by his wily maneuvers. "I don't have liquid funds," Denny had expressed in a sympathetic plea. "I guess I'm just money-poor right now." On the courthouse lawn there were shouting matches, with Louise accusing and Denny acting innocent and defensive. At the ending of one argument, Denny snarled, "You're so goddamn greedy, you know that?"

A year later, after the divorce was final, Louise—who had gotten only a small settlement—backed her El Camino into the drive. She packed her things in hard-sided boxes that irrigation motors and generators came in. The irony didn't escape her.

She loaded the boxes, knowing she had lost more than money and a husband during the whole battle—she lost part of her self. Her self-esteem melted away as quickly as a cherry Popsicle on concrete in the August sun. Cross-examining herself, she wondered just how she ever got mixed up with Denny in the first place, and then let him dominate her. She had always had dreams about a career and, eventually, a family, and had always felt she was independent enough to achieve both. *I always felt like I was a strong person,* she thought, *but how strong am I?* She pulled up to the stop sign at the end of the block and wondered what happened to that confident, goal-driven girl she used to be in high school. *Where did she go?* she asked herself as she stared into the rearview mirror. But all she saw was the neighbor woman in sweatpants leading her three kids across the street.

She moved to an apartment on the other side of town, vowing that she wouldn't tangle herself up in any relationships for a while, that she'd let things settle, like the silt at the bottom of her aquarium, where the colorful betas and angelfish flickered. Still, the town wasn't big enough to avoid Denny. She heard from Andrea that he was down at the Wildlife shooting off his mouth about Louise getting a pile of his money. Sometimes Denny would be driving in his dad's Grand Irrigation truck, and Louise would spot him from behind the bug-stained windshield of her El Camino. He smirked as he pulled out from the intersection, a young, red-haired woman giggling beside him on the seat, one strap of her tank top sliding down her shoulder. Louise wondered what kind of perfume she wore.

"You son of a bitch," she whispered, but then it would comfort her a little as she thought how that woman would get rained on, too. With guys like Denny, sooner or later women were going to get rained on.

Louise cashes a check for the middle-aged male customer—dressed in a red tie-dyed Wisconsin Dells T-shirt—and sighs as she watches him march up to the poker table. After working at the cashier's counter for a few months at Spirit Island Casino, she knows everything boils down to luck. She's seen it all: one customer drops a nickel in the slot and wins five thousand bucks. Another gambler saunters in, gets five hundred in chips for the blackjack tables, and leaves without a cent. There's always just enough hope—just a little tip of it—to keep people going. It's all a gamble, she thinks, everything's a gamble, from moving into the bungalow with Luke after her divorce to taking this temporary job at the casino.

She had dated other men after Denny, but two years ago she fell in love with Luke because of the way he looked at her on their first date, his face seeming to be lit by a glow from within. It was a thirty-five-year-old man's face, with strong cheekbones and piercing brown eyes, but the clean features of a boy's face were still visible beneath. He had a handsome aspect, with his spontaneous grin and his tousled brown hair that slanted across the corner of his forehead and curled around his ears, but she fell in love with him because of his passion for life and, she admits, even his passion for baseball. He talked about that game like a kid. She fell in love with him for the way he dropped her off after their first date. There was no heavy panting, no forcing her into something in the parked car, no fast moves like you might expect from a guy already in his thirties. Like a shy teenager, he gave her a quick kiss on the cheek and said, "Next weekend?"

"What about it?" she replied.

"How about if I see you then?" he asked. In the darkness of the car, it almost looked as if he blushed.

Though she loves Luke, lately she's begun to hate this little town of five thousand. She hates the potato farms that surround Clearwater, with their irrigation machines, their arched backs, and the maze of twisted, hollow pipes. The sprinklers, hooked up to motors, always rolled, ever so slowly, on their dull rubber wheels across flat, black soil. The town used to seem friendly, in a simple way. But she senses the talk going on around her after the split-up with Denny, whose dad was the big Lions Club president. *You hear?* the voices whisper. *She married and divorced Denny just to get his cash. Denny fooled around a little, sure, but there was no harm in that.* Louise suspects that there are rumors about her being unfaithful, too. Some days it takes all her strength just to pull free from the tangled net of gossip.

Each day, Luke gives her the strength to do that. When he first looked into her eyes, it was as if his nourishing gaze could make her feel like herself again. He was a gamble, she knew, but even on their first dates, she didn't mind letting him know her innermost feelings.

She's come to understand that Luke—complacent as he is about his future—could be what ever he wanted to be. Sometimes at breakfast she's noticed him staring in awe out the back door, as if each new sunrise—which to Louise has begun to look just like every day before it—was something to be relished, another chance. Mornings, when he wakes and kisses her, Louise thinks she can taste sunlight on his soft lips.

She knows he loves her, but he also loves this little town with his heart and soul, just like his father did. With his grandfather and father growing up here, his roots are planted deep down, too deep for Louise to ever understand. She knows him, yet there always seemed to be something more to know. He once told her a story about being a kid on his grandfather's farm and about how, each spring, he'd push his hands into the mud of a fresh-plowed field.

"And why'd you do that?" she asked.

"I was listening," he replied.

"To what?"

He seemed to ponder a few seconds, then said innocently almost, and as though she'd know what he meant, "The earth's music."

Now he wants more than anything else to make a comeback with the baseball team, and she's trying to understand that. She realizes he's doing it just for himself—to convince himself that he isn't getting older. She knows he'll be good at it simply because he wants to be. The truth is, Luke is good at so many things. He has so much potential that it disappoints her to see him, after three years of college, delivering rolls of grass around the county, then spending his spare time working on the new ball field. Each morning he seemed to reach down into the Clearwater topsoil, plunge his arms deep into it. He didn't care if the soil was musty or if it clung in half-moons under his fingernails; it was as though he wanted its fertile embrace to cover him to his elbows.

One afternoon they sat on their front porch, watching the neighborhood kids racing each other on Big Wheels on the cracked sidewalk. The kids waved enthusiastically as they passed, as they always did. Cute and impish—a boy of five and a girl of four—they often came dashing across the yard when Louise was outside, and they stayed with her a while to play and chat. She'd always loved children, and sometimes watching those two playing gave her a pang of emptiness, and she yearned for children of her own.

"Have you ever thought about just picking up and leaving?" Louise asked him.

"You mean move? Luke seemed a little perplexed by her question. "Where to?"

"I don't know." She shifted her eyes to the boy, who had stopped to adjust the small flags he'd put on his handlebars. As his face squinted in concentration, tongue out to one side of his mouth, she thought about what a great close-up photo it would make. "Madison. Milwaukee. Or somewhere. The East Coast, maybe."

"Guess I never thought about it."

"Well *I* have."

"What makes you think any of those places would be better than this place?" The way he asked it made it seem like a rhetorical question, and she didn't really have a comeback.

Luke had a way of holding on to things: his job, his faded pickup. His habits were like old T-shirts in the dresser drawer he couldn't part with, no matter how stretched out and moth-holed they became. Ever since his father's sudden death, he had been afraid of losing things. "Something's here one day, and the next day, it's gone," he told her. "You just can't count on anything."

Honest as it might be, his attitude was starting to bother her. Sometimes she felt as if both of them were caught here in a place called Clearwater. *Clearwater,* Louise often thought—*what a misnomer.* There was nothing clear about this town: it was as murky as any place on earth, the waters of the town so muddied and opaque that, if you dove under them, you'd never know which way was up or down.

The middle-aged woman steps to the cashier's desk, interrupting Louise's thoughts. Louise musters a smile for the woman, a friendly face from Clearwater she's seen here fairly often.

"You know, honey," the woman lowers her voice as if telling a secret, "I had this dream." She digs into a cheap white vinyl purse and pushes two bills toward Louise. "Quarters," she says. "Yep. Had me a dream last night."

"Oh?" Louise replies, reaching into the change drawer. "What about?"

"Dreamt I won that Whirlwind drawing. Can you believe it?" She gives Louise a wan smile. If the customer's ticket number gets drawn from a tumbler, they get to stand in the Whirlwind Money Machine—a sealed glass booth rigged with high-powered fans in which the players try to grab as many circling bills as they can in thirty seconds. They step out of the machine with anywhere from five dollars to two hundred. Louise has, at times, entertained the thought of dropping her name into the tumbler, but she knows employees of the casino aren't allowed to enter drawings. The lady waves her stash of ticket stubs in front of Louise's face. "Maybe this'll be the day," she says, the words almost singing.

"Yeah. Maybe it will." Louise pushes rolls of quarters toward the woman and recites the rote phrase she's been prompted to say after each transaction. "Good luck."

CHAPTER

4

Though it's only six thirty in the morning and he's still half asleep, Luke rakes the infield, smoothing the soil with the rusted blue rake. His limbs feel as if they're filled with sand, but he doesn't mind volunteering to do the work at this early hour. He knows that each time he scratches the earth's back with a stroke of the rake, this park is beginning to take shape. *The third baseline has to be level and even,* he thinks, *so when the baseball rolls slowly down the line, everyone can tell if it's a fair ball or not.* Somehow, day by day, this ragged lot gets a little closer to resembling a real baseball field. Luke dreams about the day—weeks from now—when he'll sprint onto the field in center, his new white Lakers uniform igniting in the afternoon sun.

But first things first, he reminds himself: he has to get himself in shape for the team tryouts the week of April 21, which he's marked on his calendar with a dark, penciled X, a mark he stares at each morning when he passes his desk. And the field needs to be finished by the end of May in time for the first home game on June 1. As he thinks about them, those important dates seem so close, and yet too far away.

Behind the storage shed, he shovels a pile of reddish-brown dirt into a wheelbarrow and carts it toward the infield. The rest of the workers—the Clearwater city crew and a few volunteers from the team—won't show up for another half hour. As he dumps the moist dirt near the place where home plate will be, it slides from the wheelbarrow with a soft hiss. After a few trips back and forth, he brushes his hair out of his eyes and looks up, admiring the progress of the field so far.

Tall posts line the outfield like a row of aluminum ribs. Stacked near them, the bales of wire wait to be unrolled. By next week, they'll wrap the cyclone fencing around the posts, and the field will have perfect symmetry, just the way he pictures it: 321 down the first and third baselines, 400 in center. Behind home plate, the taller silver pillars rise as if trying to touch the blue dome of sky; they'll support the backstop that protects the fans from the fast foul tips or wild throws from third. Luke knows Clearwater will have a good team—maybe a championship team, with a mix of veteran talent and youth. He wants, more than anything, this second chance at baseball. Wants to jog onto this field on opening day and, at season's end, to stand proudly in a team photo holding a trophy, half smiling, the way his father does in the faded photograph Luke keeps on his desk.

He strolls back to his truck, grabs his Styrofoam cup of coffee from the Rainbow Café, takes a drink, and rotates his head, trying to work the kinks out of the back of his neck. He waits for the caffeine to kick in, stares at the watery brown liquid, as if that would make the coffee less like decaf. He leans on the fender and wonders if the

28

fans that fill the bleachers before the first game will sense what he's sensing: this wide section of land, this wood, this aluminum have suddenly turned into a living, breathing being. In the silence of the still morning air, Luke anticipates the sounds he'll hear on opening day: fists thumping their heartbeats in leather gloves, the staccato of cleats clicking on the concrete floor of the dugout, the startling, resonant percussion of the wood bat cracking against the leather ball, the high-pitched note as a hard-hit liner careens off the glistening wire fence in center, the music of the fans screaming as a runner rounds third, digging for home.

Luke tosses the coffee cup into the flatbed as he starts his morning jog around the perimeter of the field. At first it feels easy, this running, his legs rhythmic and light as if they're filled with air, but after a couple of circuits, Luke's pulse is punching its small fist inside his neck, and his lungs begin to burn, even in the cool morning air. He puts his hands on his hips and slows to a walk. Though his body is still in decent shape—a hundred and eighty pounds on a six-foot-one frame—he's not in the same condition he was when he played ball regularly years ago.

Luke hopes that this field—built on the same location as the old one, with its collapsed bleachers and pitted, weed-choked outfield—will bring back the fervor of the days when the town boasted championship amateur teams year after year, like the one his father played on. He thinks about his dad—Dwight Tanner—out there at night, illuminated by the yellow glow of the lights while Luke, a young boy, watched from the stands. He pictures his dad making that legendary catch in a playoff game; Luke has heard versions of the story around town, in Elmer's Water-in Hole and at the Rainbow Café and the Farmer's Co-op. It was the ninth inning, and his dad sprinted straight toward the fence for a long fly ball hit high and deep. Dwight, in his wrinkled flannel Lakers uniform, dug fast for that ball, and as he approached the wooden fence in center, he didn't slow down. He caught the ball on a dead run, then hit the fence and kept running, breaking right through the one-by-six wood slats, flattening a five-foot section of the sign for Henderson's Everyday Drug with the Burma Shave logo on it. A little stunned, Dwight staggered in the long weeds beyond the outfield and glanced around him, surprised, as though he had broken through to another world. Then he looked down at the white leather of the ball, still in his glove, and became aware of the roar of the hometown fans, who leaped to their feet in the stands, boxes of popcorn and cups of Nehi soda flying into the air. Dwight suffered two sprained wrists and a bruised left shoulder making the catch, but he showed up for the playoff game the next night, wrists taped, ready to play. Luke can see his father's smiling face, his broad forehead with the hat tipped back as he stood proudly during the national anthem, played on a scratchy forty-five-rpm record through a tinny speaker mounted on a high post.

His father was a baseball hero every weekend, adored by the fans; his cleats barely seemed to touch the infield dirt as he rounded first, stretching a single into a double. But to Luke he always looked so ordinary each weekday morning, dressed in his rumpled gray Tanner Implement Company shirt with the name *Dwight* embroidered across the left pocket. At breakfast, Luke could see the quarter-moons of dirt under his dad's fingernails, probably from fastening a lug nut beneath the oily chassis of a John Deere. His father led the league in batting a couple of years, and people in town started talking about how he was good enough to make it to the big leagues, or at least the minors. But then Dwight's father—Luke's grandfather—passed away, and the steel burden of the implement company landed squarely on Dwight's shoulders. Dwight didn't play ball the next season, and he dropped from the team when he started working nights in the shop.

"How come you don't play baseball any more?" Luke asked once when he was in grade school.

"There's things you just do in life," his father answered in his usual cryptic way, "and there's things you just stop doing."

"But *why?*" young Luke prodded. "I mean, you were so *good.*"

His father slid out from under a thresher on an oily creeper and pointed a wrench at him. "I'm good at *this,*" he said, ending the conversation and sliding back under the sky of sheet metal.

Returning to the storage shed, Luke drags out a roll of cyclone fencing that will become the outfield fence. He sets it on the first baseline, unrolls a few feet of it, stares at the crisscross of wires. Nobody will break through this thing once it's up in center, he knows. An image of his dad surfaces again, but this time his father is gasping for air and hooked up to tubes and machines in the Madison hospital after being rushed there by an ambulance. His face the color of ashes, his damaged heart failing second by second, Dwight turned his head toward eighteen-year-old Luke as if his dry lips were about to utter a secret. Inside the oxygen mask, his voice rasped like footsteps in cinders, and he faltered. Dwight Tanner faltered, as he rarely did in life.

"Dad?" Luke gasped.

The only reply was the sound of the machines, hissing, clicking a mechanical language, the subtle blip of the heart monitor. Then the thick plastic of the mask fogged, and Dwight's eyes seemed to roll inward, as if he were looking at something far, far back in his skull.

Luke inherited his family's skills at baseball. Luke's grandfather played on this field too, decades earlier; it seemed there'd always been a Tanner, loping gracefully beneath a fly ball. In high school

they gave Luke the nickname Skywalker, after the *Star Wars* character—not only because of the way he could leap at the fence to take a
home run away from his opponent, but because of the number of
towering fly balls he sent over the fence. He was an all-conference
center fielder from this town of Clearwater, Wisconsin, population
5,421, which nobody had heard of. At the high school field, Luke
could hit the ball over the ravine in left and into the school parking
lot, where old Doc Dotworthy, the math teacher, might pick the ball
up in his jittery hand and give a scolding shake of his head. Luke was
the king of the diamond then, the center of the universe; all the girls
in school gave him longing stares in class, and the townspeople nodded at him. Now, as the years have passed, he's gradually become nobody. He's beginning to feel like just one of the ordinary adults,
walking along the gray sidewalks of the town. For years after graduation he didn't pick up a ball. His work got in the way; his life got
in the way.

This spring, his first workouts with Lance—a paunchy catcher on
the team and Luke's buddy since childhood—haven't been easy, and
he's beginning to wonder how he'll do at tryouts. His arm, after too
many throws, begins to feel leaden, the eight-ounce ball taking on
weight.

"Shit, Luke," Lance quipped, noticing the way Luke was laboring.
"It's like you're throwing a dang shot put."

"Yeah, maybe so." Luke replied, his grimace turning into a laugh.
"But at least I don't look like one."

He threw hard twice from deep in the outfield, and after each
toss it felt like he had slept wrong on his arm, the way it went tingling
and numb. When he fielded Lance's fly balls and liners, the sudden
stops and starts took their toll on Luke's ankle and knee joints, especially the next day, when he eased himself from bed and saw Louise
already brushing her long blonde hair and putting on her makeup.

Some mornings his knees seem to be made of steel alloy with sand grinding between the joints. Mornings like those, he feels like his '78 Ford 150 truck, its bearings wearing thin—he always can sense, before it happens, when that old beast is about to have mechanical trouble.

Early this morning before he left, Louise stood in front of the mirror, looking so businesslike, yet still somehow sexy, in her casino uniform—a white blouse and blue skirt—instead of the Levis and tight red cotton top she usually wore. She took a sip of coffee—black, the way she always drank it—from the cup on the dresser. He limped to the closet, letting out a soft groan as he slipped on his jeans. Luke feels it gnawing at him every day—that pain of a boy turning into a thirty-seven-year-old man, that sudden, aching realization that you're in the middle of something, that you're alive, but you're almost halfway through your life at the same time. And Louise knows he feels it, too.

"Sore from practice again?" she asked, turning from the mirror.

"No, not really," Luke said, covering for himself. "Well, my arm hurts a little, maybe."

She stepped toward him, squeezed the muscle of his throwing arm. "Hmmmm," she said with a soft laugh. "It hasn't turned to Jell-O yet."

He echoed her laugh, then slid his palms around her slim waist and pulled her close to him, her navy skirt pressing against the front of his faded jeans. "And neither have you."

He kissed her lightly on the cheek, and she kissed him back, then gazed at him sympathetically. "I know you love it, but aren't you getting a little old for baseball?" She knows he's trying to keep up with the young guys with their buzz-cut hair and their diamond stud earrings. They're the nineteen- and twenty-one-year-olds with speed and power who, Luke has told her, will be trying out for the team.

"What's *old?*" he replied.

"I don't blame you for having a dream, Luke," she said, a little concern sounding in her voice. "But you're going to hurt yourself. I mean, trying to keep up with those kids."

"I'd hurt myself more if I *didn't* try to keep up with them," Luke replied, pulling back and brushing his hand through his matted brown hair. As he did, his fingers felt thick, as if he still had his baseball glove on.

Hearing the roar of mufflers, Luke turns to see the first men from the work crew pull into the lot next to the field, kicking up clouds of dust. He recognizes Lance's recently waxed gold Citation with a squirrel's tail—courtesy of his ten-year-old son—hanging from the antenna. The same age as Luke, Lance has a wife and three kids already. He's assistant manager at the Hi-Vee grocery, a guy who might be seen in a park or a playground on Saturday mornings, kids squealing on the swings, wife planted on a blanket, while, a headset on his ears, he swings a metal detector over the lawn.

"Jesus, Luke, you're here pretty damn early. What're you trying to do? Show us up?"

"Don't worry," Luke chuckles. "I still left some work for you guys."

Lance peers for a moment at the infield dirt. "Think we'll turn up any coins?" he asks hopefully, lifting one of his overgrown eyebrows.

"Why don't you pull out that detector of yours," Luke says wryly, "and test the area."

"Hey, I probably make more with that thing than you do at your job."

"Probably do."

Dale, Mick, and the other guys from the crew pile out of their cars and amble toward the storage shed. "Hey Tanner!" Dale calls. "You workhorse!"

"Hey Dale," Luke retorts, "you lazy ass."

Feeling a blister rising on his index finger, Luke grabs a pair of leather work gloves from his duffle. There, he sees some of his favorite baseballs— with names written on them—from his high school days. Luke has noticed that some baseballs, inexplicably, fly farther than the rest or take crazy bounces on the infield. He's kept those balls tucked in the corner of his duffel, having marked them in pen with whimsical nicknames, like *Bleacher Boy* or *Fenceball* or *Goes So Far*. Luke jokingly told the guys that certain baseballs have a personality—and maybe even a soul—passed on from the animal from which the leather was made.

As the guys carry rakes to the infield, Luke rolls a wheelbarrow— piled with sod—down the third baseline. He recalls the unexplained incidents that occurred when the crew began to work on the site. One morning Dale's Bobcat died suddenly when he drove it onto the field, even though it had enough gas and the battery was good. When they towed the thing back to the shop, the mechanic shook his head, saying there was nothing wrong with it. Then there was the morning they discovered the aluminum fence poles in center field tipped slightly to one side after they'd pounded them in securely the night before. It was as though the earth itself had suddenly shrugged and shifted a few inches beneath them, causing the row of poles to tip. Luke led the crew out there with shovels and crowbars to straighten the posts. As he walked, he strummed his shovel like a guitar, swinging it left, then right, as he sang "Centerfield."

35

"I hope you play ball better than you sing," Lance quipped.

"Don't count on it," Luke replied.

The more Luke thought about it, the more he began to believe that there really *was* something mysterious about this field; it was as though, at times, the crew's presence there was somehow unwanted, their progress jinxed in some way. And he began to wake from short, recurring dreams of seeing a vapor, a misty ghostlike figure, rising through the earth in the middle of the field and then disappearing in the sky.

Near nine o'clock, Luke is the last to leave. With his leather work gloves—stained on the fingers—he lifts a section of sod and unrolls it. Each length is a piece of the puzzle, he knows, and each has to be placed exactly along the edge of the other and then flattened with the sole of his shoe so there'll be no bumps, no ridges. No places where an outfielder might lose his footing. Eventually, the sod will cover these acres, inch by inch, roll by roll, section by section. *Steady,* Luke thinks. But no matter how steadily you work, the progress always seems too slow, and to take too long. He knows that for a job like this, you have to develop patience, a patience that can't be dented by doubts.

He pulls out the pocket watch his father gave him—it's an antique, 1880s vintage, and its gold-leaf cover flips up at the touch of a button to expose the ivory face with black Roman numerals. Checking the time, he realizes that he has only five more minutes to get to work.

Before he leaves, Luke lifts his eyes and gazes at the field's face, its expanse of bare brown soil, exposed to drying sun and harsh winds, and pictures it transforming to green—a calm, seamless lake

of grass. An ocean. No ripples, no ripples, no ripples. Rich, succu-
lent green for as far as he can throw his sight. A place where, as he
stands in center, nothing can touch him. A field, waiting for him,
waiting for the sprint, the dive, the catch, the sound of the lush grass
blades cheering.

CHAPTER 5

Late at night, unable to sleep, Mayor Butch Sobieski tosses in his bed. He keeps thinking about how, though nobody knows it yet, his town of Clearwater, Wisconsin, is about to put itself on the map. A federal committee is considering Clearwater for the Top Ten Best Small Towns in America, and Butch feels that his town is the logical choice. Being a Best Small Town opens the way for new commerce, new building sites, new billboards to get the tourists in to see the historic downtown buildings. Butch turns onto his side; in his mind he rehearses the spiel he's planned for the committee members that will tour the town in June.

He'll tell them Clearwater is no less than an emerald hidden in the center of scenic Wisconsin. Here in Clearwater, he'll tell them, we have pretty much everything a person could possibly want in a town. First of all and foremost, it's a damn good place to settle down. It's a quiet place, unlike cities like Milwaukee or Chicago, with their nonstop traffic and their gangs and their guns. Nelson's Quick Corner shuts down at nine P.M. sharp, the cars thin out on the town square, and Sheriff Rollie Maas does his rounds through the downtown, checking the storefronts and looking over the neighborhoods to make sure everything's on the up and up. Sure, Butch thinks, his old friend Rollie might, late at night, mess around on the Internet at the station, but you can forgive him that. It's a lonely job, working that night shift. One night after high school graduation, the kids egged Rollie's car while he was in the café, but he more or less figured out who was responsible and had a talk with their parents. Once Rollie found a railroad bum behind Burnhart's Hi-Vee grocery store; the man was eating potato buns out of a bag that had turned green with mold. The guy was from Tennessee or Alabama or somewhere, as Butch recalls. Rollie didn't rough him up or anything; he followed protocol and gave the fellow a ride to the Sauk County line, then sent him on his way. You can bet, after that, the Hi-Vee started locking the heavy steel cover on the dumpster.

On Center there's the Daylite Bakery, Butch would proclaim, continuing his tour. The Daylite makes the best doughnuts and sticky buns you'll ever sink your teeth into. Jeannie Stumpf over there is awake around four A.M.—while the rest of the town is pretty much asleep—and she's pulling the raw dough from the mixer and making donuts and pans of rolls. When you see her crossing the street with those tight gray curls on her head, there's usually a little white confectioner's sugar just so on the side of her cheek, where she touches her face with her hand when she's surprised. You can bet that every Knights of Columbus and Kiwanis and Lions Club from around the county orders her dinner rolls for their Friday fish fries.

Two doors down, past the Curl Up and Dye Hair Salon, is the Rainbow Café, where your coffee, brewed in those big stainless steel percolators, tastes every bit as flavorful as coffee made by some fancy cappuccino machine. You spoon a little cream or Coffee Rich in there, and you're in heaven. Not too sweet, not too bitter, and plenty of Coffee Rich—that's the best way to drink it. Any morning you walk in, you'll hear the constant sound of spoons clinking in the cups as the friendly people stir their coffee. It's like music. And there's plenty of conversation. Ralph Finch might give you best bets on the annual Clearwater Steam and Gas Show, the thresher festival at the county fair. That man knows threshers better than anyone Butch has ever met. After thirty years of farming just outside of town, you'd expect him to be able—without fail, usually—to guess the make, model, and year of an old monster of a thresher roped off beneath the grandstands.

In the middle of town, in what used to be the Kraft Cheese Factory, is the Clear Day Bottling plant. There they bottle fresh spring water taken right from the town's water supply. The blue and white label—which has a silver drawing of the town's lake—boasts:

Clear Day Spring Water

Bottled at the Clearwater Bottling Corp., Clearwater, Wis. USA

Best Drinking Water in America

Of course, the company supplies bottles to the Cold Spring Brewery, the local microbrewery with that tasty Cold Spring and Hofbrau Select beer.

Further down the street, past Burnhart's, the Daylite, and the Soap Box Launderette, is the Starlight Theater. Clearwater is proud to say our theater still shows movies a couple times a week, and hasn't buckled in to the cheap cineplexes they build over in Madison. Butch knows that when there are six or eight theaters in one of those prefab buildings, the screens are so small you never get the thrill of a

Hollywood movie. The Starlight has red velvet seats, just like when it was built in 1929, and a glass chandelier that hangs from the middle of the ceiling where you can still see—a little faintly, though—the painted circle of tiny cherubs. As you'd expect, the theater is listed on the National Register of Historic Places. You get real popcorn, made from a brass machine that really kicks out the fluffy white kernels. None of that microwave stuff—burnt and half dry. The popcorn's in paper tubs, and when you grab a handful, you know by the feel of it between your thumb and fingertips that it's covered with that sweet butter from Bud's Creamery. Then there's the Monday Night Classic and the reruns of the movies with Cary Grant, Rock Hudson, Doris Day, Jimmy Stewart, an occasional Hitchcock or two, and, of course, Audrey Hepburn. Her face always looks so white and pure up there on the thirty-foot screen, Butch thinks. The kids can see all the sex and violence they want on the weekends by watching *Scream* and *I Know What You Did Last Summer* and *Freddie's Dead: The Final Nightmare* or whatever.

At the corner of the theater is the traffic light, blinking red, then green, every 120 seconds. The city crew put it in one year after a T-bone crash at that intersection. A man from Milwaukee was passing through town on the county road at a high rate of speed, Sheriff Rollie stated in his report. The man was killed in the crash, and a Clearwater resident—Mrs. Roberta Jenkins, who pulled into the lane unaware of his approach—was injured, and her new Taurus was totaled. Though no one witnessed the accident, Sheriff Rollie determined—from the length of the bug smears on the windshield of the man's smashed Lexus—that the man was traveling at a speed of least fifty miles per hour. Rollie issued him a ticket and mailed it, certified, to the survivors over in Milwaukee, but they never paid.

Other than that, there's been no traffic problem in town. It moves along at a steady pace. Even during rush hour—when businesses close—the traffic flows pretty well, people keeping a safe distance between cars, though sometimes you have to wait a little while to pull into the flow. Old Mr. Andershodt can sometimes be seen cursing inside his Buick when the traffic gets thick like that, but Butch and everyone else in town knows he's pretty much on a one-way street to the nursing home, what with his hypertension and the bad legs.

At the edge of town is Smitty's Gas and Video, soon to be part of the new Clear Way Plaza, and there you can fill up your car while you browse among the wire racks of Ripples and Corn Nuts and Fritos and air fresheners shaped like pine trees, keys, or girls in swimsuits. Farther down is a combination garage and salvage yard, Rite Away Auto, and there you might find Johnny, the chief mechanic, sliding out from under an old Bonneville on his creeper, his tan shirt spotted with oil. Johnny—in his late thirties—will always take the time to talk to you about carburetors or fuel pumps or valves, though he has that peculiar but not quite annoying habit of rubbing his grimy hands over and over on that pink rag while he talks. He claims he's building a stock car from scratch out of salvage—that it'll be a car he'll race someday over at the Golden Spike, a quarter-mile dirt track in Portage. He's often told Butch he used the water pump from Mrs. Jenkins's Olds, and that he'd love to get his hands on Mr. Andershodt's Buick after he cashes out and goes into the nursing home. He tells Butch, emphasizing his words with a pair of stainless steel pliers in his hand, that he could use a few of those 350-horsepower engine parts that old Andershodt has never put to the test. Johnny always keeps his race car under a gray tarp in the back of the shop, and if you ask, he'll proudly lift the corner of the tarp and let you peer in for a few seconds at the welded chrome grille or the hood, covered with flat gray primer, or the engine-in-progress, which always looks dark. Butch can tell just by looking that the thing is pretty hot to trot. But no matter how often Johnny works on it, late in the evening after Rite Away is closed, the trouble light glowing beneath the chassis, he never seems to finish it. "Someday," he often says to Butch, the gray smudges above his eyebrow lifting, "I'll run her in a race. Someday."

On Sunday mornings, there's Mary of the Seven Dolors Catholic Church—made of gray granite from the local quarries outside Clearwater, with a tall stone spire above the bell tower—where Father McGuinn gives an inspirational sermon. He's been the pastor there for thirty years. Though he has an occasional guitar Mass, he usually sticks with a good traditional service, with some incense and plenty of choir hymns to the accompaniment of the big pipe organ in the back. On Sunday mornings, at nine and ten A.M., you can hear the pealing of the large brass bell in the bell tower as Father McGuinn, assisted by one of his altar boys, pulls the heavy rope that hangs in the foyer of the church. That rope is thick and rough, with frizzed ends sticking out from it, and that ancient cast iron bell must weigh five hundred pounds. "Do you ever get blisters?" Butch asked once, and Father just shook his head, chuckling as though Butch had made a mildly funny joke.

On the north end of town is the park, a town highlight. In the evenings, the townspeople have taken to strolling through Goettmer's Park among the big elms and oaks along the shore of Clearwater Lake. The park's named for Karl Goettmer, one of the town's founding fathers, a German pioneer who lumbered the big pines out of the area and rounded up the Indians to clear the way for the small towns of America. Clearwater Lake is not all that big—180 acres— but it's scenic, and when the sun reflects off the lake, it nearly blinds you. On the row of swings, you'll see the little kids rising up into the air, then swinging back to their parents' hands, then rising up and back again. Maybe it's the proximity to the water, Butch has often thought, or maybe it's the city parks crew that fertilizes it so well with manure from the Gateway Dairy Farm outside town, or maybe it's just the angle of the sunlight. Whatever it is, just before sunset, that grass in the park is as green as anything.

The lake is fairly small by Wisconsin standards, and you won't find any muskies or walleyes lurking at the bottom. Little sunfish are about all that's in there, and an occasional medium-sized crappie. Not much beneath the surface, really. Butch doesn't like those big lakes—like Lake Michigan—where you can't see the far shore. When you stand at the edge of the perfect oval of Clearwater Lake, you can see right across it to the other side. Most folks in town would agree—there's something comforting about being able to see to the other shore, to the rows of pines and oaks on the far side, and the fields and farmlands of Sauk County that lead toward the rolling bluffs in the distance. And that, Butch concludes, is peace of mind.

Butch feels a stinging sensation on the side of his cheek and suddenly sits up in bed. He slaps the mosquito that must have slipped in through the window screen. He walks quickly to the window, runs his finger along the rusty screen, trying to find out if there's a tear in it. His thick finger finds a frayed edge of sharp screen. He thought he fixed that hole last year. "Damn it!" he says, stumbling toward his desk in the half-dark. He reaches for some masking tape he keeps in one corner. The roll of tape falls from the desk and lands with a soft thump on the shag carpet. He bends over, groping, but can't find it in the darkness. "Goddamn tape!" he spits as his fingers finally lift the dry roll.

An image of Luke Tanner lifting that bone from the half-constructed baseball field pops into his head again. The rumors of what Tanner found keep nagging at him. Earlier that evening, in a booth at Elmer's Water-in Hole, Sheriff Rollie spilled the story casually as dice skittering across the table. The story sounded like something Butch could just ignore. He wants the ball field construction to continue on schedule, after all; he wants to continue the proud tradition of the Clearwater Lakers, the championship team that led the town through the '50s and '60s. In August, he hopes to host the state Amateur Baseball Tournament, which should add a pretty substantial income to the town.

But more than anything else, Butch wants to push ahead with his plans to build a new road through the back acres of that property, a road that would connect to the interstate. A Clearwater exit—with the help of a billboard that reads *Welcome to Clearwater, Heart of Historic Wisconsin*—would bring in commerce, enticing travelers to the center of town. The green and white exit sign *Clearwater 4 Mi.* lights up in his mind as surely as if you shined bright headlights on it in the middle of the night.

Butch checks the red numbers on his alarm clock: it's 2:18 already. He lies down on his bed again, closes his eyes. He jolts awake, hears the sound of another mosquito near his ear, its irritating, high-pitched whine. When it lands on the side of his thick neck, he slaps it hard with his palm. *Damn little pests,* he thinks. *Don't they have anything better to do than suck the blood out of people?*

He jumps out of bed, clicks on the table lamp, lifts the phone. He doesn't care if it *is* Sunday morning at goddamn two A.M.—he has to make the call.

"Rollie," Butch says, sounding more out of breath than he intended, "you've got to talk to him."

"Who, Butch?" Rollie's high voice sounds irritated. "Who you talking about?"

"You've got to talk to Luke Tanner."

CHAPTER 6

Rollie Maas pulls his squad car up in front of Luke Tanner's rental house, the dry sticks at the edge of the street crackling under his tires. He clicks off the Johnny Paycheck song on the four-speaker radio, checks the time—8:45 A.M.—and, with a blue pen he got from city hall, marks it in his log book. On the passenger side, beneath the beige troll with pink hair that's attached to the glove compartment, is the shotgun, which he's never used except for target practice out by the Gun Club Range. The Lions Club sponsored a turkey shoot out there last fall, and Rollie, using a .22 rifle, took second prize. They set up some sod bunkers with the caged turkeys inside them, and each cage had a hole in the top. When a turkey poked its head through a hole, you aimed and fired. Rollie picked off three turkeys, which he got to keep; he baked one and froze the other two. Hans Rinehardt, who goes moose and bear hunting up in Canada every year, came in first again with four turkeys, much to Rollie's dismay, because first prize was a brand-new Arctic Cat, donated by the Lions.

Kicking out a thin wrapper from a to-go deluxe JimboBurger from Jimbo's and holding a Styrofoam cup of Rainbow coffee, lightened with his usual four packets of Coffee Rich, Rollie slides out of the cruiser. The squad car is a 2006 Crown Victoria with the works—a big 440 engine with overdrive, a call radio, a black wire cage in the back seat, lights on top and hidden in the grille, a 500-watt side spotlight, and a siren you could hear in the next county. He's been sheriff in town for nearly twenty years, and this is the best car he's ever had. In the old days, they just gave you a basic Ford, put a red cherry light on top of it, painted *Clearwater Police* on a silver shield on the side door, and that was it. That was all you needed, really, because this wasn't much of a high crime area. Rollie recalls those days when, bored on his rounds some afternoons, he'd stop at the park and hand out Kiwanis Club candy to some kids. He still does some volunteer work for the local Kid Stop on his lunch breaks, ushering the three- and four-year-olds from the park back to the old junior high gym. He feels good, doing a little community service, holding up his hand to stop traffic on Center as the children, hands linked and dressed in their stupid cartoon character T-shirts, march two by two between the lines of the crosswalk.

Rollie never thinks about murder around here; there's never been one in Clearwater during his terms as sheriff, and the only one on record—according to the files at the police station—was the case of some off-the-wall Swede farmer who went crazy in the 1930s, killing his wife and then himself. Of course, with the suicide, there was no prosecution or trial, case closed. But this thing about finding bones on the ball field bothers Rollie a little. He doesn't want any kind of ugly scene, like headlines in the *Clearwater American* saying something like *Remains from Mass Murder Found in Clearwater.* Headlines like that would make their way to the *Wisconsin State Journal* or the *Milwaukee Journal,* and it would, as Butch says, be more than just a little blemish on this town, not to mention the hassle it would cause Rollie himself. Sure, he'd get a little publicity with the interviews and maybe Madison's Channel 5 coming out with their Live at Five report, but it wouldn't be worth the stain on his reputation for keeping Clearwater a wholesome, law-abiding town. And then there are the elections coming up again in fall—he's been pretty much unopposed for the last few terms. Still, since Butch's call early Sunday morning, he's lost a little sleep. He knows that maybe his imagination is just getting the better of him, that he's been reading too damn many *Weekly World News* headlines when he buys some Cheetos at the Quick Corner.

That's why Rollie wants to get it all cleared up, to talk to this Luke fellow, whom he's never really spoken to. He's only seen him driving around town in his pickup with that slinky divorcee Louise dangling her bare, slim arm out of the passenger's side. He's heard a few things about Luke's dad, Dwight, of course, who people say was a decent guy.

Rollie stumbles on the bottom step of Luke's porch. Sloshing a little of Ruth's coffee on his blue pants with the black side stripe, he exhales "Aw shoot," then composes himself and knocks on the door.

As he waits, he studies the blue door's paint, peeling a little around the edges. He figures he's not going to like this Luke guy, not one bit.

When the door opens slowly, Rollie smells hash browns and eggs, and it makes his stomach do a left turn, because he really didn't have much of a breakfast, except for his usual bowl of cereal. There's another sweet scent coming from the house, too, one he can't quite figure out. Luke Tanner's face appears in the doorway, and his smile surprises Rollie, who was expecting a cocky, abrasive Clint Eastwood, some scowling Stallone or Chuck Norris. Instead, Luke looks pretty much ordinary—a hundred and eighty pound guy in a gray, wrinkled Clearwater Lakers T-shirt, faded jeans, and bare feet. Luke is a couple inches taller than Rollie, and it bugs Rollie to have to look up at him. His brown hair curls around his ears. A smile sort of lights up his face, and he looks years younger than what he must be, which, Rollie figures, is around mid-thirties.

"Morning, officer," Luke says.

Rollie is distracted for a moment by the wooden bird feeder hanging on a chain from the porch roof. He presses his index finger into the layer of seed at the bottom. "What kind of birds do you get with a feeder like this?" he asks.

"All kinds," Luke responds.

"Hummingbirds, even?"

"No, not hummingbirds."

"They can fly in one place, you know. Can even fly backwards."

Luke gives him an impatient stare, his smile draining from his face. "So what can I do for you?"

"Sheriff Rollie Maas," Rollie introduces himself with his high, nasal voice. He notices Luke glancing at the coffee stain on the side of his pant leg. "Got time to chat?" Rollie asks. Rising to his tiptoes, he peers into the dining room, where he sees a wicker chair with a lacy pink cushion on it—Louise's touch, no doubt—and an oak desk scattered with books and papers.

"What's this about?" Luke crosses his arms, his muscles showing. "We were just sitting down for breakfast."

"Just want to ask you a question or two about what you found," Rollie recites the words stiffly, as if they're being read from a rehearsed speech. "Over at the ball field, I mean."

Luke's face seals over with a blank look. Rollie can't tell what it means; it's like looking at a granite statue and trying to figure out what it's thinking.

Rollie shifts his weight to his left leg, leans his wiry arm against the wood siding of the house. He's picking up another scent from the house, too. It's not food. It's something he can't quite identify. "The mayor sent me over to ask a few questions."

"How'd you know I found *anything*?" Luke asks.

"Well maybe you did, and maybe you didn't. The thing is, I'm just here to clear a few things up." Rollie takes a sip of the cooling coffee in the brown-stained cup as he waits for a response. He doesn't want to use a harder line of questioning, which might put Luke off. "Say," Rollie utters casually, mustering his small lips into a smile, "Heard your dad was a real good ballplayer."

"Yeah?"

"Sure. The mayor mentions him. Told me he had a live arm."

"So they say." Luke glances quickly over his shoulder, showing that he's checking on the breakfast.

"So, about what you found . . ."

"What about it?" Luke runs his fingers through his matted hair.

"I just need to know if you found bones out there. On the city land, I mean. And if they're bones, then what kind of bones they are, that's all," Rollie adds. "I mean, if it's dog bones or deer bones, well then, shit."

Luke doesn't reply, and during that pause, Rollie identifies the other smell—it's the wafting scent of perfume from inside the house—Louise's perfume. For an instant, he can picture her fingers, dabbing a little in the curve of her neck with jasmine or Chanel or whatever she would put on in the morning. He wouldn't mind leaning into the doorway a little, getting a glimpse of her long legs coming out from under her nightgown. When he makes his rounds, he's noticed that pink spaghetti-strap nightgown and some of her bras and panties hanging on the line in the backyard. He likes the way they sway real nicely in the wind.

"I found it on *Tanner* land, you know. My grandfather owned those acres where the new field's going in. He let the city use them for a ball field."

"Wait just a minute," Rollie says, mustering a chuckle, his narrow chest shaking a little beneath his white shirt and lint-speckled blue jacket. A black leather belt with a large square stainless steel buckle hitches his pants up a little higher than they should be. "I'm gonna have to differ with you there. It's city land now."

"My dad and the mayor didn't exactly agree on that land deal, you know."

"The mayor says he can locate the papers," Rollie states, making himself suddenly in the know. "That's what counts. So," Rollie tries to sound casual as he shifts the subject. "I don't need much this morning. I just need to see what you found, to know if it's an animal bone or what. You know, routine investigation. Run-of-the-mill." His left cheek twitches. He hates it when it does that. "So, you have it handy?"

"No, I don't," Luke says abruptly, though without anger, and with one smooth motion, he takes a step back, slides behind the door and shuts it in Rollie's face. Rollie hears the *click* as the door locks from the inside.

Rollie feels his high forehead flush with heat. It burns like that time he stood too close to a heat lamp to try to get his face tanned before last year's Firemen-Policemen's Ball at the Legion Club. He has a notion to rap on the door with his knuckles again, hard. He has a notion to keep rapping, to make the glass in the diamond windows vibrate, and wait there until Luke opens it again. He has a notion, if no one answers, to go back to his cruiser, pull the thick, long crowbar from the trunk, and pry the door open until the frame cracks and splinters. Then he'd rush in, where he'd see Luke, standing in the middle of the dining room with his fists clenched, and Louise—a fine glimpse of cleavage showing—huddled behind him in a sheer pink nightgown, just like on the cover of some damn romance novel. Rollie has a notion to run in there and train his shotgun on them—though it's not loaded—and scare the living daylights out of them. That would ruffle their goddamn feathers.

Instead, he pivots on his black, shiny shoes and heads back to the cruiser, the stiff heels clicking on the uneven sidewalk. Sliding into the extra-cushioned front seat, he checks the time. He picks up the blue pen and writes in the black logbook: *Tuesday, March 27. 8:58 a.m. Questioned Luke Tanner about bones found in lot between 12th and 15th streets.*

He pulls his new Nokia cell phone from his belt, dials the mayor's office; Butch answers. "Yeah, Butch," Rollie says. "Rollie here. I talked to that Luke Tanner guy. Got it all pretty much cleared up. Nothing to worry about. Nothing at all. Some goddamn chicken bones, is all."

CHAPTER 7

Luke pulls up near the hollow faux-marble pillars at the Vegas-style entryway. Two men in tuxes and chauffeur's caps wait to open the doors below a sign that reads *The Potawatomi Band of the Indian Nation Welcomes You.* As he passes through the tinted glass doors, the scent of trapped smoke assaults his nose; he hears the *bing bing bing* of a thousand slot machines, each of them chiming for attention.

He makes his way across the geometric brown and gold carpeting. The place is dim except for the illuminated fronts of the video slots—Caribbean Gold, Lucky Sevens, and Red, White and Blue, and those slots made especially for this casino—Spirit Island Treasure, with an image on the lit glass of a mist-shrouded island piled with stacks of gold coins. At the dollar slots, heavy brass tokens clank into the metal bin of a machine as a gray-haired man, face as blank as a worn coin, cashes out. No clocks on the wall, Luke notices. No clocks anywhere. *It could be 4 in the afternoon for all these dazed players know,* he thinks. *It could be midnight. The only clock they know is their inner clock, which tells them, "Keep playing. Even if you're losing, keep playing."* He slides past the change carts on wheels with their yellow flags, pushed by dark-haired women wearing the casino's customary white blouse and blue skirt; then, in the back corner, he reaches Louise's cashier's cage, the bars cutting her sweet, sad face into segments.

She looks surprised to see him. "What are you doing here?" she asks. "I was planning to catch a ride back with Andrea."

"Thanks for the welcome," he says with a twist of humor. "I don't suppose I could arrange a date with you after your shift?" He raises one eyebrow expectantly.

"Not 'til six." Her face tries to smile as she stacks some plastic cups with the blue and gold Spirit Island logo on them—a silhouette of a stereotypical feathered, loin-clothed brave on an island, his campfire smoke rising in a swirl. "This is my night for tutoring."

"Oh, yeah, that's right."

Luke knows how excited Louise was about volunteering to tutor a group of seven- through ten-year-olds on the reservation. On her first visits, though, she found that it wasn't so easy. She told him the students were suspicious and withdrawn, and it took a lot to get them to trust her. Lately, she's been returning from tutoring feeling exhilarated and thinking that maybe she is making some progress.

Luke admired her commitment, liked the way she set goals and worked so hard to reach them.

As he lingers in the casino, he drops six quarters into the Home Run slot machine, wins a few ten-quarter payouts. He feeds it all back into the machine, decides he would have been better off—and ten bucks richer—if he had waited for Louise in the entryway.

"You a ballplayer?" a voice asks. Luke turns to see a guard nodding at his Lakers T-shirt. He's a Native American man in his late fifties; his long gray-streaked hair is tied behind his head in a ponytail. A little shorter than Luke, the man has a good build, judging by the way his barrel chest bulges against his blue suit jacket.

"I guess you could say that."

The man's tawny face widens into a smile as he sticks out his large hand, introducing himself as Ray Youngbear. "I watched some Lakers games when I was a kid."

"Really? My dad played with the Lakers once," Luke responds.

When Luke says his father's name, Ray twists his lips slightly to the side; parallel lines of wrinkles carve themselves into his forehead as his brown deep-set eyes seem to look right past Luke. "Sure. Dwight Tanner. An outfielder. Damn good one, as I recall."

Picturing his father in a Lakers uniform, Luke feels a sense of pride. He remembers when he was eight years old and watched his dad play. Luke sat alone in the grandstands, the aroma of cigars and buttery popcorn and strawberry sodas wafting around him. He used to lean against the backstop during batting practice, where he felt the sharp cracking sound of his father hitting the ball, a sound that seemed to resonate inside his chest.

"They had a hell of a team for a few years there," Ray continues. "Star pitcher was a guy from the reservation."

When Ray gets a call on his walkie-talkie, Luke thinks about how he had a number of Native American classmates in grade school, but most of them were the quiet type, always keeping to themselves. That was the way it was in the Clearwater schools—there were unwritten rules about whites and the Potawatomi kids. The two groups were separated by an indifferent but icy silence. In high school, at the

55

teen dances, the Native American kids always hung out at the rear of the school gym, and the white kids closest to the dance floor. No white boys ever crossed that distance to ask a Native American girl to dance, and vice versa. The only time that distance was crossed was behind the power plant during the Friday night skirmishes between the white and Native American boys. But he was never involved in them.

"So. Tell me more about this pitcher," Luke says as Ray slides his walkie-talkie back into his belt.

"He was the only Indian in the league, I guess. And a really good one. Chief Bender, they called him. Great athlete—a regular Jim Thorpe, this Bender guy. His real name was Jim Whitebird." He leans his shoulders—the blue sport jacket stretched tightly across his back—against the limestone facade of the entryway. "Yep. People on the reservation thought he was going all the way to the big leagues. The elders even did a couple prayer ceremonies for him." He nods his head. "We all thought he'd make it." Ray pauses to check IDs as a young couple enters. He studies the cards, then motions the couple in. They wear Packers jerseys, and their wide-eyed stares fix on the glimmering crystal chandelier's reverse reflection in the glass ceiling. "I hope those two don't lose *all* their cash," he says, shaking his head.

"So," Luke says, "was Whitebird as good a pitcher as everybody thought?"

"Well, he had a great curve ball, that's for sure. That thing broke a couple feet." Ray makes a quick hand motion, exposing a beaded wristband on his arm, to show the curve of the ball. "Scouts from the Milwaukee Braves farm team checked him out. Even came asking about him after he was gone. That would have been something, eh? A real *Indian* on the *Braves*?" Ray's mouth curves into an ironic grin. "But the guy was too damn cocky. Thought he was God's gift to the game. Yeah, he stirred up a little resentment, all right. He'd mouth off during practice. Sometimes he'd come to games half-drunk. White-bird was pretty much at odds with those damn hot-shot white boys on the team." He looks slyly at Luke out of the corner of his eye. "No offense," he says.

"No offense taken," Luke smiles, brushing off the comment.

"There weren't exactly good feelings between the whites and the tribal people those years. You know, between the fighting and those spear fishing rights." Ray steps to the doors and opens them for two senior women in matching mauve and white jog suits who dig through their purses for loose change. The aluminum and glass doors wheeze as they slowly seal.

"Anyways," Ray continues, "during those Lakers games, we pretty much had our own section in the stands."

When Luke gives him a puzzled look, Ray says, "Yep, we always sat on the first base side. That was our place."

"Guess things are different now."

Ray lifts one eyebrow. "Depends. The elders, like my father, say everything's changed, changed for the worse. Casinos popping up all over. Says money is the new tribal god. The ancient ways are forgotten. Says I should stay close to my source and be proud of the old Potawatomi ways. But hey," he gestures toward the glittering Island Gold sign hanging over the entryway, "this place pays me the bucks."

"So, you're not into the old ways, then?"

"I'm still in touch with them, I guess." He stares down at his shined shoes for a moment. "It's kinda funny, but I remember one day in seventh grade, my father told me I needed to go on this vision quest. You know what that is?"

Luke nods.

"So one afternoon, I walked out into the trees behind our place. Stood there with my eyes closed for a long time."

"Then what?"

"I waited for the spirit voice, any voice, to enter me. Or some such thing. Waited a long time. But all I heard was the sound of the stupid little dog next door, yappin' away. Went back to my room, popped open a couple cans of beer, cranked up Led Zeppelin on my stereo." His body shakes with a deep laugh. "Yep, I got a good beer buzz and lit up a Kool. So much for my vision quest."

Louise sidles up next to Luke and asks him to pick her up after she's done tutoring. He glides his arm around her waist.

"Hey," Ray says. "Why didn't you tell me you knew this fabulous woman?"

Luke gives him a humble smile.

"She's none other than the nicest lady working in this whole place," Ray adds, making Louise blush. "Well, except maybe for Lady Luck."

IN THE PARKING LOT, Luke opens the door of his pickup for Louise. A duffel bag rests in the middle of the seat. He unzips the duffel, exposing fried chicken in ziplock bags on an ice pack, a container of coleslaw, a loaf of French bread, a bottle of Chardonnay, and a six pack of Miller Genuine.

"A picnic," she exclaims. "How sweet."

"Don't jump to conclusions," he jokes. "You haven't tried my coleslaw yet."

The metallic blue Ford 150 follows the narrow highway out of town, the engine hesitating a little as Luke shifts from second to third gear.

"How'd tutoring go?"

"Not bad today. I gave Rita some help with her math. She was really lost at school. When she added fractions, she just totaled up all the numbers." Louise tucks one slim leg beneath her as she rides in the passenger seat. "So where are we going?"

"It's a surprise. You'll just have to wait."

"What if I can't wait?"

Luke sees the impatience he's noticed lately behind her smile. "You have to trust me—that's all."

As they drive a few minutes in silence, Luke watches the low sun in the west sending up spokes of light, like a huge pink hand opening. The farms ignite, half lit by the setting sun, and barns and outbuildings stretch their long, narrowing shadows across the fields. Silhouettes of horses stand motionless in wood-fenced corrals. The plowed furrows of farm fields carve the hillsides where Clearwater Valley sweeps toward the bluffs. In the Ice Age, before the glacier melted and receded, it gouged kettle shapes and pushed the land into wide valleys and ridges. Local lore says that before the glacier shaved it down, the quartzite bluffs south of town used to be as high as the Rocky Mountains, but Luke figures this is an exaggeration. He watches the silos and the large skeletons of windmills seem to rise on the horizon, then shrink back into the earth behind him.

Luke turns right at County A—a worn asphalt road with weeds overgrowing its sides—and his pickup follows the gentle undulation, the rising and falling of the wooded hills. Haze appears, a whitish veil wrapping around a row of trees on a ridge. "Almost there," he says as he eases his foot off the gas pedal. "But you have to close your eyes."

"Luuuke . . ." she playfully protests. There's something girlish in her voice as she exaggerates the sound of his name, and Luke loves that. She closes her eyes as he turns into the parking lot of Man Mound Park, a county park outside Clearwater.

He flings the door open, helps her out, and leads her across the gravel of the lot. Eyes still closed, she walks unsteadily. He eases her slowly up a wooden stairway that leads to a viewing platform ten feet off the ground. Climbing tentatively on the splintered wood, she laughs lightly, stubbing the toe of her sandal on one step. "Luke, this is really dumb," she chides, though he can tell by her tone that she likes it.

"Okay," he finally says, squaring her shoulders. "Open your eyes."

She peers down at a large mound of earth, not sure what she's looking at. Luke points out the shape of a human figure with buffalo horns on its head. The Native American mound—a figure of a walking person—spans between the highway and the woods behind it.

"Wow," she exclaims. "I never knew this was out here."

"Yeah. It's at least a thousand years old."

"Amazing. So what do you know about it?"

"Not much. Only that it might be a burial mound. Or a tribute to a god, or some great tribal leader. My dad once said it was a historic landmark worth preserving. Another time he said it was just a pile of dirt, but I don't agree with that." He leans against the rough wood post of the railing. "There's only a couple of these left in the whole country."

Back on the lawn of the park, Louise sits down on a blue and white picnic blanket and starts to unpack as Luke paces off the effigy. "Almost two hundred feet long," he calls, "and fifty feet wide." He strolls back to her, takes a sip from a wine glass she unwrapped from a paper towel.

"But what happened to the legs?" she asks.

"Cut off by a road crew, I heard." Luke glances at the south end of the effigy, which crumbles, at the knees, into gravel near the county road.

"They *could* have angled the county road. Instead, they cut right through it, just to keep their square grid."

"That's the town fathers for you."

After their picnic they sit in the middle of the effigy mound.

Luke stretches out on the grass, and the green tide buoys him up. The grass blades, damp with dew, caress his bare arms and the back of his neck, relaxing him. "I wish we could stay out here all night," he says.

"All night?"

"Yeah. After all," he sighs, "this is sacred ground."

When Louise closes her eyes a moment, Luke notices how her eyelids are like pale moons. When she opens them agaiFn, her blue eyes darken in the dusk, but he can still see the highlighted flecks in them.

Louise tips her head upward. "Ever think how tiny *we* are?" she asks. "And what a huge universe is out there?"

"Sometimes." He sips his wine. "The stars look really close to-night, don't they?" he muses. "Like sparks from a campfire. Only they never burn out."

"You're quite the poet tonight. Or is it just the wine?"

"Maybe both," he laughs, his head spinning as they finish the bottle of Chardonnay. "No matter. That doesn't change how close the stars are." He tilts his head toward her. "And I love you like I love the stars." He reaches over for her hand, props himself on one elbow. Absorbing the moment, he leans close to her face, his eyes riding the smooth hillside of her cheek.

"I love you too," she echoes.

He kisses her—the long kiss blossoms inside him, spreading to his fingertips and toes. Luke feels the passion rising in him steadily, something primitive and beautiful between them. He reaches to touch her long neck, his bare forearm grazing her breasts, silky be-neath her white blouse. *Water, earth, stars,* he thinks. *That's what the ancients worshipped. And something else.* The next thing he knows, he's gliding his body on top of her. His ears fill with the music of the first crickets, their high-pitched song rising from the grass. He feels as if he could climb that high-pitched song all the way to the sky. Luke imagines the two of them taking off their clothes, their pale skin glowing in the moonlight, making love to a beat—the earthen effigy's persistent, ancient heartbeat vibrating through the grass. He pictures their child, growing wild, wild in Louise's womb, and imbedded deep within the child is the memory of this night, this soft, endless heartbeat, this tribal rhythm that reaches to the center of the earth, and all the way to the farthest stars. He presses against her, feeling the heat, the fire of her body through his jeans, until he hears a gasp, a sound like the distant wind moving closer through the grove of trees behind them.

"Luke," her voice whispers, though it sounds loud in his ears, "not here. Not now."

"Why?" The word sounds ragged as he exhales it. "Why not?"

"We're in a park," she says in a more practical voice. She slides out from under him and, lying on her side, pulls her knees up to her chest.

"Okay," he says, "okay." He rolls over and lies on his back a few minutes. The first, small leaves on the oak trees flutter, and the light breeze cools the heat on Luke's face.

A few minutes later, he speaks. "I've been thinking about something," he says tentatively. "I mean, wondering about . . ." He pauses a few seconds, trying to capture the right words that seem to be flying away from him like lightning bugs at the edge of the woods. They glow for an instant, then go dark a few seconds, then glow again. Finally he blurts out the words he's been planning to say for weeks: "I think maybe we should get married."

For a few agonizing seconds, she doesn't respond.

"Did you hear what I said, Louise?" He sits up from the grass, crosses his legs. Still on her side, she lowers her eyes, like she's sleeping, and she still doesn't answer. Luke hears only the sound of the night around them—the steady shrill of the crickets, and beyond that, the silence, the blackness. "I heard you," she finally says in a far-away whisper.

"But you're not answering." He studies the side of her face, noticing her lips pursed in a line straight as the horizon. He thinks he can see her shivering.

"I don't know," she finally replies. "I just don't know, Luke."

Her long pause makes him feel anxious. "*What* don't you know?"

"I really don't know if marriage means anything to me right now. I mean, Denny and I . . ."

"To hell with Denny," Luke interrupts, surprised by the sudden bitterness in his voice. "We can *make* it mean something, you and me."

"And what would we do?" Louise sits up, tugging at the sleeves of her T-shirt like she's beginning to get chilled. "Get married, spend our life in Clearwater?"

"What's so wrong with that? We've got jobs. We could look for a house. A house to buy, I mean. Not just some old rental place . . ."

"So," she says, her voice tightening, "you'll stick with your job at the sod company, and I'll be at the casino, breathing stale smoke eight hours a day? You'll go to your Sunday ball games while I sit in the bleachers with the wives and girlfriends? So that's our future?"

"I didn't say that," he replies defensively. "I didn't say that at all." He looks down at his fingernails, their frayed edges.

"But you're *thinking it*," she says. "In the back of your mind, that's what you've planned."

He squeezes his fist, his nails digging into his palm. He's confused by her reaction, wants to reach out and grab her wrist and pull her close to him, but he doesn't—he can't. "So, okay—so what is it that *you* want?"

"I'm not sure," she says, and he sees the sadness surfacing on her face. She pauses, brushes the blades of grass from her bare arms, her eyes fixed on the darkened county road. "Maybe going to Madison. Taking photography classes. A town besides *this* town."

He gives her a hurt, puzzled look, then lowers his head. He hates it, hates it that, even at their age, neither of them seems to know where they're going. "Maybe part of me thinks that, too," he admits. "But another part of me loves this place."

"I understand."

"And there's more to it than that. I just can't say what I feel . . ."

"No, you can't." She shakes her head, her long blonde hair swaying on her shoulders. "You never seem to know what you're feeling." She stands and lets out a long sigh. "And maybe that's the problem."

He chews his lip, wondering how this conversation has quickly erupted into conflict, ruining this perfect night. "Damn it, Louise." He stands and gestures aimlessly in the air. "I'm *trying* to explain it to you. To tell you how much I care about you. About us."

"I know." He can hear the anguish in her voice as she says the words. "But don't you understand?" she continues. "Lately I just feel torn. I *do* love you. But the whole world's out there."

She turns and walks to the edge of the park, past the paint-peeled picnic tables and toward the sound of the brook. Luke watches her as she slips through the dense shrubs and disappears into the trees. Suddenly, the whole night goes silent. No sound at all from the water, the wind, the earth. Luke senses his flesh going silent, too, growing older second by second. He stands up; he wants, more than anything, to run toward Louise, to catch up with her in the woods, to whirl her around and kiss her hard on the lips. But at that moment, he feels a strange sensation: it's as though his legs have gone numb. He can't feel the ground beneath them, and he stares up angrily at the stars, their clear light which suddenly seems so close, and so far away.

CHAPTER 8

Before going to work at Feld's, Luke plunges his shovel into the dirt at the far edge of the infield, and the tip clinks against a hard object. He bends down and picks it up, turning it over and over in his fingertips. It's tan—earth colored—and its surface is curved. Yesterday, he had uncovered a spearhead and a small, carved talisman, made of flint, shaped like a crude bird. He wrapped the pieces in tissue paper and stuffed them into the oiled pocket of his baseball glove, and the glove's thick fingers seemed to curl slowly around them. As he picks up this piece and dusts it off, he realizes it might be another bone fragment. Whatever it is, he thinks, it doesn't belong on the infield of a ball diamond. Some of the other guys on the work crew are saying that the field is probably built over an old landfill. But Luke knows it's more than that.

He sets down his shovel, stands motionless, closes his eyes. *What do I hear*, Luke wonders, *through the soil of this field? It's a vibration, a voice. But what is it saying?*

Luke never thought much about the supernatural, but now he's begun to wonder if it might be the voice of the ancients, their words sifting upward through the soil. Is it the voice of the Native American man who made the perfectly chipped beige spearhead, or the soft syllables of the woman who shaped a clay pot—now broken to triangular shards—with her fingers? Is it her fingerprint Luke sees on the rim of the curved, reddish-brown shard he found—a print he's supposed to follow around and around to the center, the heart of her index finger, the heart of the earth?

Or is it the voice of his father he feels through the soles of his Nikes, the growling voice, sometimes angry with the world, with its headlines of wars and accidents and deaths, other times complacent about it, but always puzzling in its tone? Whenever he had his mind set on something and gave an order, his voice was a turbulent river flowing downstream—either you stopped struggling and went with the current, or you tried to swim against it, which didn't get you very far.

Perhaps it's the voice of Luke's mother, a voice so far back in his life that he doesn't really remember hearing it. He pictures her soft words climbing up through the grass blades and tickling his bare ankles, then floating upward like swirls of fragrant incense. A thousand times he's tried to imagine her voice, his mind straining for it: Was it faltering and hesitant? Was it encouraging, like a gentle hand nudging his back? Or was it harsh, perhaps, after too many cigarettes, her words sounding as though they were sliding over the legs of crickets? With his father gone, he can only guess about her and the disease that, as his father told him, ate away at her until she got narrower and thinner, and eventually he couldn't even tell if she was lying in the bed.

Then he thinks of Louise's voice. *Where's her voice in all this?* This morning he envisions her, standing at the edge of the outfield, whispering his name, the word sliding from her lips. Louise is so real: she's the only one who seems to know what he thinks even before he thinks it, what he feels even before he's aware of his own emotions. At one glance, she makes his thick exterior transparent. She always claimed he was a dreamer, and she loved that. But sometimes, when he leaps too high into the dream-smeared sky, trying to defy gravity, it's Louise who brings his feet back down to the solid and loving earth. If she weren't already at work, he'd like to tell Louise everything he's been thinking. He wishes he could slip his hands around the small of her back and pull her close.

He wonders why these things he's found on the field keep distracting him, keep nudging him in his sleep. Last weekend, he woke suddenly and couldn't stop thinking about that section of a jawbone—the first object he found on the field. Unable to doze off again, he slipped out of bed and in his blue boxers walked downstairs to the basement, where he dug the bone fragment from the bottom of his duffle bag. He held it in his palm a few seconds, felt that odd, tingling, almost stinging sensation again. But it was more than stinging—it was almost as if something was rising inside his body—a fire, maybe. He closed his fingers around it, climbed the stairway to the kitchen.

Just then Louise padded down the stairs and turned the corner to the kitchen.

"What are you doing?" she asked, turning the dial of the dining room dimmer switch, which sent a filtered light into the kitchen.

"Nothing."

"It's three in the morning. You're coming up from the basement. It can't be nothing."

Luke was silent a few seconds. Then he held his hand up to her. "Not nothing. This."

Louise squinted at the object, partially obscured by Luke's big hand.

She reached over and took it from him, clicked on the fluorescent kitchen light. When the bright light fluttered on, hurting his eyes, he bumped his knee against the leg of the table, the box of Wheaties wobbling.

As Louise studied the object, she lifted one shoulder in a shrug, a shrug that Luke would have found sultry and sexy any other time but now. And, if he wasn't so preoccupied, he might have appeared sexy to her as he—bare-chested, his brown hair tousled—leaned close to her.

Louise lifted her eyes and stared at him. "What's so important that you're looking at this in the middle of the night?"

He rubbed his forehead, felt it crisscrossed with a hieroglyph of creases. He had a thousand answers for her. A million. Instead, he finally mumbled, "I don't know."

Today Luke opens his eyes. There's work to do, after all, he knows; there are mounds of dirt piled along the first baseline, where the rake, its rusted teeth pointing toward the sky, waits for him.

Luke wonders, was this field a magical place, or a sacred one, or just a field like any other field with its ordinary indentations and sinkholes, its subtle, imperfect rises and falls? Checking his pocket watch, he realizes he's almost late for work again, and he heads toward his truck. As he does, he knows one thing is certain: the field seems to have a voice. But he just can't figure out what it's saying. It speaks only once in a while, catches you off guard at that very moment when you should be listening, but your mind is spinning off in a day-dream.

CHAPTER

9

A few minutes after five o'clock, Butch Sobieski stops at his two-story Tudor-style house to let out his dog. "Hey, Dutchess, you have a good day?" he says to the black Labrador as he walks onto the porch. "I had a damn good day. Can't complain. Nope, not one bit." The dog cocks its head sideways as if it's trying to translate Butch's words. "Run, girl, run!" he calls as he lets the dog out the back screen door, watches it sprint in quick circles in the backyard. Funniest thing, he thinks—the darn dog always runs clockwise in the backyard.

Stepping back into the house, he glances at the mantle where his twenty-year-old self stares at him from a framed black-and-white picture. In the photo, he's in the middle of a wind up, about to throw the ball and shatter the glass of the frame. *Jeez*, he thinks, *I was good back then. One lucky break and I could have been in the majors.*

Next to that is a picture of his wife, Dorothy, and when he sees it, his smile fades, and he feels that familiar pang. It's ten years since the diabetes finally took her. In the portrait, taken years ago on their anniversary, Dorothy, her hair in a flip, cheeks dabbed with orangish rouge, smiles a wan smile, as if she knows something is going to catch up to her in a couple years. And a younger, thinner Butch stands near her, holding her arm as if to steady her from tipping to one side.

Everything started to shut down inside her, and the next thing Butch knew, she was gone. *Damn awful disease*, he thinks. He doesn't talk about her much to the people at city hall, or to Rollie, even. He's got a job to do every day, after all. After she died, he held himself together; those years, he poured himself into his obligations—first as sheriff, then on city council, and then eventually as mayor. It's what you do, he thinks—sometimes you just have to bury the hurt, then you move on; you think about what's next. Brick by brick, shrub by shrub, streetlight by streetlight, sidewalk by sidewalk, you're building a town, he thinks—you're building a life. You sign papers, set them on a stack, and sometimes you just have to put your past on there along with them.

The screen feels a little rough and scrapes his elbow as he holds the back door open, calling the dog back. "Good girl," he says, "good, good girl," ruffling the black fur on top of her head, her tail swishing away his loneliness. It's what you do, he thinks. Keep the dog happy. Keep it running clockwise.

After he changes out of his blue three-piece suit to a tan button-down shirt and casual tie and slacks, he strolls down to Elmer's for the Friday afternoon happy hour. He's pleased that the planning commission passed his new I-94 access plan at this morning's

meeting. County Road 16 is tailor-made for an interstate exit, he figures; the road will lead to Clearwater through the back section of
what once was Tanner land, but Butch knows that it's city land, from
the annexation that Bob Sewell researched. He thinks about the
commerce the new access to the interstate will bring; Clearwater's
the ideal halfway point between Milwaukee or Chicago to the south
and the fishing and hunting resorts to the north. After the meeting,
when Butch pushed through the doors of city hall, he glanced up at
the clock tower atop the building. At night, the big face of the clock
is lit with a yellowish glow, and at first some folks, glancing up
quickly in the evening, might confuse it with the full moon, caught in
the tall oak trees.

At the Water-in Hole, Elmer usually leaves the screen door open
when the weather gets warmer so the smoke filters out. Butch pauses
outside, notices the few dead moths, their wings crumbling on the
sill just below the eight block windows that face the street, opaque
so kids can't peer in. The usual Friday afternoon happy hour crowd is
inside; Fridays the bar features two for one on Hamms and Cold
Spring Specials. Butch sticks with the Cold Spring, as do most of the
regulars, except maybe Cyrus, who hits the harder stuff in the bottles
lined up on the lit glass shelf behind the bar.

Sliding onto a stool, Butch gazes at the glass display case in the
corner of the wood back bar, where, sitting at a miniature wood table
in a miniature tavern, a stuffed badger—wearing a cowboy hat and
tiny holster and gun—plays cards against a squirrel. The diorama
makes him smile every time he walks in.

Elmer, the fireplug-shaped bartender, looks up at Butch. "Usual,
Butch?" Butch nods, and Elmer pulls a Cold Spring from the cooler.
He pops it open, sets it on the bar in front of Butch, a tear of conden-

sation sliding down its green and white label that depicts a geyser of water spewing into the air, though there are no geysers in Clearwater.

"I s'pose you've heard the latest talk," Cyrus says, suddenly standing right next to Butch, his oversized head twitching to the side as he speaks. He worked in the mayor's office with Butch for a couple years before he retired.

"All *what* talk?" Butch pastes on an inquisitive look. He figures Cyrus is referring to the accident out on the interstate, where a truck jackknifed and slid over the median into an oncoming car, closing the westbound lane for three hours.

"About those bones. The ones turned up on the new ball field."

"Oh, yeah. That," Butch says, showing he's in the know. "I had Rollie check it out a few days ago. Nothing to it. Just some animal bone, is all."

Cyrus shifts his weight in his long-sleeved red flannel shirt, purses his lips like he's about to spit. "Not what I heard. Not what people say."

"So what are they saying?" Butch raises his voice irritably over the whine of a country music song that begins on the jukebox. *Merle Haggard?* a part of his mind wonders. *No. Johnny Paycheck. Definitely Paycheck.*

"That they're finding more stuff out there," Cyrus says, circling the last inch of liquid in his glass of Beam and water. "Tanner and his crew turned up spearheads and more bones."

"More, eh?" Butch tries to maintain a matter-of-fact tone.

In the meantime, Hans from the Rainbow Café and a couple of other men gather around Butch's bar stool and listen intently, as though this is a breaking story on Fox News.

"You bet," Cyrus nods, though the twitch in his head makes him say *No.* "Folks say they're *human* bones."

"Human?" Butch feels his teeth bite the inside of his lip, then fixes his eyes on a surprised bass that leaps from an oak board hanging on the wall.

"Yeah, human." Cyrus leans toward Butch as if he has a secret. "And that's my personal theory, too, if you ask me."

"Aw, come on," Butch says, trying to dismiss it. "That's all just gossip. Shoot, old Mrs. Zantow takes a little tumble down the stairs in the morning, and by afternoon, everybody in town thinks she's got two broken legs. You know this town, Cyrus." Butch tries to minimize things, though heat rises from his starched beige collar as he wonders why nobody told him about this development. His blue tie is a snake, squeezing his neck a little. He takes a long drink of the Cold Spring to ease the sensation.

"Yeah," Cyrus says. "I know this town." After a pause, he adds, "So, you gonna set up some kind of investigation over there?"

"I don't think that's necessary," Butch says, trying to sound casual, but irritated that Cyrus seems to be telling him his business. Though he likes Cyrus, Butch resents the fact that a couple of drinks makes him an expert at almost anything. "Right now, nothing is *confirmed*. Not when it's just some old *animal* bone. I'm on top of this, boys," he says, lowering his beer to the soggy Hamms coaster. "After all, I *am* the goddamn mayor."

Cyrus polishes off his whiskey, slaps the glass down on the bar, gestures for another one with his thick fingers, and states flatly, "Yeah. You're the goddamn mayor."

Leaving the Water-in Hole in a huff, Butch blinks as the sunlight glares off the windshields of parked cars. Pausing at the corner at the edge of Old Man Coborn's lawn, he leans over, and sees them— the first tiny green shafts of grass, growing in the moist earth near the sidewalk. It calms him down, staring at this sight a few seconds. He bends low and admires the blades, one by one—fragile green stalks, God's spring exclamation points. Then he notices, at their base, a line of small black ants. The row of tiny ants moves as one, like a writhing black thread. Fascinated, Butch bends closer, studying the row as it glides across the loam of the yard. He scowls when he realizes that the line of ants leads to the remains of a half-eaten Daylite Bakery caramel roll someone tossed out, the hundreds of ants, crawling clockwise, covering the sticky roll's surface like pepper.

CHAPTER 10

Luke pulls the cord on the lawn mower, and the mower sputters and stalls, coughing out a cloud of smoke. He pulls again, and when it doesn't start, he unscrews the gas cap. Empty.

As he rolls the mower to the garage, the wheels squeak, and suddenly he's sixteen again, hearing the creaking wheels of his father's mower that evening. His father rolled the lawn mower from the garage just as Luke was about to go out with his buddies on a Friday night. "I thought we'd mow the lawn," Dwight said matter-of-factly. His father always seemed to have that uncanny knack—or maybe it was a conscious plan—to start the lawn detail just as Luke was about to go somewhere. Luke thought of it later as a test of his loyalty, a measure of his dedication and work ethic. But that night, when his father—lean and muscular in his white undershirt and his khaki work pants—pushed the tan mower to the center of the driveway, Luke only felt resentment.

"What about tomorrow?" Luke offered. In those days, not only did Luke dislike the weekly lawn mowing detail, he simply didn't have the patience for it, for his father's methodical routines.

"No. I want to get it done before the weekend," his father countered. His voice was harsh, and Luke knew by the tone that there would be no debate. His dad leaned over the machine with a kind of coiled expression on his face. He seemed to be studying the frayed cord of the old Briggs and Stratton motor, then uncapped the gas cap and peered into it. "Did you know this thing always starts on the first pull? Amazing, eh?"

"Yeah," Luke said, having heard his father say this before. In his head, he anticipated the next sentence: *Even after sitting in the shed all winter.*

"Starts the first time. Yup, even after sitting in the shed all winter."

As his father rolled the mower to the shed to fill it with gas, Luke dug into his pocket and pulled out the keys to his late '70s Pontiac. It was a car with over eighty thousand miles on it and rust leaking on both sides of the chrome strips that ran the length of the car. Dwight had bought the car at an Army surplus auction. Luke gave it a tune-up and repainted it, covering its army green with a layer of metallic red so the car had some semblance of coolness for a sixteen-year-old. The door of the car, parked behind his father's second-hand Chrysler, beckoned him. Luke thought of his buddies, waiting for him out at the lake; he thought of the girls, toweling themselves dry as their long legs stepped out of the water and onto the beach. He spun around, jogged to the car, slid behind the wheel, and started the engine.

Backing out, Luke saw his father round the corner with the lawn mower and stop abruptly at the edge of the driveway. His father didn't look up—just kept his eyes fixed on the ground in front of him, as if he'd just come onto a patch of bristling weeds made of iron.

Luke drove alone for a few minutes along the deserted county roads near the lake; the sun had set, and the glow of his headlights seemed to be leading him where he needed to go. He turned the radio volume up, rolled down the window, and sang along loudly with Springsteen and Bon Jovi and Foreigner.

Then he saw a pair of lights flare up behind him. The car gained on him quickly, and he expected it to pass him, but it didn't. As the car edged closer, he recognized its silhouetted shape. It was the Chrysler, and inside, that lean form hunched toward the steering wheel was his father. He stayed behind Luke, flashing his brights. Luke took his foot off the accelerator, and his Pontiac coasted to the gravel shoulder of the road. For a few seconds, Luke felt short of breath, as if he'd just run the mile in gym class. Dwight stepped out of the car and, like some big-shot sheriff, stalked toward him, following the white line at the edge of the asphalt road. As his dad reached the car fender, Luke, without even thinking, floored his car, spinning up a cloud of gravel dust around his father. At that moment, Luke remembers, he didn't care where he was going; he was just trying to lose his father—lose him, leave him far behind with this world of orders and duties and lawn mowers.

In the rearview mirror, Luke saw the headlights of the powerful Chrysler closing the gap of darkness behind him. In seconds, the headlights edged within inches of the Pontiac's bumper, and Luke began to sweat as he glanced into the rearview mirror, then back at the speedometer, which read almost ninety, then into the mirror again.

It was at that moment Luke noticed another set of headlights behind them, and, a few seconds later, a red cherry light stung his eyes.

Luke gasped and yanked his foot off the accelerator, as his father must have done at the exact same moment. Both their cars, as if doing a dance, coasted gradually to a stop, keeping the same even distance between them.

Stepping from the car, Luke walked on shaky legs back to his father, who stood on the shoulder of the road next to the cop.

"What's going on here, Dwight?" he asked Luke's father. He was a county cop named Vern Wascotch they'd known around Clearwater for years.

Luke's father looked guilty, the shadows carving deep creases in his skin. When the cop pointed the flashlight upward, Luke saw his father's face become suddenly fragile, apologetic.

"Nothing, Vern," Dwight replied, his voice calm, controlled. "The boy here," he said, then paused, faltering a moment, "the boy's having carburetor trouble with his car. Tried to fix it, told him to take it out for a run on the road. Told him I'd follow in case the car killed again."

"You had to go that damn fast to test it?" Vern puffed. "Sure looked like some kind of race to me."

Luke could feel the arteries in his neck throbbing from the adrenaline. He knew a speeding ticket—especially at this speed— would cost him a big fine, and his license. His father knew that, too.

"Well, you see, the engine only killed at higher speeds," Dwight said, continuing his fabrication. "Runs like a top on city streets, though." He managed a throaty chuckle.

The cop shook his head as he shined his flashlight at their licenses, making them both appear thin, translucent. Luke saw his full name printed in black—the name his father gave him out of pride when he was born, a middle name Luke was sometimes embarrassed to admit: LUCAS DWIGHT TANNER. "I don't know who the heck to ticket here, the lead car or the one who was following." He paused.

"So I'm not going to ticket neither one of you." He shifted his stare toward Luke's father. "Just take this as a warning, Dwight. Better take care of this boy, and clear up that engine problem some other way. You can't be out racing like a couple of teenagers."

After the trooper pulled away, Luke's father didn't say anything, just looked at the opaque sky, the thick, impenetrable layer of clouds where no stars or moon appeared, then laughed a quick, sharp laugh. Luke felt that maybe everything was okay. "Thanks, Dad," he said, trying to sound confident, though his nerves were tangled and sparking like crossed distributor wires. "I mean, for bailing me out."

His father opened his callused palm. "Give me the keys," he said, his voice flat and hard like a piece of tin.

"Huh?"

"Give me the damn keys. You're walking home."

Luke lifted the keys, attached to a leather strap, from his pocket, lowered them into his dad's palm, and Dwight clenched them. But Luke didn't let them go, feeling a sudden rush of resistance. Thinking about the five long miles back to town, he held onto his end of the leather strap.

Those few seconds, as they both pulled on the keys, Luke could feel the whole world pulling on them like a tug of war—the whole world pulling them together, pulling them apart at the same time.

Then the strangest thing happened. His father released his grip, and the keys jingled into Luke's fist. Dwight closed his eyes with an expression Luke couldn't quite understand; in the dim light, Luke tried to read his face, but he just couldn't figure it out. That was the thing about Dwight Tanner—Luke was always on the verge of understanding him, but never quite could.

His father pivoted toward the Chrysler, then slipped behind the wheel. Luke thought for a second about the lawn mower his father left in the middle of their front yard. He pictured that mower, stained with oil, low on gas, sputtering, his father trying to cut a straight path through the long weeds of a field.

As he drove, Luke glanced in the rearview mirror, and the asphalt road looked pitch black. He clicked the radio off and followed closely behind his father's car, their lights cutting a column through the darkness. At one point, his father's Chrysler seemed to hesitate a little, and Luke concentrated on keeping an even distance between their two cars. Not too far back, not too close. All the while, Luke couldn't help but focus on the taillights, and wonder just how long he'd follow them, and how far, their steady red eyes neither angry nor forgiving, but simply watching him all the way back to town.

TODAY, LUKE FILLS the tank with gasoline, the amber liquid gurgling from the red can's spout, and tightens the cap. But before he pulls on the mower's cord again, he strolls back to the house. Inside, on a shelf in the den, he spots it: the bank, in the shape of a Model T car.

His dad gave it to him for his eighth birthday.

"Do the wheels spin?" young Luke asked excitedly, thinking the car, its bronze buffed to a dull shine, was a toy he could push across the linoleum kitchen floor.

"Well, no," his father explained. "They don't spin. They're stationary." Luke remembers being a little puzzled at the gift, a car with its wheels molded to the frame. Taking the car from his hand, his father turned it over, showing him a coin slot in the base. "It's a bank. See?" He handed it back to Luke. "Your job is to fill it."

Now Luke turns the bank over, stares at the stamp on its base: *Sauk County Savings and Loan.* He thinks about how his father hefted the weight of that loan around—like a heavy stone—for the last years of his life.

If his father were alive today, Luke thinks maybe he'd learn to appreciate his routines, his responsible work ethic, his practical words, like nails hammered through aluminum siding. *His goals were simple,* Luke thinks. *A lawn mower that starts every time. A toy bank to fill, as if collecting enough coins would make the future all right.*

"Thanks for the present, Dad," Luke says, his voice choked with emotion. "Stay close." Before he places it back on the shelf, Luke rubs his thumb over the rear wheel of the Model-T, and, for a moment, it's almost as if the smooth, polished wheel is spinning.

CHAPTER

11

When Sheriff Rollie needs a quick meal before he makes his early evening rounds, he stops at Jimbo's—Clearwater's only fast food place, if you can call it that. Rollie parks his squad car in front, squints at Jimbo's flaking metallic window-mirrors that you can't see through. After dinner, he'll head to the west side of town and talk to Tanner again. He figures that questioning Tanner will clear things up for Butch, who seems all ruffled up about this ball field thing and has been bugging him all afternoon on the cell phone. It is a big thing, Rollie supposes, especially if those really *are* human bones. But right now, Jimbo's is the main thing on his mind.

Inside the ten-by-twelve lobby, whitewashed wood counters line the walls, and two black telephones hang on opposite sides. Rollie knows the routine, though he's seen his share of out-of-towners who walk up to the main counter, where big Jimbo himself or Dolly—his heavy-set wife of twenty-some years—would be standing, and attempt to order. Jimbo promptly tells the patrons to order through the telephones, pointing a chubby finger just to make sure they know what he means. "Why can't I just order here?" a man asked one day, and Rollie—feasting on a JimboBurger with the works—just had to chuckle. "It's policy," Jimbo answered with enough authority that the man slunk back to the phone and picked up the receiver. Jimbo had been taking orders this way since the place opened in the early '80s, and he wasn't about to change now. Rollie knows it's the way you do things here. When the man picked up the phone, Jimbo, eight feet away, lifted his phone on the other side of the counter, held it up to his good ear, and said, as close to pleasantly as possible, "Welcome to Jimbo's. Can I take your order?"

Above the phones are the two faded French travel posters mounted on the wall, as if Jimbo's is in the middle of Paris or somewhere. Rollie shifts his eyes to the handwritten signs—pieces of cardboard held up by masking tape—that let you know you're in Jimbo's world:

If you want you're food faster,

> *go elseware.*

And next to it: *No Drinking Aloud.*

Rules, Rollie confirms. *That's what makes Jimbo's place what it is. And that's what makes my job what it is. You believe in them. You follow them. And, hopefully, the world's a little better place because of them.*

Rollie lifts the telephone receiver to his ear. "Chicken basket to go."

Rollie goes through the usual litany with Jimbo—white meat or dark, slaw with that, beverage, large or extra large, to stay or to go—even though he knows Jimbo has his order memorized.

84

"Window two," Jimbo puffs. "Eight minutes sharp." Rollie hangs up the phone, sits down to wait on a stool, trying hard not to get riled up about the ball field. It's just that Tanner and the grounds crew keep finding more things—bones, pottery, and such. Rollie knows the rumors are racing around town like a wildfire, but they don't always mean anything. There was once a rumor about Old Man Ebersole being robbed of his antique clocks and vases; he swore up and down that somebody must have a key to his house. A few weeks later, in the middle of the night, his wife caught him taking her jewelry up the attic stairway. Turns out he'd been sleepwalking and putting things in the attic; Rollie found the clocks and the whole works in a box up there.

Rollie waits, drumming his fingers on the veneer of the paneling. After fifteen years, Rollie's learned how solitary this sheriff's job can be. There's lots of routine to it, like circling the grain elevator after the boys on the second shift knock off work at nine P.M., or doing his nightly checks on the back doors of the town businesses, even Jimbo's, with its duct-taped patch on the screen and the big padlock holding it shut as though there's something really valuable inside.

This sheriff's job isn't one that attracts many women to him, and that bothers Rollie. He always thought that if he became a law enforcement officer, he'd have the women crawling all over him. But it hasn't been that way. These past couple years since he's turned forty, his job occasionally gives him a lonely feeling inside.

He recalls what it was like that January afternoon during the ice-fishing contest on Clearwater Lake in '95. He was off duty that day, and the Kiwanis Club hired him as security guard for the event. The club let him use one of their snowmobiles, and he cruised around the lake, checking for trouble, radioing back to the first aid tent when somebody passed out from too much Cold Spring and cracked their skull on the ice. He remembers how the women loved him in that black snowmobile suit and black helmet and visor. He cruised the ice all afternoon, revving the engine of that Arctic Cat, and the women smiled at him. He even gave a couple of the good-looking gals—Barb and her friend Emily—a ride from one side of the lake to the other, but when he was back in town, the helmet and suit off, those same gals didn't even give him a second look.

He could use a woman, though—a good woman. Sometimes he thinks about the sexy women he sees on TV, like Shania Twain, or Faith Hill, with her blonde tresses swaying in the spotlight. Once, in the sheriff's office, late at night, he clicked his computer to the Shania Twain Fan Club site, just to check it out. He peered at the screen, watching Shania's sexy pop-up video come to life, pictured her dancing right out of the screen and into his office—Shania, swaying with a microphone, her syrupy voice pouring over Rollie as she sang a private concert right there in the Clearwater police station. Now that would be the day, he thought.

One night, bored with his late shift, he logged into an Internet site called LoveConnection.com and entered the chat room for lonely hearts. There were no calls on the squawk box that time of night, and his deputies were off duty, so he had the place pretty much to himself. He began chatting with the woman, and since she was on Pacific time, he typed messages to her way past midnight. *Vanessa,* she called herself, and he pictured her, dark and slinky. Still, she wouldn't send a picture, wouldn't give much information about herself, except for describing her *auburn hair* and *five foot eight* and *one hundred twenty shapely pounds.* Rollie figured she might be some housewife whose husband was at work, and she had nothing to do but flirt on the net. But then, how could she trust him, either? He introduced himself as "Joe Connery," and told her he worked in high-level security. Told her he worked for the Secret Service for a while, that he actually got to guard George Bush, Jr., when he toured Wisconsin before the '04 election. He added some extra height—five inches—to himself. He told her he had black hair—not brown streaked with gray—and was *six-three* and *a hundred ninety muscular pounds.*

The thing was, when Rollie chatted with the woman, night after night, he actually started to imagine that he *was* that person: Joe Connery, Secret Service. Late at night, when they met privately over the invisible connections of the web, he actually began to feel taller, sensed his muscles bulging, saw himself wearing mirrored sunglasses and an earphone, glancing quickly left and right as he jogged beside the presidential limousine. The thing about the net was, if you could so much as point your index fingers at a keyboard and click out a word, you could be whoever you wanted to be. No one would ever hear your voice or see your face. No hard addresses, no real names. No wonder there were so many crazies and crimes on the Internet, Rollie figured; it was a great place to hide, to cover your tracks.

Then one night, when Vanessa's messages got friendlier and friendlier, Rollie typed the words *What about sex?* He was sorry the minute he keyed those words in. Her screen just went blank. She didn't answer his question that night, or any of his other messages, like when he typed *Just kidding.* Rollie figured she must have just jumped right out of that chat room, as though her husband or her minister unexpectedly walked in and peered over her shoulder. Rollie rationalized that she was probably overweight after all, with a couple of little kids running in the living room and a basket of dirty laundry next to the computer.

He never heard from her again, though he wrote her a couple more times. That was the thing about modern technology, Rollie figured. Everyone was brave, and everyone was scared at the same time. Nobody really ever knew who was dealing with whom. It was perfect, in a way, until someone broke the perfection, said something to short-circuit things. Rollie still checks his screen once in a while, looks wistfully for a message from Vanessa, as if he might someday see the words *What about it?*

"Order ten's up!" Dolly interrupts as she makes her way with his order, taking dainty little steps for such an overweight woman. It's been fifteen minutes, at least—Rollie checks his watch—but he wouldn't dare mention the order took longer than *Jimbo's Eight-Minute Guarantee* proclaims on the wall. Dolly's permed reddish hair puffs out, and it seems to add even a little more to her round, fleshy face.

"Got any of those mud bars?" Rollie asks. He has a hankering for Dolly's famous mud bars, those chocolate and caramel bars baked in a wide, flat tray.

"Nope," Dolly says. Her high-pitched voice might be musical, if it came from another woman, and no matter what, she looks everywhere but your eyes. "We're fresh out."

As Rollie leaves, another customer—no doubt an ignorant out-of-towner—struts in and tries to order at the front counter. Rollie smirks and lets the door shut behind him just before Jimbo chides the man.

While eating the chicken in the silence of his squad car, Rollie gets that lonely feeling again. His throat feels thick, as if a piece of a chicken bone was stuck there. He gulps his super-size orange soda, but he can't wash it down: the vague sensation of a dull lump, lodged somewhere in his windpipe.

Rollie stops the cruiser in front of Tanner's house. As he saunters up the front walk, the image of Louise slides through his mind, the curve of her body in those tight jeans she wears. Her long smooth neck leading to those firm, upturned breasts. Now that's a real woman. Rollie's had a little crush on her, seeing her at the Hi-Vee. He couldn't help but notice her blonde hair, tied back in a pony tail, and her spunky personality as she checked out while Rollie pretended to study the bologna-and-lettuce deli sandwiches in the glass case. The last few times he was at the casino, Louise always said hello with that friendly voice when he stopped at her cashier's booth for change, then smiled and slid some chips to him with her slim, pretty hands, saying, "Have yourself a nice evening."

He rings the doorbell, waits for an answer. He's not thrilled about talking again to Tanner, not with his surly attitude. It's already dusk, and the neighborhood is quiet—a few lights inside the gray and white wood-frame houses, a small sliver of moon cutting the horizon. To his right, he can see the vague yellowish glow from the downtown, with its antique street lamps around the town square and the two floodlights that light up the crème cupola on top of city hall. Butch said the electric bill was hell for those floodlights, but it was worth it: everyone who drove through town, even if it was three A.M., would see the top of city hall all lit up as if it were noon.

Rollie rings the doorbell again but gets no answer. He knows somebody's home, because he can see a light inside, so he follows the driveway toward the back door. The cinders crackle beneath the hard soles of his shoes. When he notices a small back window, which looks like a bathroom, he pauses, raises to his tiptoes, leans toward it. The window is cloudy, and he can hear the faint, low-pitched sound of water rushing through pipes, the higher-pitched sound of water spraying from a showerhead. He peers between the blinds, feeling his heart start to thump like a quail flapping. He takes a ragged breath, holds it. He thinks he might see the vague shape of Louise in the shower stall—he pictures her smooth body surrounded by billowing steam. He stands there a while, staring, straining his narrow-set eyes until his legs begin to shiver from standing on tiptoes. But all he sees, when the water stops and the shower door slides open, is a quick shadow—slim and lithe—moving across the wall. Then the light goes out, and the room dims, and Rollie keeps staring hard at all that steam, that damn steam that almost hurts his eyes. Then he feels the lump again, like something stuck deep in his throat, like one of Jimbo's chicken bones got caught going down.

What am I doing back here? a voice in his head suddenly asks. *What the hell do I think I'm doing?* He quickly pulls back from the window, brushes the wrinkles on his shirt from where he pressed against the siding. Hurrying around to the front, Rollie raps on the door again. This time Luke appears in front of him, and Rollie says, almost with a gasp, "Got time for a few questions?"

"More questions?" Luke crosses his arms in front of his tight gray T-shirt.

"We're starting an investigation." He gives Luke a nod to show he's confident. "About those bones." He glances behind Luke, hoping to get a glimpse of Louise in the background. "I'm gonna have to come in for a minute."

Luke shakes his head side to side in disbelief. "All right, all right," he acquiesces, and slowly opens the door. Rollie thinks he can smell the faint perfume of shampoo wafting through the room.

"Sit down, if you want," Luke motions to the table.

"Nope," Rollie says, notepad and pen poised in his hand. "I just need to have a look at what you found out there, is all."

"I'd like to show you," Luke says, stuffing one hand in the pocket of his worn jeans. "But there's one problem. That land's technically *my* land. So what I found was actually on private property."

Rollie doesn't reply for a few seconds, just sucks in his small lips so they almost disappear.

Just then, Luke recalls the scene, almost twenty years ago, when Butch Sobieski, the newly elected mayor, came to his father's house.

Butch had insisted that the land was annexed by the city in years past. "Jeez," he said, trying to appease Luke's father, "We'll call the place Tanner Park. What the heck else do you want?"

"I don't care what the hell you call it," Luke's father said. "It's still *my* land."

"But your family defaulted on paying taxes. That land was tax forfeited," Butch countered.

Luke's father glared at Butch and spoke with a calm but steel-solid voice: "You get out of here."

"Hey, let's not get that way, Dwight." Butch forced a smile. "Let's not get hard feelings here."

"You heard me." Dwight, his index finger jutting from a clenched fist, pointed at Butch. "Just get the hell out of my house."

"There's no way that's private property, Luke," Rollie is saying. "That land's public domain. The city can do with it what they want. The mayor says . . ."

"I don't give a damn what the mayor says," Luke cuts him off. "I've heard what they're planning. And there's no way they're going through with it."

"Hey, that access road's a darn good idea."

Luke's jaw tightens as he pictures bulldozers, gouging into the ground, the sod folding like a green accordion.

"But hey, let's not get sidetracked here. I just need to see whatever you found on that ball field," Rollie insists, his head bobbling. When Luke doesn't respond, Rollie puts his hands on his hips a few seconds, then finally reaches into his back pocket, pulls out the yellow, folded receipt from Jimbo's. "This is a search warrant," he says, his voice becoming scratchy and threatening. "I could turn this place inside out if I wanted to, you know." Rollie hears some rustling in the back bedroom; his eyes flick over Luke's shoulder, and he catches a glimpse of Louise's reflection in a wall mirror—she's wearing cutoffs and a blue T-shirt, a pink towel wrapped around her head. The back of her neck looks moist, damp; the hallway light gives it a sheen.

"Is somebody there, honey?" she calls to Luke.

"Nobody," Luke answers.

She turns and disappears into a back room.

The way Luke says *nobody* infuriates Rollie, and he wonders how such a gorgeous woman can put up with a bullheaded guy like Luke.

"So let's have it," Rollie commands. "I need to see that evidence. Now."

"Go ahead and look. But it'll take you all night, and you still won't find it."

Rollie swallows hard as if to clear some sawdust from his throat. "So you're not cooperating, then, I take it."

"I'm cooperating." Luke grins smugly, holding his arms out to his sides. "I'm saying go ahead and look, if you want to."

Rollie scowls, hears the high-pitched whine of a hair dryer through the closed door. "I don't have time for all this right now," he finally says, waving his receipt in the air. He raises himself on tiptoes so he's almost Luke's height. "I've got another call to take care of." He pauses for emphasis. "But I'll be back here." Rollie wishes his voice was lower, more booming, so it would have more authority. Still, he likes the way the words sound, and though it could be a little melodramatic, an image of an Arnold Schwarzenegger movie flickers through his mind, so he goes with it and plays it to the hilt. "You damn well better know that I'll be back."

CHAPTER 12

How is a son supposed to follow the rules of his father? Luke wonders as he sits alone eating dinner tonight. With Louise on the late shift, he's made his own meal: mac and cheese, a Kaiser roll, microwaved peas on the side. *Is he supposed to follow them at all? And what if his words and advice always seemed cryptic, or just plain contradictory?*

"LIFE'S A CIRCLE, I s'pose," his father sighed one afternoon as he was repairing a combine in the shop, "and you'll find yourself at the same place on it once in a while. Then you go around it again." He gave a tight smile to the green sheet metal, the Lucky between his lips wiggling as he spoke. "Or so I read in an article in the barber shop the other day."

Luke tossed him a puzzled look; at eight years old, he wasn't sure what his father meant. "Sounds like one of those Indian sayings," he said, having read some books on Indian lore in grade school.

Dwight looked up from trying to loosen a tough bolt, took a long drag from the cigarette, and then pulled it from his lips. "What do *you* know about Indians?" he asked.

Luke shrugged.

"Don't ever trust an Indian," Dwight grumbled. "At least most of the time." His words clicked harshly, like ball bearings.

"What do you mean?"

Dwight took a final drag on the cigarette, exhaled, and flipped the butt outside onto the stained concrete past the double-wide garage doors. Beyond that, the back lot loomed with the tin dinosaurs of crippled, steadily rusting John Deere corn huskers and hay balers. "It's not that they're swindling you," he told Luke. "It's just that they make promises they can't keep. They know what they want, but they just don't have what it takes to back it." Luke knew his father was referring to some of the men from the reservation who had come in to buy a snowblower or Lawn Boy from the store on time payments and then failed to pay their bills.

Dwight grabbed a shop vacuum, clicked the button, and began vacuuming some iron filings beneath the bench, the motor's roar filling the small room.

When Dwight switched the vacuum off, Luke offered, "I know some Indian kids in my class. They're not that bad."

His father's jaw seemed to tighten, like when his teeth bit down on a bone in a fish fillet. He picked up a dulled wrench and pointed it at Luke. "It'd be a good idea to just stay away from them. A real good idea."

Dwight grunted as he went back to loosening the bolt on the sheet metal. The wrench kept sliding off the bolt, and his father's arm

jerked suddenly as if he were elbowing someone in the ribs. "Shit,"
he said under his breath. "Gol damn. Gol damn it all." Luke thought
about how those wide pieces of sheet metal, leaned in the corner,
made a sound like thunder when he picked them up and shook them.
And if you grabbed them the wrong way, their rusted edge cut your
palm.

"So, what about that circle?" Luke asked. "I mean, where are we
on it?"

"Don't know." His father stood up and looked toward Luke, but
not really at him. His stare was aimed more at the parts boxes, oil
stained and stacked on the wooden shelf in back. His red and beige
Dwight name patch on the front of his shirt was smudged. He
strolled to the gouged wooden workbench, leaned over, studying the
contents of a corroded red toolbox. Finally he grabbed a bigger
wrench. "What I do know, I guess, is that wherever we are, it's surrounded by a shit load of sheet metal." He chuckled, as if pleased
with his analogy. "Yeah, sheet metal, and lots of stubborn bolts."

Later that fall, Luke hunted for grouse with his father, who strode
through a dried cornfield cradling a shotgun in the crook of his arm.
They walked up and down the dry symmetrical rows of yellowed
corn stalks, his father wearing an oversized army-green hunting
jacket with pockets on the inside where you could keep the game.

A large grouse burst in front of them, the thump-thump-thump
sound of its wings drumming the air. Dwight instinctively raised the
rifle to his shoulder, trained the barrel on the arc of the bird's flight,
and fired. The bird's wings stopped mid-flutter, and it dropped in a
twisting spiral to the field, a few feathers circling behind it.

Luke jogged excitedly toward the grouse. "You got it!" he yelled
as he ran. "Good shot, Dad!"

Luke bent over the bird and suddenly felt a little disturbed by its feathers, spattered with blood from the shotgun pellets. He watched as its small eye seemed to stare at him a moment, and then a translucent sheath slowly closed over it. His father stalked up to him from behind, the dried husks of corn cracking beneath his leather boots. "Think we should say a prayer for it?" Luke asked.

"Now why the heck would you do that?"

"Because. I read that's what the Indians did."

"Is that so?" the skepticism in his dad's voice was like a file on a rough edge of metal. "Well, I think I'll skip the prayer. We're taking the bird home. Then we'll clean it and eat it for dinner."

"But what about the prayer?"

Dwight straightened and stared at the flat line of the horizon beyond the ragged rows of cornfields. "I used to pray, sometimes." His voice dropped. "Before your mother was gone."

Luke blinked like there was a speck of corn chaff in his eye. Those past years, his father—once a devout churchgoer, Sunday usher, and volunteer for Catholic Charities—had been taking him to church less and less often, and when Dwight did attend Mass, he seemed to go through the rote motions of kneeling, of reciting the Mea Culpa, of bowing his head for the benediction.

Dwight ran his palm over the polished wooden stock of the rifle. "I don't know what those Indians were praying for. Seems like it didn't get them very far. Look where they ended up."

"Where?" Luke asked naively. "The reservation?"

His father shook his head and chuckled, the sound coming out raspy from one-too-many Lucky cigarettes. He bent to one knee next to the grouse.

"Dad, remember that arrowhead collection?" Luke asked as his father picked up the bird. "Those points are pretty cool, right?" Luke thought about the way he and his father used to hunt for arrowheads in the fields around town, about how his father proudly displayed the beige and pink arrowheads in a glass display box on the wall. He remembered his father's face glowing with amazement when, after sifting through some soil in a nearby field, he turned up a perfectly symmetrical arrowhead amid all the plain, round stones. Dwight held it up like a prize fish he just caught and rubbed the caked dirt from it, tracing his fingers along its notches and back and forth across its frozen rippled surface.

"Yeah," Dwight conceded. He slipped the limp grouse into the inside pocket of his hunting jacket. As they walked the half mile back to the truck, Luke thought he could see a faint blood stain spreading through the front of the jacket.

Tonight, finishing his dinner, Luke thinks about his father's words, his rules, his riddles. He stands from the table, and as he does, he catches a side glimpse of himself in the dining room mirror. For a few seconds he sees his father, thirty years ago in his office. Sees him gazing at the wall, lifting a dull pencil, and then leaning toward the newest in a series of yellowed Tanner Implement calendars dating back to the '50s. Sees him marking off, with a thick X, another square.

CHAPTER 13

Luke and Louise sit watching the ten o'clock news on opposite sides of the blue floral sofa. Small and dark, the living room of their rental house seems to close them in. The windows, facing the street, are askew, their park-bench green painted frames slanted slightly. Luke often thought that if there were no carpeting, he could drop a tennis ball on one end of the living room, and it would roll to the other side. Ever since their picnic at Man Mound Park, there's been a lingering tension between them. Luke hates it that they haven't spoken much for a few days, and when they do, their words—steering as far away from emotion as possible—are businesslike and curt, cutting the days into small, manageable chunks.

As a breeze billows the translucent gauze curtains, Louise tucks one bare foot under her thigh and crosses her arms. It's a motion that seems languid and practical at the same time. "I suppose you're getting up early again?" she asks. The seemingly idle question has a slight edge to it.

Luke stares at the Motorola, a TV they bought one Saturday morning at a garage sale. Images of an earthquake flicker across the screen.

On the news, a rescue crew pulls someone—coated with dust so you can't see his face—out of the rubble. Luke can't tell if the limp body is dead or alive. "Yeah. I've got to drop off some fencing at the field. Before work." He picks up his glass of milk from the blonde Formica end table, takes a sip.

"You and that baseball field." She glances down at the stains on the carpet, then at the framed Monet print on the wall, a print that always looks crooked because of the lines of the walls. In the painting, gold fish swim inside a thick glass bowl. "It's all you talk about lately. You're out there every day."

"So?" The word is heavy and solid. "I'm trying to get it done." He clicks the TV off with the remote, the images of a collapsed city disappearing from the screen. "And you're on the late shift at the casino. Or you're tutoring."

She turns toward him with a frown. She's looking at the creases on his forehead, he knows it. It's those creases that seem to dig deeper—infinitesimally—each day, those creases that rob his forehead of its smooth pond of skin. And some times he feels that, because she sometimes traces them with her fingertip, she's pushing them in deeper.

Luke leans toward her beneath the yellow glow of the wicker lamp. "The team needs a field to play on, you know." He wants her to feel his desperation, to understand it, but he can't quite put it into words. "And I want to be on that team. Not want to, really. *Have to.*"

"Boys and their games," she exhales. Standing, she rinses the dinner plates in the kitchen sink. He hears the hard surface of the dishes clinking. "And I suppose you and your buddies are going out again tomorrow night?" She lets the question hang in the air.

"Maybe for just one or two," he admits, justifying his weekly night out with his buddies. "We play cards. We have a good time."

When she doesn't respond, he steps into the kitchen. "I'll clean up the dishes later," he offers, thinking that maybe it's time for this glacier of an impasse to begin to melt. He knows he's perpetuated the iciness as much as she has. Hurt by her rejection, he's been stubbornly putting up a roadblock whenever she hinted at a compromise. "Okay?"

"Did it occur to you that I was watching the news when you clicked it off?" she says.

"Oh." He holds the remote toward her. "Here." He smells the lemony scent of Joy detergent mixed with a faint musty scent from the garbage disposal.

"Never mind," she says, stacking the dishes in the cupboard and drying her hands on a paper towel. "I wasn't paying attention anyway." She tosses the towel in the waste basket, then whirls around and faces him, her face flushing with emotion. "Luke, I want it to work," she says, almost pleading. "I want us to work all this out."

"So do I. Then what's stopping us?"

"I don't know," she replies, her voice frayed with sadness. "What's stopping us?" The question lingers a few seconds in the diffused fluorescent light of the kitchen.

Through the open window, he hears the low moan of the train whistle on the south side of Clearwater, and he feels it again—that distance between them, like they're riding on two separate boxcars pulling in opposite directions. He can sense, right through his shoes, the scraping, the aching of the steel wheels against the tracks.

At the Wildlife Bar and Grill, Luke and his buddies slap cards—aces, kings, queens—onto the beer-sticky surface of the table as they play poker and sheepshead.

"I fold," Lance says as they finish the last hand.

"Same here," says Luke. "Anybody for some ball?"

"Sure," Lance says, and the rest nod.

The four of them chug down what's remaining from their glasses of Old Milwaukee, exit the bar, and cross the street to the courthouse lawn for what has become their Wednesday evening ritual.

In the darkness, with Luke standing over the plate—a city hall dedication plaque—Lance does an exaggerated wind-up, then hurls the phantom ball. Luke takes a quick swing with an imaginary bat. Dale and Mick, playing the outfield—which is really the green area by the WWI cannon—dash to their left. One of them calls for the ball, catches it with his imaginary glove, then throws it back in to Lance, who one-hands it casually. "Easy out!" Lance calls.

Old Cyrus, making his way home from Elmer's Water-in Hole after his nightly dose of Jim Beams, wavers on the sidewalk and peers at them, his head shaking sideways. Not able to see a ball flying in the air or a bat in Luke's hands, he slurs, "What the hell? What in the *hell?*"

"Hey, Señor Smoke!" Luke goads Lance. "I need a better pitch than that!" Luke feels dizzy and is a little wobbly, having had a couple more beers than he intended to. "Give me one over the heart of the plate," he says, pointing to the bronze plaque in front of him.

"Okay, Lukey," Lance says, taking a deep breath and puffing his cheeks in mock concentration. "One Nolan Ryan laser beam, comin' up!" He peers in at the phantom catcher, shakes off a couple of signs, then winds up, throws another one.

Luke watches the imaginary fastball zip toward him, takes a quick, hard swing, connects, and then points to the sky, laughing, as he watches the ball rise up, up, and over the courthouse roof in an impossibly high drive.

"Nobody catches that one," he says, as Dale and Mick, laughing, scramble backward, waving their arms and bumping into each other in an exaggerated collision, "Nobody."

When Luke returns at eleven o'clock, Louise is already in bed, but she's not asleep. When he appears in the frame of the bedroom doorway, lit only by the night light plugged into the wall, she climbs out of bed, floats close to him, and kisses him softly.

Pulling back, she says, "You taste like alcohol." After a hesitation, she adds, "And it reminds me of something."

"What?"

"The way Denny used to smell when he'd come back late."

"I only had a couple beers," Luke says, more defensive than he intended to sound. "And I'm *not* Denny."

As she studies him, Luke notices that her face, in this dim half-light, looks almost bruised, though he knows it's not. Then, without another word, she turns, her silky nightgown sighing, and slides back into bed, pulling the sheet halfway over her face.

Alone in the living room, Luke sits in front of the dark screen of the TV. The pilled fabric of the sofa feels scratchy on the back of his shoulders, through his worn T-shirt. He finishes a glass of milk, lowers it to the end table, stares for a few seconds at the residue, clouding the side of the glass.

The next morning before work Luke lingers in the front doorway.

"I guess I'm off," he says to Louise. "See you."

"Yeah," she replies as she slides her casino uniform from a hanger. "Bye."

"We'll talk things out tonight. After work. Okay?"

She looks up and gives him a tentative smile.

On the top step of the porch, as Luke inhales the sweet, moist air of the warm morning, he feels a sensation of an energizing sap rising through his body and into his limbs. It's a sign of a fresh start, as spring always is, he thinks, and he has the notion—however idealistic—that things are going to change. In the early light just after sunrise, the tulip buds nudge through the soil in the flowerbed in front of his house, their light green, tentative points surprising the black soil. He leaps over the two steps, lands gracefully on the uneven sidewalk, and jogs to his truck.

There he sees his duffle bag stuffed behind the seat, thinks about how he had pulled the ancient bone from beneath his ball glove late last night. He leaned close and studied the bone, thought for a moment about the ancient person, a chieftain, maybe, wandering through the densely wooded bluffs and then making camp in the lush, verdant valley near the Clearwater River. Luke wondered: *Why did this person's bones end up, of all places, beneath the soil of the ball field?* He stared at the yellowed surface of the bone—hardened like porcelain by centuries—and wondered about its secrets. At that moment, the bone seemed to become heavier and heavier in his hand, and it took all the muscles in his arm just to hold it up.

Today, riding along the bumpy, cinder-coated alley, he notices the way the morning light reflects off the small crystal dangling from the rearview mirror—a crystal Louise bought for him on a trip to the Black Hills. "Look," she had said as she held it up in the kitchen window. "It's so tiny, but it catches the whole sun."

He knows what needs to be done this morning at the ball field before he heads for work. He'll finish the sod in center field, flatten out the coiled, concentric green and black rolls, then he'll pull out the sprinklers and watch the arcs of water spurting their rainbows into the air. Next, he'll unroll the fence wire along the baselines. Five weeks from now, the bleachers will rise, tier by wooden tier, from the ground behind the backstop. The fans will climb on them until their foreheads touch the sky. *Beautiful*, he thinks.

When the field is finally finished, baseball will begin, and he'll have his second chance at playing the game he loves. Everyone deserves a second chance; he embraces that thought, believes it deep down in his gut. He pictures himself running so fast across center that maybe he'd grow younger with each step. He'll be a smooth-faced kid and a thirty-seven-year-old all at once.

As he approaches the place where the road dead-ends at the ball field, he sees the sky as clear as he's ever remembered seeing it. So deep blue, he could stare at it all day.

Then something—a thin, yellow bar—cuts his vision. His eyes sting, and he blinks and looks again: the line cuts into the deepening green of the ball field. He slams his foot on the brake, steps out of his truck to get a better look. The yellow plastic tape snakes all the way around the outfield, wrapped clumsily around aluminum posts, and on the pilings where the backstop will be. Luke gasps as he sees the whole field is sectioned off. He sees the tape vibrating in the breeze, can hear the fluttering sound it makes as it vibrates. He notices them in the parking lot, leaning against the side of the blue and white sheriff's cruiser: Rollie, dressed in uniform with his black patrolman's cap, a deputy next to him, and, nearby, paunchy Mayor Butch Sobieski in his too-tight blue polyester suit, smoking a cigarette.

Luke feels anger coiling inside him, and the next thing he knows, he's leaning his body into a run. He's sprinting across the back of the park, ducking beneath the low branches of the pine trees, and crossing the clearing toward the place where the outfield fence will be. Then, gasping, he raises his arms and breaks the yellow tape with the words *Police Line Do Not Cross* printed on it in thick black letters. He runs onto the field, racing like he's trying to get under a high fly ball dropping toward the ground. It's when he slows to a jog in the center of the field that he feels it. A hand grasps his shoulder, an arm clamps his midsection, and though his legs keep churning, it's as if he's trying to run through thick, sucking mud. His knees buckle, and he falls hard to the soil; the air is crushed from his lungs, and they squeeze out a painful sound: *Uhhhhh!*

"You're under arrest," the brawny deputy is saying as he leads Luke toward the squad car and pushes him into the rear seat.

"What the hell? Why are you arresting me?" Luke says incredulously, panting hard, though his bruised ribs make it hurt to breathe.

"For crossing a police line," Rollie says smugly, looking him straight in the eyes. "You broke right through it. Don't tell me you didn't see it."

"You can't do this!" Luke shouts as Rollie slams the car door shut, and suddenly Luke feels smothered, surrounded by the silence of the police car: the heavy black enameled doors with no handles, the smudged panel of Plexiglas that separates the front and rear seat, the thick, tinted windows that turn the whole blue sky gray.

CHAPTER 14

The jail cell smells like cheese puffs. Burly ex-football linebacker Arnie Bronson reaches into the super-sized generic Cheetos bag with his thick fingers, pulls out the puffs, and gnaws on them one by one. The chomping sound irritates Luke and makes him want to chuckle at the same time. Then Luke notices another scent—one rising from his shirt collar, and it's a scent Luke hates: his own uncertainty, his fear—the pungent smell of not knowing what's happening next in his life.

"Did you make that phone call?" Luke calls to Arnie.

"Huh?" the big man says, walking toward the cell, his mouth rimmed with yellow-orange dust.

"The phone call. Did you make it?"

Arnie wiggles his pug nose like a rodent. "Oh. Yeah, I sure did." Luke hears his footsteps in the foyer and the beeping sound of him dialing his cell phone.

Luke leans over the sink and wipes his temples and the back of his neck with a wet paper towel, as he's done repeatedly since Sheriff Rollie threw him into this place. He pictures Rollie, filled with self-importance as he escorted him to the jail, strutting in front of the townspeople by the courthouse. He puffed up his little bony chest like one of those birds, inflating its feathers to impress the other birds on the prairie. *The nerve of him,* Luke thinks, *threatening to lock my wrists together with handcuffs. Rollie, the big-time crime fighter.*

The cell is spartan: a stainless steel toilet with no lid, a cot with a thin mattress pad—its cover yellowed with odd-shaped stains Luke prefers not to think about—and a wall sink with a cloudy plastic glass and a small stack of industrial brown paper towels. *It has Rollie's touch, all right,* he thinks. *That small-town Alcatraz décor.* The Lava soap balanced on the edge of the sink is worn to a smooth-edged lozenge. There's nothing you could use for a jailbreak or hurt yourself with, Luke muses, except maybe the three walls themselves, with their huge solid grayness. The initials of a few petty inmates—probably tossed in here for driving without a license, drunk and disorderly, or minor theft—are etched into the concrete, barely visible beneath the thick layers of paint, and Luke idly runs his fingers over them.

At the top of one wall there's a second-story window that faces the town, and if he stands on his tiptoes, Luke can see across the treetops and all the way to the field. *His* field. He squints and thinks he can make out the shapes of the mayor and a few bigwigs from city council. He'd do it again, Luke tells himself—he'd rush out onto the new sod of the field and dare them to arrest him. They seem to be pacing off the field in their black street shoes—these paunchy men taking methodical, measured steps. *No athletes, these guys, that's for sure.* He couldn't picture any of them tracking down a fly ball. He shakes his head, thinks about the stupid arrest scene for the hundredth time. Thinks about Butch and his damn commission, planning to build a county road through the back acres of his family land. He balls up a paper towel, throws it at the wall. He picks it up, throws it again, hard, but it just flattens against the concrete with a damp *slap.*

A woman's voice from the dispatch room filters down the hall—he recognizes the resonant voice, saying his name. *Louise.* He can't tell exactly what she's saying to the deputy, since she speaks in a low murmur, but he loves that voice, needs its melody to fill him right now.

"Louise?" Luke calls out as he grips the bars of the cell, their coldness penetrating to the bones of his knuckles. He feels almost primitive in this place. He wishes he could, like King Kong, rip the bars apart and break free. He'd lift Louise in his hand, falling in love with her as he studies her like a precious jewel.

Louise appears, stuffing her checkbook back in her handbag as she follows the large form of the deputy to Luke's cell. Luke thinks he sees her smiling, but her lips are pulled taut—nothing close to a smile. Arnie unlocks the cell, creaks the door open, and motions Luke out.

Luke reaches his arms toward her, but Louise's stare stabs him like the point of a scissors. "I can't believe I had to come here from work to bail you out." She clenches her car keys. "Luke, what the heck's *going on?*"

Luke smiles at her sheepishly and, for a second, tries to make light of his situation. "Tanks for springin' me, kid," he says, doing a bad imitation of a '40s movie convict.

"This is unbelievable," she says, in no mood for his humor. "You got *arrested* for crossing a line?"

Luke's first impulse is to grab her and hold her tightly, but not the way she's standing there, arms stiffly at her sides, as if her body is made of titanium. "Yeah, I did," he says. "But it's that idiot Rollie . . ." he stammers. "And Butch. They're blocking it. The field, I mean. They're . . ." As he tries to explain, the words, on the way to his lips from his brain, get all jumbled up, boxcars of a train derailing.

"Never mind the explanation," she says curtly.

Luke lowers his gaze to the gray disks of flattened gum on the concrete floor. "I really *am* glad you came," he says appreciatively. Again he reaches to hug her; this time she hugs him briefly, then pulls away with an awkward twist of her shoulders. For an instant he wonders if Louise notices the scent. It's Luke's own, disgusting scent, not the aroma that emanates from him when they make love—that aromatic, yeasty smell—but an acrid scent of someone burning from the inside out.

She pivots on her low black heels and walks briskly down the hallway.

After Louise steps outside, Arnie slides behind his desk with the half-empty bag of cheese puffs and a mini television set tuned to the soaps. Unlocking a scratched black safe, he pulls Luke's belongings from it. He lifts them ceremoniously in the air with a smirk. He hands them to Luke one by one, as if he's distributing Halloween candy: his father's pocket watch, a few coins, a concave wallet, a leather belt, a gold-leaf high school class ring, and a shriveled Rawlings batting glove with a hole worn through the palm.

When Luke pushes through the tarnished bronze door and hurries down the granite steps, Louise is already behind the wheel of her El Camino. Before she can back out, Luke jumps into the passenger's side.

"Luke, I've got to get back to work."

"Listen, I really am sorry . . ." He wants to veer this conversation back to the old tenderness they once felt.

"I'm sorry too," she interrupts, "sorry you don't care as much about *me* as you do about your baseball. And that field." Her fingers open and close on the steering wheel. "Don't you see? You're letting it take over your life."

"I just don't want to lose that field. Not an inch of it."

"The field isn't everything, Luke."

"Maybe it is. To me, anyway."

"You know, there's a whole world going on outside this stupid little town."

"I realize that," he sighs. "But I have to figure out my life here. What's mine and what's my father's. I can worry about the rest later." He rubs the biceps of his right arm. "I don't understand why you can't see that."

"I do see that," Louise responds. "But what you don't see is that you never finished your degree, and maybe you're okay with that. Maybe you're okay with settling in Clearwater and hanging out with your buddies. Maybe just sitting on the porch reading the damn paper every night is what makes you happy. But I need more than that."

"Why are you so restless all the time?" Luke says through his teeth.

She clicks the ignition with a quick motion of her wrist, and the El Camino revs. The radio crackles on a faraway country station. "Restless?" Anger draws pink circles on her cheekbones, and her voice magnifies to a near shout. "You call me *restless* because I want to better myself? Don't you get it, Luke? I just feel like . . . like I'm suffocating here."

"Maybe I don't get it," he snaps back at her, matching her volume. "I guess I don't get it at all!"

"Just go, Luke," she says, her voice shaking as she pushes back tears. She swallows hard, then chokes out the words slowly, as if she really doesn't want to say them: "Just go. I can't talk to you any more."

"Good," he spits. "Fine with me. I'm sick of talking to *you.*"

He jumps from the upholstered seat, slams the door, which bumps against the seat belt and stays ajar. When he reaches to close it again, she speeds off. Trailed by dust and a bluish exhaust that makes Luke blink, the car disappears around the corner on Center Street.

Luke is hours late for work at Feld's Sod Company. Clifford, his foreman and the owner of the business, grunts, "Where the hell you been?"

"Nowhere," Luke says, and he stalks to the back lot, jumps onto a forklift, and begins loading rolls of sod onto the back of their delivery truck.

Clifford follows him to the forklift, a stub of a cigar in his mouth. "Next time," he says, raising his voice over the motor of the forklift, "try calling when you're going to be this goddamn late. We got deliveries overdue."

Luke doesn't answer, just stares at the roll of sod as he lifts it above a truck, lets it fall to the flatbed with a *thump.*

"Hear me, Tanner?" Clifford demands, irritated.

"Yeah," Luke finally says. "I hear. I *hear.*"

For the next few hours, Luke talks to no one, though others from the crew work close by. He thinks about what Louise said about not finishing his degree. He excelled in his classes in college, and though he couldn't really explain why, he just simply lost interest near the end. "Ever think you're a classic underachiever?" Louise asked him once, and maybe she was right. Maybe he *couldn't* finish things; maybe he always dropped out at that very moment before he reached his goal. *And now I'm here,* he thinks. *Taking orders from some hick boss in a sod company.* He considers how long it's been since he picked up novels like *Farewell to Arms* or *Moby Dick,* books he'd read and reread, books he used to love. The day he returned from college, he dumped them into the donation bin at the local Goodwill. That day, jumping back into his pickup, he felt the oddest sensation, as if the bumper of his truck was attached to a thick rope, and downtown Clearwater was a deep sea. *Don't leave again,* the town seemed to be calling to him as it pulled him in. *Stay.*

Now, as he maneuvers the forklift, he stares into the rolls of sod; their green and black spirals keep drawing his vision to their centers, their core, where everything is silent. Then he hears the same sounds he hears each day: the boss's radio playing scratchy country music on WCLR, the muted ringing of the black rotary phone on the office desk, the hypnotic purring drone of the fork lift's motor.

After work, Luke drives home with a small bouquet of wild flowers he picked behind the back lot—they're a token of apology for Louise. Not a big token, but something, at least, to give her before they talk. He's not sure what kind the purple and white flowers are, but she'll know their name, he figures; Louise always knows things like that. When he pulls up in the alley behind their house, the weathered, asphalt-shingled garage doors are propped open with two-by-fours, just like they were this morning. As the wind picks up, one door sways, creaking against its hinge. Maybe she parked in front, he thinks.

As he steps into the entryway, he notices the scent. He inhales it, taking it deep into his chest: the scent of Louise, filling the house with its sweetness. He bought her a bottle of the lavender body wash for her birthday, after he noticed her gazing at their framed dining room poster of a field of purple lavender outside a picturesque medieval village in Provence, France. "Take me there some time," she had whispered to him one evening, to which he had replied, "I will."

But when he reaches the bedroom, he realizes something's wrong. Her closet doors are open. Hangers cling to the corroded pole, their black wire mouths straight and expressionless, mocking him. He opens the dresser: no knit tops, no silky nightgowns, no underwear, only specks of lint, and the empty rose-colored wood, dovetailed and interlocked in the corners. He hears himself gasp the word *Shit!*—a sound like the tip of a rusty shovel pushing into the earth.

He stands in front of the bedroom mirror, glancing at himself, then into the drawer, then back at himself again. Louise's words bounce back and forth through his skull: *I feel like I'm suffocating here.*

He grabs the bouquet from a table, the stems still wrapped in wet Kleenex, tosses it into the waste basket. All that remains of Louise is a scent that permeates the house, a scent that's so overpowering now that it's beginning to nauseate him. The aroma gets stronger and stronger as he nears the bathroom, where he finally finds its source—her bottle of body wash, shattered in the bathroom sink. He picks up a few pieces of the broken glass. *Did she accidentally drop it?* he wonders. *Or did she throw it down hard, shouting "To hell with you, Luke!"* He stares at the flowers of red blood opening in the white porcelain sink, their thin stems meandering across his palm from the cuts where sharp shards sliced his fingers.

PART

1

CHAPTER

15

When Luke presses the Play button, the red light stops blinking, but there's no voice on the answering machine. He had hoped it was Louise, calling him to explain; instead, there's just a kind of hissing sound, grating in his ears like sandpaper. After a few seconds, there's a sigh and a click as the caller hangs up. He plays the message again and again. "Louise?" he says aloud, as though she would answer. The sigh is flat, indifferent, and he can't detect the emotion in it. He leans close to the machine, putting his ear right next to the speaker, and he's not certain if it's a sigh at all, or just a sound on the worn tape as it winds around and around itself. Then the message ends, the five high-pitched beeps drilling into his skull.

Luke drops the stick shift of his pickup into first, and it makes a low-pitched clunking sound, the gears not quite meshing. Driving down the block, he sees the picture windows throw yellow squares of light onto the lawns. Inside the living rooms—couples, sitting on sofas or La-Z-Boys, talk and eat snacks from TV trays. As he passes house after house, there's a crush of loneliness inside the cab of the truck; he grips the thin steering wheel a little harder. *Where would she go?* he wonders. *Her mother's house in Portage? Her sister's in Madison?*

He passes through an intersection beneath the diffused glow of the streetlight. Or maybe, he thinks, she'd just drive and drive to the west until she disappeared, dropping right off the edge of the flat-lands. As he pulls to the stoplight on Fifth and Center, he takes a drink from a can of Cold Spring Special, finishes it, tosses it to the floor mat, then opens another from the six-pack on the seat beside him. When he clicks the pop-top, the beer splatters the windshield. He stares at the pattern on the glass and, beyond it, beyond the town lights, the faint sprayed pattern of the stars in the clear night sky. He takes a long drink, the rim of the can clinking against his teeth; the beer, confined too long to its aluminum can, tastes bitter and metallic.

He wants more than anything to talk to her right now, to find the words to tell her he's sorry about everything—about her having to bail him out of jail, about making her feel like she's tied down to this town.

"So," he said tentatively to Louise two nights ago as they ate in the dining room, "maybe we should talk about our plans."

"Plans?" she uttered after a few seconds, then stared down at the last few strands of spaghetti on her plate, the noodles intertwined in a pool of tomato sauce. She knew he was talking about his proposal, though, by the hesitant look on her face. Inside the pause, the branches from the shrubs outside the window scratched their fingernails against the panes of glass in the gusting wind. "I've got a lot to get ready for work tomorrow," she finally said, lowering her fork to the plate.

"Like what?"

"I made a mistake adding some totals yesterday, and I never do that." Weeks before, she never would have been so businesslike, so curt. Weeks before, she might have pushed the work aside, cupped the sides of his face with her sleek hands, and pulled him to her waiting lips. "I love you, Luke Tanner," she might have whispered. But that night she pushed herself away from the table, and it rocked a little on its uneven legs. In the bedroom, she clicked on the lamp above the desk, then reached back to close the door. The door Luke had promised to fix stayed open a few inches. She pushed at it again, and it sprang back. "I thought you fixed this hinge."

"I'll get to it," Luke said, "Soon." He stared at the print hanging in the hallway, a flock of geese caught inside the dark wood frame.

"*Soon* means *never* for you."

"Hey," he said defensively, staring at her tight-lipped face, framed in the narrow rectangle between the door and the dark wood molding, "I've been busy with things after work, you know."

"What things?" The way she said the flat wafers of those words, he knew this conversation wasn't just about doors.

"We're measuring the dimensions. For the outfield, I mean." He knew how overly practical his words sounded as soon as they emerged. They weren't about the way he was feeling; they weren't about romance or love, but he said them anyway.

Her eyes narrowed as if she were looking through blowing dust. "Is that all you care about? Just some field where you pace off the dimensions?"

Luke crossed his arms, a roadblock. "It's not just *some field.*"

She stepped close to him as if she wanted to reply, to say more, as if she wanted him to say more. She looked at him with vulnerable, pleading eyes, then turned, stepped back into the bedroom, and pushed the door shut, hard.

There it was again, he thought, the broken record of their argument. He could hear her drag something in front of the door—a chair, maybe, or the wood table, keeping it shut.

"Louise," Luke called, but she didn't answer. For a moment, he thought he heard her sobbing lightly. He leaned his cheek against the hollow-core door, waiting for her to say something, waiting to feel the vibration of her voice through the wood, but there was no sound—only the faint, high-pitched wheeze of the springs as she lay back on the bed.

As HE REACHES the town square, he glares at the town clock, its round yellow face caught in the tips of the elms. Eight thirty already, and no sign of her. Coasting slowly past the theater, the light bulbs on its marquee darkened and cool, Luke recalls the times he and Louise saw movies there. He remembers, on one of their first dates, feeling embarrassed by the high school kids making out behind them in the back row, but, at the same time, when Louise's hand found his in the dark, he wanted to kiss her passionately, to moan softly like those high schoolers. The next thing he knew, he *was* leaning toward her like a sixteen-year-old; he *was* kissing her. And like a passionate teen, she was kissing him back.

After the movie, as they strolled in the park, she joked, "I guess we're competing with the teenagers. So, how do you think we *made out?*"

Luke smirked, grabbed her around the waist. "Oh, we took first place. I'm sure of it."

He passes the two-story rectangles of the downtown stores with cardboard *Closed* signs hanging from strings inside their windows. No cars parked inside the yellow paint of the stalls; no El Camino. It's just Luke, drifting like Ishmael, clinging to the wheel of his dented pickup on a wind-blown street.

He takes a sip of beer, wonders how long he should drive, moving from stop sign to stop sign, block after block, looking for her. *An hour? Two?* He should have a plan, he knows, but he'll probably just end up driving around this abandoned town all night, wasting gas, wasting time. He stares at the fuel gauge on his dashboard, slowly lowering toward E. He wonders how long before it runs dry.

The Wildlife is closed Mondays, but down the street, at Elmer's Water-in Hole, the red and blue neon beer lights glow through the opaque block windows. He takes a deep breath, gathering his strength, stands for a few seconds in front of the three triangular windows of Elmer's door, then pushes against the peeling veneer surface. As it opens a few inches, he wonders if she'll be in there. He remembers another time, after an argument last summer, he found her sitting at the bar, drinking Captain Morgans and talking to her friend Andrea. He peers through the half-opened door; the air in the room moves toward him in waves: stale popcorn, cigarette smoke, spilled beer, and Pine Sol from the bathrooms. Louise isn't there—just a half-dozen regulars whose heads all pivot toward him. Their heads seem large, their mottled red faces distorted. "Hey there Luke!" Cyrus calls out to him. Luke turns to leave, and Cyrus calls after him. "Heard you had a brush with the law this mornin'. A real outlaw, eh?"

Yeah, a regular Jesse James, Luke wants to say, but instead, he lets the door spring shut behind him, muffling the men's laughter.

Luke's truck comes to a halt at the railroad crossing near the Farmer's Co-op. The black and white crossing gates lower, their warning lights flashing. A train rolls slowly by, its whistle moaning with a monotone middle C, its cars rumbling past, wheels grinding, metal on metal.

It reminds Luke of the time when he and Louise, on an impulse, jumped into an empty boxcar in the freight yard on a humid summer evening. They discovered names and initials—scratched on the brown steel interior. They talked about who the people might have been. *Drifters?* They wondered. *Steinbeck characters? Gypsies?* Or were they lovers, like themselves, who impulsively climbed inside the boxcar and jokingly dared the train to pull away. "Hope this train's headed to someplace awesome," Louise smiled. "San Francisco. Or New Orleans."

"Or scenic downtown Fargo," Luke added ironically. "Or maybe just the east side of Clearwater."

It was strange how their voices reverberated off the steel walls and high ceiling of the boxcar. Luke broke into song that night; his full baritone voice serenaded her with Elvis Presley's "Are You Lonesome Tonight?" Then he switched to Springsteen's "Born to Run." Louise clapped as he performed brief imitations of Elvis's gyrations and Springsteen's intense throaty vocals. Louise's laugh resonated as the diesel, coupling the cars a hundred yards down the track, caused their car to suddenly lurch, sending her off balance. Luke caught her and then held her there in the freight car as if he never wanted to let her go.

As Luke waits at the crossing, it seems like forever before the red and yellow lights of the caboose finally slide by. Luke accelerates into the darkness of the country road. He finishes another beer, drops the can out the window, its clanking quickly swallowed behind him. He feels lost, just plain lost out here without Louise.

A couple miles from the interstate, he pulls into The Oasis truck stop, with its faded green palm tree décor; it's a place he and Louise sometimes went to have coffee and lemon meringue pie. Luke used to dip his spoon into the meringue on the top of her pie, and as he put it in his mouth, she'd laughingly slap his wrist. Pausing by the row of empty stools, he sees, behind the counter, a shrine of James Dean photos, and above, mounted high in the corner, the TV flickers with a NASCAR Winston Cup race, where sleek cars follow one another around and around the track. The audio is set on mute, and the announcer's commentary appears in captions: *A good driver's got to be patient. A lot of drivers have been too anxious in these races lately, and, you know, it's caused some pile-ups.* For an instant, Luke believes they're talking about him. *Is it my own damn fault?* he wonders. *Have I caused this wreck?* As if mocking him, a stationary red plastic race car in the arcade growls its recorded engine and screeches its tires every few seconds.

On his way back to Clearwater, he feels the heat from the floorboards; the drive shaft makes a grinding sound when he shifts gears, and the gauges, set into the metal dash in their square plastic cases, wiggle tentatively. There's a sudden splatter of a rain shower, and he clicks on the wipers; they swipe across the glass in syncopation but leave streaks of liquid in the middle. *Everything wearing down,* he catches himself thinking. *Need to get new wipers, check the oil, the engine coolant.*

"Severe weather for Sauk County tonight," the radio announcer's crackly voice says with a moderated urgency as Luke idles at the stop light. "Tornado watch for Madison and the southern half of Dane County . . ." Luke clicks the radio off; he's sick of warnings, sick of news. He's sick of empty theaters and lemon meringue and boxcars, sick of driving, sick of sitting still.

CHAPTER

16

She pulls into the lot by a small park where an old wooden swing creaks in the breeze as if an invisible child is sitting on it. The silhouettes of the play equipment—teeter-totter and slide and jungle gym—rise from the ground like iron skeletons. Louise wonders if she made the right decision, leaving the man she loves. Or was it just a senseless, impulsive action, the junior high rebel surfacing in her again? Staring out at the lake, she faces the narrow, stony beach, as if that would give her some answers. But the lake keeps its huge liquid mouth open, gaping at the sky, and doesn't say a word.

Sliding onto one of the swings, she's careful not to let its weathered wood give her a splinter. She glides forward and backward slowly, arching her long legs outward, pulling them back, gaining momentum as she does. For a moment, as she rushes upward, blonde hair twirling behind her back, she feels like a schoolgirl again on the playground, and then the same thoughts that have been haunting her all afternoon intrude. What is it about men that they can't say what they're feeling? she wonders. What is it about them that makes them grunt and mutter about their daily routine, but never talk about what's inside? Why does Luke tug at the tattered sleeve of his blue work shirt at the dinner table, saying things to her like "We leveled out the first base side today" or "I ordered some bags of lime for the chalk lines," as if those things would ever matter to her. As if piles of earth and ball fields mattered. As if jerseys and boys' games—the little winnings and losings of a small town team— mattered. "We matter," she wanted to say to Luke in a pleading voice. "We matter—you and I. I feel like we've lost *us*. Can't you just once stop talking about your little world?"

What's certain is that she can't go back to Clearwater, not right now. She's got to discover whatever lies beyond the city limits. She knows she'll keep her job at the casino, at least for the time being. And she'll keep tutoring those children on the reservation, knowing she needs them as much as they need her.

As the swing slows, she brings herself to a stop, scraping her sandals on the worn dirt oval. Back in the parking lot, the El Camino mocks her with its boxes filled with her belongings—hastily filled boxes of blouses and jeans and books and shoes. Through a clear plastic container, she sees the chaos of cosmetics—lip gloss, eyeliner, a curled toothpaste tube, toothbrushes, and a half-dozen bottles of makeup. A couple pink plastic hangers stick out from the top of one box like question marks.

So this is my life? She muses. *Sagging cardboard boxes of clothes? Plastic bins of bottles that make my face look polished?*

She remembers her mother's words: "Boys won't like you if you don't wear makeup," she advised one day at Hilldale Mall, when Louise balked at buying lipstick and blush.

"Why not?" Louise questioned. She had just turned thirteen that Sunday. She was tall and willowy in junior high, with a pretty face.

"Because they might see what you really look like," her mother replied, leaning her perfumed wrist against the cosmetic counter with its rainbow trays of Maybelline, Revlon, Cover Girl. "Men like illusion," she smiled, half kidding, "not reality."

This evening, as she slides back into the front seat, the boxes stacked in slanting piles against the rear window, Louise doubts if there's anything that will create the illusion—or the reality—of what she's feeling.

CHAPTER

17

Luke bumps the tires of his pickup against the curb in front of his boyhood home. He didn't plan to drive back from work in this direction, but here he is, on the south side of Clearwater, gazing at the gray clapboard house.

On this, the anniversary of his father's death, Luke wonders if it wasn't the house that finally killed his father. The house seemed to be sinking, ever so slightly, into the soil; each year the narrow cracks in the basement foundation seemed to gradually widen, the shingles of the sagging front porch slanting more to the right.

Those days after Luke's mother died, his father would return from the implement shop, lower his lean frame into the La-Z-Boy chair—the dark brown imitation leather sighing—and open his *Popular Mechanix* books. The rims of his fingernails were still stained faintly with grease. Under that beam of yellow light from a small lamp, beneath the round plastic wall clock with a cord that meandered to a socket, he'd sit and read. Once in a while he'd say to Luke, "You should see this invention. This car would save a ton of gas." Or: "Huh. Who'd believe you'd get to the moon and back in this dang contraption?" Between pages, his pack of Luckys on the end table next to him, Dwight would bring a cigarette to his lips, inhale deeply, and hold it in, his face seeming to fold in on itself with pleasure as he did. Then he'd exhale slowly, the streams of smoke billowing from his lips and nostrils and curling over the rug in the living room, where young Luke sat, playing with his Lincoln Logs. Those years, Luke was convinced that his father could have been a great inventor, that, if he had the time, he could have come up with life-saving inventions, things that could benefit humankind for the next hundred years. Luke believed he could have been the next Thomas Edison, hundreds of ideas bubbling from his brain, it if weren't for the demands of that implement company.

Luke often wished his father would give up his job at the implement company, but the reality of Dwight's life was that threshers and combines had to be repaired; so did tractors and riding mowers and snowblowers. Machines, young Luke began to understand, were made to break down. Blackened parts wore thin, carbon clogged pipes, fuel lines cracked, axles bent, ignitions failed, and the big sheet-metal and cast-iron beasts were worthless until his father resurrected them.

His father wasn't some great inventor; he was just a man who, after reading for a while, would go downstairs to tinker with his clock collection. He would amble down the wooden steps to that cavern of a basement, the walls half-finished with poured concrete, half with old stones, their puzzle shapes held together with dank, musty cement. Because the work bench he bought at an auction was too big for the narrow stairway, Dwight had to take the stocky legs off it, lug them down the stairway, then reassemble them onto the heavy, four-inch-thick tabletop, which was covered with gouges and deep scratches smoothed over with coats of sticky varnish. For hours, Dwight would sit at that workbench beneath the small fluorescent light and work with the clocks he'd purchased over the years at auctions and salvage yards: small grandfather clocks with chipped wooden casings or cracked glass, wind-up alarm clocks, '50s wall clocks with green plastic starbursts spoking outward, cuckoo clocks shaped like Alpine chalets. He'd take them apart and try to repair them; he even bought a jeweler's loupe—a mini-magnifier attached to a head strap—so he could see the clocks' mechanisms better. It always amazed Luke that the big hands that could fix the axle on a thousand-pound hay baler could perform a delicate operation on the tiny cogs and wheels of a clock. For young Luke, the basement was filled with hope: it was a place where stilled parts came alive again, a place where things, long motionless and crippled, somehow began to move.

As Luke peered over his shoulder, Dwight leaned close to a decorative brass clock with a tiny screwdriver, exhaling smoke from his cigarette into the shiny meshed gears and the coiled mainspring. "What're you doing with that one?" Luke would ask, and his father would chuckle, always answering with the same tired joke: "I'm buying some time."

When his father was busy with yard work, Luke occasionally tiptoed down the stairway and paused, halfway, where he could hear the chaotic ticking of the dozen clocks Dwight got to work, none of them set at the same time. It was like someone shaking a handful of small stones in their palm. The sound comforted him, and it bothered him a little at the same time, the way the ticks were at different pitches, and out of syncopation. Upstairs, lying in bed in the darkness, Luke sometimes believed he could still hear that ticking, rising all the way up from the basement.

Dwight didn't talk much to Luke those years after his mother died; most of his words were practical, instructional, outlining what tasks he had to get done at work, what they might eat for dinner, which was usually hamburgers or hot dogs or, if he got fancy, a noodle and tomato sauce casserole of some kind. "How's dinner?" he'd ask Luke.

"Good," Luke would inevitably reply. "Real good."

"That burger done enough?" He'd raise his eyebrows so the parallel lines furrowed on his forehead.

"Yep."

When Luke would wake on Saturday morning and creak down the stairs, his father, looking up from a magazine, would say, "Up and at 'em, eh?" At bedtime, he'd announce, "Time to hit the hay."

During Luke's high school years, as Dwight left in the mornings, he'd say, "Well, off to the tin mines, I s'pose," and then ask, "When's your ball practice done?"

"The usual," Luke would answer. "Five thirty."

"I'll pick you up, then."

Sometimes Luke longed to have his father say other things, things he felt and wondered and dreamed about. Words that came from deep down. Like how his father felt about his mother being gone. That way, it would open a door so Luke could ask about her, or tell Dwight that he missed his mother. But for years, the door stayed closed, locked. Other times, Luke decided, it was best not to discuss those things, best to leave them where they were. In that way, Luke's world remained a secure and predictable place, with no surprises or upsets, a foundation of words that held up a level, unwavering wooden floor beneath him.

Until his father's sudden stroke, which changed everything. His father couldn't buy time after his heart went bad, and no oiling or replacing of parts could change that. It wasn't just the fault of the smoking, like the doctors said, Luke knew. It wasn't just the inhaling of all that smoke and tar and nicotine that, Luke imagined, circled inside the hollows of his heart. The real reason was that his heart was a machine that, one day, simply wore down and decided to stop working.

Sometimes, when Luke drives past the old house his aunt and uncle sold shortly after Dwight died, he pulls his truck to the curb and stares at the sagging front porch, held up by the arms of the paint-chipped pillars, the wood siding that begs, year after year, to be repainted, the slightly askew windows, the yellowed shades pulled down from the inside. Luke thinks about the people who live there now, if they ever walk down the bowing stairs to the cellar, see that work bench, its thick legs and heavy, gouged top, and wonder what the previous owner used it for, and how anyone could ever have gotten it down the stairs in the first place.

Luke recalls the times he'd come home from school and see his father, sitting at the thin railing of the second-floor porch and studying the town.

"What are you looking at?" Luke asked him once.

"Nothing," Dwight mumbled. He swirled a whiskey sour in a glass, the ice cubes clinking. "And everything."

This evening, Luke rolls down the window of his truck, thinks he can still hear the house ticking, somewhere deep inside it. *What did kill my father?* He wonders. *Was it staying here, in one place? Or did that just make him stronger?* Luke starts his truck and pulls away. Seeing the big house shrink smaller and smaller in the rearview mirror, he wishes he had the answers.

CHAPTER

18

He sees them—pale, thin, and rising, one by one, at the edge of the outfield. The thin bones lift from the grass in a row like a small, yellowed picket fence. The bones make a sharp, menacing sound, like a snake's rattle. Then a bone topples over, striking the one next to it, and that one strikes the next. Like dominoes they fall, tumbling steadily one after the other. Butch panics, knowing he has to do something about it, but it's hard to move, his body wrapped tightly in black electrical tape. Somehow he pulls his arms free and struggles to his Concorde, manages to start it, and floors the car at the objects. The car seems to pass right through the bones without touching them, and when he slams on the brake and looks in the rearview mirror, he can see them still toppling, one by one, all the way toward town.

Butch sits up in bed, writhing as if he still has the tape around his body, and the dream's images fade and are slowly replaced by the familiar silhouetted shapes of his mahogany desk, his bicentennial lamp, the old radiators with their curved ribs. He rushes to his second story window, parts the drapes. In the light from the moon, he can see the empty ball field in the distance, the tips of the backstop posts rising into the air. He fumbles for his cell phone, clicks it on, its green numbers glowing.

"Rollie?" he says.

"Yeah?" Rollie's groggy voice answers.

"Butch." His name rises up in his throat like a dry leaf.

"Why the hell you calling at midnight? For chrissakes, I was trying to get some sleep between shifts, and . . ."

"Just listen," Butch interrupts, his voice steadier now. He sits down on the edge of the bed. "Just shut up and listen. Something happened back there, Rollie," he blurts. "Where the field is built."

"Yeah, I know," Rollie answers offhandedly. "A lot of stuff happened back there. With the old Indian villages and burial grounds and . . ."

"No, Rollie," Butch cuts him off again. "That's not what I'm talking about." He pauses, clears his throat, squeezes the small cell phone between his thumb and index finger. "That's *not* what I mean." Then he bites down on the words and holds them tightly.

JUST AFTER FOUR A.M., the field is dark, and a big car—with its lights off—inches forward in the parking lot. The car rocks to a stop near the pavilion. The trunk pops open with a clunk, springs upward on its hinges. Dressed in polyester slacks and a gray sweatshirt and wearing leather work gloves, someone slides from the driver's seat and lifts a shovel wrapped in an army blanket from the trunk. He raises a pint of brandy, takes a long swig, winces from the liquor's sting, then steps carefully over the yellow tape that's strung between the half-finished dugout and the supply shed.

At the edge of the infield, the dry dirt crackles under the hard black heels of his shoes; though he's only a little overweight, his shoulders sway left, then right as he walks, like a man who weighs much more. He pushes the shovel into the soil, empties a couple of scoops on the grass, then drops to his knees and brushes through the dirt with his gloved fingers. He tosses aside chips of rock, slivers of wood, rusted bottle caps. He stands and digs into the dirt again, puffing as the crickets lift their shrill curtain of sound around him. He clicks on a small penlight, circles its weak beam around and around, seeing nothing. "Sheezes." The word is like a curse—or a prayer. He sifts through the dirt, then moves a few feet down, trying another spot. He pushes the shovel hard with the heel of his shoe. He kneels again and leans toward the pile. "Ah sheezes," he whispers again, keeping his voice soft, as if someone might hear him, though at this time of night there are no cars on the adjacent street, no lights in the houses of the nearby neighborhoods.

As he digs, sweat stains the collar of his sweatshirt; dark circles appear under his armpits. He pauses a few seconds. There's a quarter moon, a sliver in the sky, the low, fast-moving clouds scuttling across it. He's glad it's not full, or he'd be illuminated, his body casting a faint shadow, as it might have that night years ago. He was a young deputy then, a good, fair cop who had already gotten the town's trust and admiration. He was a pitcher on the town ball team, a man on his way up in a career, a public servant. He remembers his squad car's headlights illuminating this field. He pictures himself sitting in that squad car as he stared out at the scene. Then he pressed on the accelerator and, like pressing a fading memory into soft soil with his heel, pushed the images further and further away from him.

He recalls returning that night to the dispatch trailer, taking his three A.M. break, drinking a couple cups of Folgers and eating from a king-size bag of Sugar Babies. The Sugar Babies were sweet on his tongue, and he ate the whole bag as he fixed the short on the dispatcher's microphone cord with some electrical tape, winding it around and around, around and around. Afterward, he told the story so many times he began to believe it himself. He knew he had taken an oath to protect the community, but about that night, he told everyone, "Nope, I didn't see a thing out there."

Now he straightens, slides his bulky sweatshirt off his head, exposing a beige tank-top undershirt that clings to his pasty belly. He pictures himself running the bases years ago; he was thin and lean then, an All-American kid, the town's favorite son. He remembers how flat the land was across the field and all the way to the farms on the outskirts of Clearwater. That old ball field was fine just as it was, he thinks. It was solid and level, everything on an even keel.

He wipes his forehead, the grit on his leather work glove scratching his skin. Taking another drink of brandy, he leans into the shovel, grunting as he pushes its rusty tip deep, the shovel slicing through a couple of pale roots. He pictures Luke Tanner's fingers, and he chops them off, one by one. He'll dig and keep digging, if he can. He'll dig all night if he has to. He'll dig all the way to the center of the earth.

Just then, a spotlight flares, shining in his face, pushing him off balance. He staggers backward a couple steps, then freezes, as if he's turned to stone or ice. He parts his lips but can't make a sound, the bright white light filling his mouth and throat, numbing it.

A car door opens, someone steps out, and he hears a familiar scratchy voice. "What the hell. Butch? That you?"

It takes a few seconds to gather an answer. "'Course it's me."

"Thought maybe I caught Tanner digging out here." Rollie's voice sounds a little disappointed but still incredulous. "Thought we'd nail him and lock him up for sure. But it's *you*."

"Yeah," Butch says, mustering a chuckle. "It's me."

Rollie clicks the squad car's spotlight off. "What the hell you *doing* out here, Butch?"

"What am I *doing*?" Butch keeps his voice from sounding flustered. "What's it *look* like I'm doing? I'm digging. I need to figure out what's out here."

"So," Rollie says, his voice hesitant as a gearshift stuck in neutral, "what's out here?"

"Dirt," Butch says, dusting off his work gloves. "Mostly goddamn dirt."

Rollie fiddles with a button on his uniform, gives Butch a skeptical squint. "Weren't *they* the ones supposed to dig it up, though?" Rollie questions, referring to the state archeologists who have been called in to investigate. "Don't they have their methods, and all that?"

"Not necessarily," Butch picks up his sweatshirt, throws it over his shoulder, trying to seem casual. He pulls out a bag of Sugar Babies, pops a couple into his mouth. "Those state boys can mess up a local investigation pretty good, from what I've heard."

Rollie nods, acknowledging that Butch has a good point.

"Besides," Butch continues, gesturing toward the dry clumps at his feet, "this whole area was tilled, years ago. It's been plowed and stirred up dozens of times. Nothing's the same under there. Nope," he says with finality, "nothing's the same."

CHAPTER

19

The late afternoon sunlight paints a bright orange across the tops of the old tarpaper garages. Luke is aware of the sounds of the neighborhood filtering through the open window screen: the echoing bark of a dog, giggling children next door on their swing, the clatter of dishes from the neighbor's kitchen, the *clack* as someone lets a screen door slap shut. Tonight, without Louise, those usually familiar, pleasant sounds just make him feel lonely. Louise's little walk around the block—which is what she did some times when they had an argument—has lasted several days. *She'll come back*, he told himself a dozen times the first hour, and the next day, and the day after that, but now he's not so sure, not so sure at all.

He thinks about the first night after she left, when, on a hunch, he lifted the cordless phone from its cradle and called her sister's place in Madison, hoping she'd be there. When Luke insisted, her sister reluctantly put Louise on.

"Yes?" Louise said.

"I thought we should discuss . . .," he stammered, "you know . . ."

"I think we've talked enough." Her voice seemed small, thin, narrowed by the black wires between Madison and Clearwater. Still, its thinness couldn't disguise the tension in her voice.

"So what are you doing?" he asked. "I mean, at your sister's?" He knew, as soon as it escaped his lips, that the question was meaningless, missing the point he wanted to make, as though he was some awkward high school kid chatting with a new girlfriend.

"Nothing," she replied.

He waited a few seconds for more, but she added no words. His ear felt hot where it touched the receiver. "Is that all?" he asked, feeling short of breath. "Dammit, Louise. Say something else."

"Like what?" Her words were concrete slabs, immovable.

"Like anything." He closed his eyes, could see tiny white sparks of pain. A constellation. A galaxy. "Just *talk* . . ."

How many times did Luke know what he wanted to say but just couldn't say it, the words like fish line tangled on the bale of a fishing pole? For an instant he pictured making love with Louise the weekend before she left, saw the red spaghetti-strap of her silk nightgown sliding slowly off her shoulder, a shoulder smooth as cream pouring from a pitcher. Static electricity on the sheets sparked in the dim room. He heard the tender words they spoke to each other, their lips just a fraction of an inch apart. "You're a song, Luke Tanner," Louise had exhaled. "I hear you all the time." Didn't those words mean anything?

"It's just not that simple, Luke," Louise said, her voice shattering his memory.

He squeezed the phone hard in his palm, and his anger pushed out a sarcastic reply. "Sorry it's not so goddamn simple."

"I've really got to go," she said.

"So I guess we're done?" he blurted. "It's over? Just like that?"

"I *said* I have to go, Luke."

"So do I," he blurted stubbornly.

With that, he heard the click of the phone as she disconnected. For a few seconds, he listened to the static hissing through the receiver. The sound seemed to get steadily louder and louder, became more of a roar, like a tornado that could tear through the dining room. He threw the phone hard against the wall, stopping the sound. He stared at the broken plastic pieces in the corner, the twisted knot of red and green wires, the tiny, silent pinholes in the receiver through which her voice had just emerged.

An hour later, a knock on the front door jolts Luke. The knock is soft, tentative. *Louise?* he wonders. He starts toward the entryway in bare feet. Then, pausing and checking himself in the hallway mirror, he frowns at his unshaven face, his chin bristling with whiskers, his rumpled, faded blue work shirt with a tear on one pocket. His lips appear chapped, his eyes a bloodshot pink from lack of sleep. He runs a comb through his unkempt hair, pulling it back from his forehead as he hears another knock.

He takes a deep breath and turns the brass doorknob, the door opening, a sliver of light widening to a narrow rectangle. He sees, at first, only a silhouette. He blinks as he realizes it's not Louise, not her at all; a wave of disappointment rushes through him.

A woman, who looks to be in her thirties, is dressed in a dark blue business suit. She's not as thin as Louise, and she's shorter, with thick black hair pulled back from her face. Luke heard an archeologist from the university might be stopping by to interview him sometime this week, but he didn't know it would be this soon, or this late in the day, or that it would be a woman.

"I'd like to ask you some questions," she says tentatively, extending her hand to him and introducing herself as Virginia Marquette. "Unless this is a bad time."

"Every time's a bad time, lately," he says, half jokingly, but the joke falls flat.

"I'd like to talk about what you found."

A simple enough request, Luke thinks. But somehow he senses that the answers will just generate other questions, and he's not sure if he has the energy to explain anything right now. He thinks of saying, flippantly, "Ask me about what I've lost, not what I found," but he holds his tongue.

As he leads her to the dining room table, she has to step over the broken phone he never bothered to pick up. "Phone trouble?" she questions.

"Bad connection," he replies curtly, kicking the plastic pieces out of her way.

Virginia sets her laptop on the table and opens her knapsack, looking for the form she needs. Luke, not in the mood for this, fixes his eyes on the oak table, losing himself for a few seconds inside the concentric lines of the knots.

When she begins her questions, she seems shy, a little awkward about this meeting, but her brown eyes are intense as she asks Luke for details about where he discovered the bone, the date he found it, how far it was beneath the surface. Her voice, flat and practical as brown cardboard, seems to hold back any emotion. She scribbles notes on the printed form, then transfers them to her laptop, her hands thin and surprisingly smooth for someone who, Luke figures, might sift through dirt. Luke studies her face—attractive, in a way, with her dark, arched eyebrows and pronounced cheekbones, and he's fairly sure she's of Native American descent.

"So," Luke says, changing the subject, "when you start a dig, what do you do?"

She looks up at him and blinks, as if she's never been asked that question before. "Well, first we measure the site," she says. "Then I record the dimensions, and then I mark off the area."

"Oh," Luke sighs, thinking it sounds like a rote job. "Sounds almost dull."

"Dull's what you make it," she retorts.

She rummages through her worn canvas knapsack. A compass drops out and circles on its rim. A yellow tongue uncurls from a large spool of measuring tape. She finally pulls out some orange flags she uses to mark the perimeter of a site. "These are my marker flags," she says with a pleased look on her face. "When you see them from a distance, they look like little fires."

She lifts out a digital camera. "I'm going to need to get some shots of the artifacts."

"Well," Luke stalls, "let me think about that."

"*Think* about it?" With that, she just stares at him a few long seconds, her large brown eyes not blinking.

Luke just shrugs and leans back in the pressed-back chair. He's not really sure why he's resisting her; maybe it's just that, after all that's happened lately, he's unnecessarily defensive and ready to put up barriers around the field whenever he can. Her lips press together, slide sideways slightly on her face. "I hope you plan to cooperate," she finally says.

A part of him wants to ask her outright, "Did Butch send you? Or that self-important sheriff? Are they the ones you're reporting back to?" But then again, Luke thinks, maybe he's being a bit too paranoid and reading too much into this woman's visit. After all, she's an archeologist. She might not be another bureaucratic roadblock; maybe she's just doing her job. Maybe she just needs the truth. *But what's the truth?*

"I take it this is a touchy subject," Virginia says.

"That's an understatement."

"So. Care to tell me what's going on?"

He contemplates not answering her prying question, just ending this conversation, showing her to the door. Finally he relents. "City hall's trying to claim my land. How would you feel?"

She pauses. "Same way you would, I guess," she says, her lips pursing on the words. "Bitter. Defensive."

After she finishes her interview, they pause in the entryway.

"I could be on your side, you know," she says tentatively.

Luke just tosses her an indifferent look.

"And I *am* Native American," she adds, "which is what I assume you're thinking."

"I wasn't assuming anything."

"Well, good, then." Luke can't tell if she's being sarcastic or not. "So," she adds, "when can I see the field?"

"Whenever you want, I guess. Tomorrow, even. I suppose I could take you out near deep short."

"Near *where?*"

"Deep short. That's where I found the bone fragment." He can tell by her puzzled expression that she's not sure where that is, so he adds, "You don't know much about baseball, do you?"

She just gives him a flat look and turns to leave. He notices one of the orange flags she left on the table. He retrieves it and hands it to her, saying, "You forgot your little warning flag."

Her lips twist wryly to one side. "You mean my *marker?*"

"Yeah. Whatever."

"You don't know much about archeology, do you?" she asks.

When he doesn't reply, she says, "So, I'll need to ask you some more questions." She holds the wobbly screen door open—her fingers with clear, unpainted nails. "And I'll have to make a visit to your city hall. To research the records, locate those deeds."

"I stay as far as I can from that place," he scoffs.

A smile floats to the surface of her face, and she catches him off guard, replying, "Well, you won't be staying away. You're going there *with* me."

CHAPTER 20

"You have an appointment?" the woman blurts to Virginia at the reception desk of city hall. From behind, Luke notices how the secretary, whose name tag says *Phyllis Dietermann*, peers skeptically above her pink half-shell glasses, scrutinizing Virginia's worn jeans, her khaki T-shirt, the multicolored bead bracelets she wears on her wrist. Phyllis's face is ruddy and puffed out, as if someone cut a potato lengthwise and inserted one half under each cheek.

"As a matter of fact, I do. I'm here to look at the land deeds."

"Hmmm." Phyllis acts put out, as though, at Clearwater city hall, she's had hundreds of visits from pesky archeologists. Luke figures it's all part of her daily routine, this making strangers feel uncomfortable. Phyllis puts down her copy of the *Inquirer*, pages idly through an appointment book, then slowly lifts her plump body from the padded swivel chair, her burgundy blazer bulging at the hips. "I don't know what we got, but I guess you can have a look." She waddles down a varnish-scented aisle between shelves. A '50s bouffant hairstyle rises from her head, and as she pauses between the stacks, the scent of her Liz Taylor perfume catches up with her in sickly sweet ripples. A bare bulb hangs from the tin ceiling of a dim room; its walls are covered by warped oak bookshelves. She pulls on the cord, and the bulb jumps to life with a yellowish glow. She nods at some faded file boxes. "You can look there, I s'pose."

Virginia leans over to glance at some file tabs.

"What's *he* doing here?" Phyllis gives Luke, who lingers at the back of the aisle, her best disapproving look. "Don't know if just anyone's allowed to be back here. Except by appointment. The mayor said . . ."

"It's okay," Virginia interrupts. "He's assisting me."

"*Assisting* you." Phyllis repeats the words as though they were profane.

Luke likes the way Virginia handled this little resistance by Phyllis, who has, he notices, become quite territorial about her job. Under Phyllis's reign, everything at city hall seems to have taken on more significance than it deserves. As she heads back, she still manages to keep a watchful eye on her desk, with its row of pens, its perfectly stacked manila file folders, its cut-glass case filled to the brim with paper clips. Luke has known Phyllis for years; she always seems to be talking about the local accidents or disabled people, and he's overheard her at the drugstore saying, "They might just as well pull the plug on her, what with those burns she got in the fire," or referring to "that poor boy with the bright purple birthmark all over his face," or, "Old Stanley, he'll end up with stumps for legs. Can you imagine?"

Virginia reaches toward a shelf marked with the yellowed label *1850–1860*, pulls down a file box of papers, carries it to the table in the corner, and begins paging through deeds and land records one by one. Her fingers move nimbly through the pages, which seem to sigh as she lifts them. When she finishes with one box, she pulls down another. Her oval steel-rimmed glasses glimmer, and it surprises Luke how clear her eyes are this early in the morning; his eyes are usually bloodshot and swollen until noon, but hers are wide open, her brown irises gliding left, right, left without tiring. He admires her diligence, her tenacity, and hopes maybe she's just the person he needs to cut through all this red tape. Maybe she'll be the one to discover something that will free him from these narrow, suffocating aisles of deeds and records and land tracts.

"It could take a year to get through all these files," Luke mutters.

"That's what researchers *do,* Luke. What did you think? I could find something in ten minutes?"

"Guess I'm not that patient."

"You *learn* patience when you're in my field. It's like putting together a puzzle, I guess." He can detect the enthusiasm in her voice. "But the puzzle has all sorts of layers beneath it. And there are always pieces missing."

"What do you do when you find one?"

She gives him a fleeting smile. "My job is to figure out not just where the piece fits, but on *which* layer."

"Sounds like my life," Luke quips.

A woman's silhouette appears on the frosted window of the door. Luke figures it's Phyllis, checking up on them. He elbows Virginia, and when she looks toward the door, Phyllis backs quickly out of sight, as though she wouldn't be noticed.

"Starting to feel like we're in grade school?" Virginia whispers.

"I had nuns at St. Cecilia's who used to hover in the doorway of the boys' room, just to make sure everything was okay in there."

"And *was* everything okay in there?"

"Not usually," he says, blushing a little. "But hey, they never knew the difference."

Virginia smiles and spreads some pages across the varnished bird's-eye maple table. "Look at this one," she says pointing to details on a deed. Luke can tell that she's fascinated by these deeds—these descriptions of lands, of buyers and sellers, these indentured workers who signed on to labor on the farms for pennies a day. He can tell, from watching the way she scans the details, that she could easily fall into their lives, their histories.

"She's back," Luke whispers as Phyllis's shape reappears at the frosted window again.

Virginia pulls off her glasses. "You don't have to check up on us," she calls to Phyllis with a slight song in her voice. "We're not stealing anything in here."

The unexpected comment catches Luke off guard, and he stifles a laugh.

Foiled in the middle of her covert spying operation, Phyllis pivots, and Luke can hear the sound of her tennis shoes squeaking away.

Moments later she opens the door, sidles in, and crosses her arms, the puckered flesh dangling from her forearms. "I guess there's only one person allowed in the reference room at a time," she states.

"And who made that rule?" Virginia questions.

"I did," a husky voice echoes in the hallway. It's Butch Sobieski. He steps forward, blocking the light in the doorway with his too-tight blue suit. "We want to keep our records in order."

"We're putting everything back here, Mr. Sobieski," Virginia replies. Luke detects an edge beneath her politeness.

"So, Miz . . ." Butch stammers, obviously not knowing her name.

"Ms. Marquette." She holds out her hand, her beadwork necklace swaying.

"Oh, um, sure." Butch steps forward, taking her hand awkwardly. "Real pleased, miss." His other hand dabs at the side of his slicked-back hair.

"So, is this a new policy, or an old one?" Virginia counters.

"Standard one, I guess," Butch says, his face smudging over with a scowl as he tosses Luke a side glance.

"Okay," Luke says under his breath. He has no desire to get into a confrontation this morning. "I'm going for coffee." Luke moves toward the door, giving Butch a shake of his head. Butch pulls his weight aside slightly, but Luke still has to turn sideways to squeeze through the narrow doorway that leads to the main office.

HE SITS ALONE in one of the Rainbow's red vinyl booths, drinking a cup of coffee beneath the dime-store picture of two deer frozen in a meadow. He appreciates the way Virginia seems to be standing up to Butch. He hopes she'll find an answer in those musty boxes, that somewhere there's a piece of the mosaic that will make the whole picture of Luke's past clearer. But how long will it take? His past and his ancestors are so removed from Luke—his father rarely mentioned his own father and mother, much less the generation before them.

TAKING A BREAK, Virginia stretches the kinks in her neck by tipping her head back and gazing at the stamped pattern of the ceiling, the tiny tin squares within squares. When she reaches for the next file box and pulls it off the shelf, she pauses for a few seconds. It's marked *1880-1890*. It occurs to her that she never checked the box with the 1870s deeds; she studies her notes, the columns of numbers she's scribbled in her notebook to make sure. She turns and reads the labels on the file boxes, searching for the 1870 to 1880 box. She runs her finger along the labels, whispering the dates aloud to herself, certain that she's seeing each one. Then, with a quick inhalation of air, she realizes that there's no box, no deeds at all for the years 1870 to 1880.

"Do you know where I could find those?" Virginia questions.

Phyllis looks up from her outdated Zenith computer screen, filled with the black and white cards from a video poker game. Next to it, a tabloid headline reads *Appalachian Child Born Without Mouth*. "Don't know for sure." She puffs out her cheeks as if Virginia is interrupting a very important administrative task. "Everything we got is back there."

Within seconds, Butch appears at the door, primping a little as he straightens his wide blue plaid tie—a tie last in style during the '70s. It's apparent he's overheard her question to Phyllis. "Need something else, ma'am?" Butch asks, tossing her an upbeat I'm-at-your-service smile. The room fills with the scent of Butch's freshly applied English Leather cologne.

After Virginia explains, he says, "Let's have a look-see, then." He shuffles back to the file room, his black shiny shoes creaking. "We sure do want to cooperate with this thing the best we can." He studies the stacks, peering at their labels, his nose close to them. "Nope," he says. "Guess not." When Virginia gives him a questioning look, Butch twists his mouth to one side. "That file must be ashes."

"Ashes?"

"Yep. We had a fire in town back in the twenties. Part of city hall burned, so I guess that file got burned along with it." He pinches his lips into a tight smile. "Sorry, ma'am. Can't help you with that one." Then, through the walls of the courthouse, she can hear the slow, loud rise of the noon whistle. It begins as a low growl, then crescendos and rises in pitch, louder, louder, until it almost hurts her ears. Butch glances at his watch. "Sheesh!" he exclaims. "Lunch hour already. Time flies, eh?" After the whistle falls back to a metallic purr and stops, he turns to her and says, confidentially, "Do you know that in thirty years, that ol' whistle's never been late?"

"Never?" she replies, though Butch doesn't catch her sarcastic tone. "In thirty years?"

"Not one single day," Butch says, his wide face glowing with pride. "Can you believe it?"

"So," LUKE ASKS later as he meets Virginia in front of the courthouse. "You didn't get anywhere in the archives?"

"No," she says solemnly. "But those missing files might have had what we need."

Luke likes the way she says "we"; he's beginning to believe she's on his side. "So what next?"

"The state capitol keeps duplicates of county records in their archives. Your missing link might just be there."

On his way home, Luke approaches the radar speed indicator sign near the city limits—Sheriff Rollie's newest addition to Clearwater law enforcement. The lit yellow letters read:

Speed Limit: 25
Your Speed: 28

Out of habit, Luke eases off the gas pedal and slows. But the next moment, his foot presses on the accelerator, and the digital numbers on the sign quickly change: *36. 41. 45.*

CHAPTER

11

Luke feels self-conscious, driving with a woman other than Louise in the passenger seat. He follows Highway 12 toward Lake Wisconsin and Merrimac, his arms moving awkwardly as he steers around a gradual curve by a broken-down farmstead. He thinks about how he took a road trip with Louise on this very highway last spring: she sat with one leg propped under her, her window always rolled halfway down, Jimmy Buffett's "Margaritaville" playing on the cassette. They shared a thermos filled with lemonade and laughed at the black and white plaster cow ornaments in the front yard of a farmhouse they passed. Luke glances at Virginia, who rides silently, staring out the window at the ruins of the log buildings and the windmill with the blades missing. He appreciates that Virginia is helping him out, and he's hopeful that this trip to the state archives in Madison will turn up something he needs.

"So," Luke asks, "how do you like Madison?"

"Let's just say it's a lot different than Clearwater," she says.

"Really?" he smirks. "Now what would lead you to that conclusion?"

"Well, pardon me for saying it, Luke, but you live in a rather unusual town. I mean, some people are very nice. But a few others, well . . ."

Outside Merrimac, they pass a few aluminum trailers clinging to the land. In tiny rectangular yards, lawn chairs cluster around plastic tables amid wood torches, burned at night for bug repellent. The pickup reaches the crest of a hill and a vista opens up. Though Luke has driven this road before, he's almost forgotten the majesty of the Wisconsin River valley spread out before them: the river—like a great, glistening blue snake—meanders and pools at the base of steep green bluffs.

As the truck bounces over a section of rough road, Luke is surprised when a laminated ID badge falls from the visor to the console between the seats. It's Louise's spare photo ID from the casino. He feels his face flush as Louise's image seems to be staring at him. Virginia doesn't seem to notice the ID, and Luke hopes she won't; he'd rather not discuss it. *There's this woman,* he'd explain. *She and I are, well, we're . . .* and then his words would trail off into nothingness, evaporate like mist. *Are what? Are what?* It seems to him that Virginia is not the type to pry anyway, so he feels safe in that regard.

"So tell me, Luke," Virginia says, breaking into his thoughts. "You said you never finished college. Why is that?"

Luke tries to come up with a really good reason, but all he can manage is, "Not sure." *My usual Neanderthal answer,* he thinks. He steadies the wheel as a Winnebago motor home whooshes past them in the oncoming lane, the wind in its wake making his pickup sway, and he shifts the subject back to her. "What about you, Virginia? What got you into this field?"

She had told him, earlier, that she's a member of the Turtle Lake tribe and that her ancestors were confined to a reservation in South Dakota. "I love the past, I guess," she says. "We all have a history. I never used to acknowledge mine."

Luke adjusts the radio dial, trying to pick up a Madison station. "Maybe mine's still waiting to be written," he says.

For the last half hour they ride in silence; when they reach the stately white dome of the capital building, Virginia steps from the truck, and Luke grabs Louise's ID tag from the console. There in his hand, Louise gives him a cordial smile, and he winces as he stuffs the ID into the glove box, burying it beneath the clutter of receipts and a broken cassette, a length of its thin brown tape pulled loose and tangled.

Inside the capitol archives room, Luke and Virginia view Sauk County records from 1860 to 1870 on the yellow microfilm screen, the print blurring. Some of the records are handwritten in black script. As she spins through the years, property is sold, farms foreclosed at the twist of her wrist.

Luke imagines crops sprouting high and green during good summers, withering and dying as a drought cracks the parched land. One farm is purchased for four hundred dollars, then sold, five years later, for only a hundred. Broken fences, broken bodies, broken hearts. She keeps turning the wheel, time moving too fast. *It's the Civil War now*, thinks Luke as she reaches the mid-1860s. *North struggling against the south. In another month, Lincoln will be shot.*

The deeds from the 1870s are located in thick, gray books in a room adjacent to the microfilm section. Virginia opens the cover, softly reciting, "Joseph Frederick Tanner, Joseph Frederick Tanner," as if the mantra of saying Luke's great great grandfather's name will help her find it. Each deed is arranged in the book by sections—or square miles—of land, and then those sections are divided into four quarters, and then divided again. In some listings, the definitions are broken down into even more confusing pieces: "the southwest quarter of the northwest quarter of section 12 . . ." As he sits, his foot falls asleep, and the black ink blurs, and Luke begins to wonder about the futility of this search. At the same time, he appreciates Virginia's perseverance as she studies the books, her face intense behind her reading glasses. He's amazed she can pore over hundreds of pages without reaching a point of tedium. He takes a deep breath, inhales the stale dusty scent of the archives room, with its shag carpet, its taped steam pipes, its moisture-bubbled paint chipping off the wall, its varnished bookshelves lined with unopened books that imprison lost homesteads, lost families. In this room, time crumbles like a brittle eggshell, and Luke can almost hear the incessant clicking of his father's old clock collection in the basement.

Looking up, Luke notices Virginia gazing at him from just a few inches away. Seemingly flustered, she blinks a few times with her dark brown eyes, slides her glasses back on her face, and leans toward the text.

A half hour later, Virginia stops on one page and points to a deed. "Here," she says. The word bursts from her lips. Then she says it louder: "Here!" A male student in the next booth, his worn backpack splayed next to him, looks up, annoyed. Virginia begins reading, quickly, in a quieter voice, the details of the deed, and it's a description of the sections of land belonging to Joseph Frederick Tanner. "And look," she says, "there's the word 'squatter' in the corner."

"So what's that mean?" Luke asks anxiously.

Not answering at first, she hurriedly scribbles a few sentences into her notebook. "It means your great great grandfather lived on the land long enough, apparently," she explains, "so it became his."

"All right!" Luke calls out in excitement; then, noticing the student scowling at him, he covers his mouth and whispers, "All right!"

"But wait," she cautions. "We're not done yet."

When he looks at her questioningly, she adds, "We have to follow this land through the months and years. We have to see what happened next."

She continues looking through the documents, then pauses on one of the pages. "Hmmm." Her lips twist sideways, and her index finger follows the meandering of the hand-scripted text. She turns toward Luke.

"What?" he asks. The page is tipped sideways, and he can't make out the tiny print. "What did you find?"

"This," she says, pointing to a line. "This deed is thirty-two years later. And it lists Clearwater Township as the owner."

"What?" Luke says incredulously.

"There's no mention of sales or transaction on these. It doesn't even say how the ownership changed hands." She leans back in her chair, slips her glasses off. "Deeds can switch hands without a record of how it got from one party to another."

"Damn," Luke exhales. "I thought my ancestors *owned* the land."

"Apparently they did. At one point, at least." Virginia takes in a slow breath.

"So what happened?"

"I wish I knew."

That night, Luke drives up to his small room at the Campus Park Motel. He opens the door to a run-down room with battered chairs, a Formica nightstand, stained orange carpeting—from post-Badger game reveling, he figures—and a sagging double bed pushed next to the window. Still dressed in his jeans and T-shirt, he flops on the bedspread, marred with a couple cigarette burns, but can't fall asleep.

When he looks up at the clock, he realizes it's already two in the morning. He climbs out of bed, parts the green room-darkening drapes, and looks out on an asphalt parking lot. The rows of streetlights lead to the fluorescent blue and red glow of a twenty-four-hour Food 'n Fuel gas station, its illuminated plastic sign held high in the air by posts. Beyond it, more neon signs, leading toward the highway, the beltline, and the interstate. He stands motionless in front of the window, mesmerized by the sight. *That's America,* he thinks. *Even at night, we're never in darkness. The superette sign is our twenty-four-hour sun god.* He imagines that, a thousand years from now, if someone digs up our civilization's remains, all they'll find is plastic. Our monuments, left behind for the ages. He stands there, looking but not looking, leaning closer to the window, his breath steaming a small circle on the glass.

CHAPTER

22

The stocky middle-aged man slides a plastic bucket of nickels toward her across the brown and white marble counter. He clutches his Velcro wallet in one hand and his Island Gold gambling card in the other as he watches Louise dump the coins into the change machine. Sticking his card in the pocket of his polyester pants, the man licks the side of his lip and leers at her, listing slightly as if he's had a few too many beers. He wears a washed-out T-shirt with a logo of the Gatlin Brothers against a background of howling silver wolves and eagles taking flight over an American flag. The coins filter into the bin with a sound like hail on a tin roof. It's a sound Louise has begun to hate lately. "Played here a dozen times," the man is saying to her above the rattle, "but never got lucky 'til tonight." She looks at his total, pulls open the drawer, and slides the money toward the man, the bills dry beneath her fingertips. He picks up the cash, he leans toward her and whispers flirtatiously, like they're sitting close together in a darkened, smoky lounge, "I'd be way luckier if I had a woman like you to spend it on."

"Does your wife know you're here?" Louise says with a pleasant lilt, and he withdraws in a sheepish shrug. When he turns and stuffs the money into his wallet, she drops his plastic bucket on the stack with a hollow *clunk*.

Ray Youngbear, taking a break from his duties at the entryway, appears in the doorway behind her. "Say," he says. "Talked to your boyfriend a couple weeks back. Nice guy."

Louise, not knowing how to respond, just feels a gnawing pain as she grabs the rolls of nickels and stacks them in a bin. The reality of having to put their breakup into words suddenly hits her, and she doesn't want to talk about it, so she busies herself by stepping to a side counter and grabbing a pile of invoices, their edges sharp enough to give her paper cuts. *Nice guy. Boyfriend.* The words echo in her head.

Ray's eyes follow her as she goes through the motions of checking the invoices. "So," he prods, "you're not talking tonight, or what?"

"No," she stumbles, "I mean I guess I'm just somewhere else. You ever wish that?"

"Hey, doesn't everybody?" He squints at her. "You're not thinking about pulling up stakes here, are you?"

"Maybe."

"C'mon Louise. What would we do without you?" he gives her his trademark wink. "And the kids, they'd miss you. Talked to little Eddie today, and he called you '*Weeze*, that nice teacher lady.'"

"Weeze," she repeats. "Nice name." The sound of it makes her giggle, and she realizes it's the first time she's laughed all day.

Ray strolls into the office for some coffee. Louise looks out at the Friday crowd, their shoulders rounded over machines. She knows her life is mundane here, which makes her plan to quit that much easier. It's not that it's a terrible place; the tribe has been good to her, and so has Ray. Her hours are flexible, and the pay has been good. It's just that she never thought of herself handing over money day after day so other people could chase their dreams. She never pictured herself at the end of each day, leaning over the ladies' room sink washing and washing off the gray smudge marks on her fingers from the thousands of coins she's handled. At home, she still turns a bar of soap over and over, trying to get her hands clean, though once in a while she notices small crescents of gray beneath her fingernails.

Louise has her dreams; most often she fantasizes about being a photojournalist and having her own gallery show. She thinks how amazing it would be to capture life's passion—and maybe its anguish.

As she dishes out change to the customers, she imagines what an eclectic gallery of photos these odd people would make. She takes mental snapshots of them and invents stories: That sad-looking, frail woman in the lavender sweater is battling cancer; she's out here on a lark, knowing she only has a few months to live. The twenties-something guy with a tongue stud and a tarantula tattoo on his arm is an environmental lawyer who rode a Harley up here from a suburb of Chicago. The young Hispanic couple in green and gold Green Bay Packer jackets just pulled the tab on a lottery ticket at the Clearwater Quick-Mart, winning twenty bucks, and now they're trying their luck at the quarter machines. A white-haired couple looks into each other's eyes as though they're still teenagers while they play the nickel machines; they reach toward each other and hold hands. *Click,* she thinks, freezing their image in her mind. Louise thinks about how everyone's portrait has a story, a tale of loss or gain, or something in between. She slides the invoices back in a drawer. *But what about me,* she wonders, *the woman behind the lens? Am I really seeing things clearly?*

Yesterday, after tutoring ten-year-old Shawna, Louise ran to her car and brought back her Nikon camera. Shawna had bonded with Louise over the weeks when Louise read chapters of *Bridge to Terabithia* to her. Louise leaned in close with the camera, trying to capture the innocent charm and sadness of Shawna's large brown eyes. But the girl shied away and turned sideways, trying to block the view of the small scar on her face each time Louise moved in for a close-up. Finally, Shawna covered her face with her hands. "Why do you want my picture?" the girl asked. "I'm nobody."

"No you aren't," Louise responded, upset at the way this little girl's self-image was bruised, even as a fourth grader. She kneeled next to her and peeled her hands from her face. "You're beautiful, Shawna."

The girl smiled fleetingly, then ran from the classroom and closed the door behind her.

An hour passes, and her shift moves along agonizingly. The lines at the cashier's desk grow longer and shorter, snaking back and forth, hissing with plastic bins of coins. During a lull, a woman in a blue wool blazer strolls past her desk, reminding Louise of her mother.

Her mother, Donna—who passed away five years ago—used to drive her to Lake Wisconsin on summer afternoons. Louise loved the lake, and she feared it, too. Her mother taught her a healthy fear of water because she herself had never learned to swim. "Not too deep," she'd caution when Louise was a young girl. She once told Louise that if you jumped into the middle of the lake from a canoe, where it was sixty feet deep, you'd sink all the way to the bottom. It always irked Louise that her mother—who worked as a receptionist in an office—subscribed to a series of illogical notions and sayings.

Donna was overly protective, whether Louise was walking to school, learning to ride a bike, or getting into a car for the junior prom. One afternoon at the lake when she was in seventh grade, Louise waded into the water. On the shore, her mother had unfolded a blue and white chaise lounge and sat on it. She wore her usual low-cut black one-piece suit with the gold straps, a suit that never touched water because Donna never waded out any deeper than her ankles. "Don't go out too deep," her mother warned. "You just ate, you know."

"I won't," Louise replied dutifully, though she always longed for the waters at the center of Lake Wisconsin, a lake you couldn't see all the way across in some parts. She thought about how deceptive the deep water looked. Its glittering surface seemed no different from the shallows, yet it might be fifty or one hundred feet deep out there. As Louise swam along the red and white buoys, she heard her mother's voice, calling out nervously, "Can you touch bottom there?"

"Yes," Louise lied, and then she lunged into a crawl and swam out even deeper. She did the breaststroke in the colder waters close to the buoys, then, with an impulsive but smooth motion, she flipped the plastic rope over her head and swam beyond them.

She hadn't thought about that day at the lake for a long time. Now it seemed to parallel her feelings about Luke: She had to push off from the shore, to be alone out there, free. She had to swim away from the roped-off beach where the bottom is too soft, where the gray mud sucks at your bare toes each time you touch down on it.

Ray interrupts her thoughts by sliding a cup of cappuccino toward her. "You look like you could use this," he says.

She thanks him, gives him a weak smile.

"Something wrong?" He leans one elbow on the countertop. "Bad day, or what?"

"Yeah." She takes a sip of the cappuccino.

"Same here. It's been crazy. Must have thrown out a dozen underage kids today. They try to slip in without IDs." He chortles, his big teeth yellowed. "Must be the full moon." He straightens and gives her a smile. "So, Luke picking you up tonight?"

"Not tonight," she says, dodging the question.

She leaves through the back entrance of the casino. Outside, the hot temperature—unusual for this time of year—makes it hard to breathe. When she crosses the heat-rippled asphalt toward her car, it feels almost as if she could sink through its softening surface. Then she hears her mother's voice, calling from a distance, "Can you touch bottom there, Louise? Can you?"

I don't know, she finally replies. *I don't know if I can or not.*

CHAPTER

13

Butch sits on a wooden plank and leans against a stack of concrete blocks while Rollie, wearing his Walkman headphones and listening to the new Faith Hill album, paces, bobbing his head to the music. When a car pulls into the parking lot, Butch, out of habit from his days as sheriff, checks the make and model of the car. An '84 or '85 four-door Cutlass Ciera. Brown, silver-dollar sized rust spots around the wheel hubs. The car looks vaguely familiar, but then he's seen beat-up cars like this up near the reservation on weekends. The city made quite a bit of revenue on DWI and speeding fines those nights, years ago, when Butch was on duty covering County Road 12. Lately there were fines Rollie managed to collect—and then there were the tickets where the fine deadlines came and went, and the city never saw the money, and that angered Butch. You break the law—you pay the consequence, Butch always believed. It reminded Butch of grade school, when a tough, sneering Indian kid kept borrowing money from him and never paid him back. "Where's my money?" Butch would ask, and the kid would always echo his question, saying "Where's *my* money?" Butch has asked Rollie to keep a list of names and the delinquent fines on a spreadsheet in the sheriff's office, and some day, when he has a mind to it, he'll send Rollie out to collect.

The older man stepping from the Cutlass Ciera is dressed in jeans, a dark denim shirt with flap pockets, and cowboy boots. His gray hair is tied back in a pony tail, and his necklace—with a bead-work pendant—sways as he walks.

"Here come the big kahunas," Butch says to Rollie, lifting his weight from the bench. "Better pull off that headset." Rollie, right in the middle of a song, looks irked but acquiesces.

A large, muscular man in his forties follows the first man; his hair is a little shaggy, and he's dressed in a white shirt and tie. The chief, Butch figures. A third man, the driver, paunchy and standing bow-legged, hangs back and leans against the fender. Butch tries not to picture these three Indians dancing at a powwow, dressed in feath-ers and headbands and loincloths, wearing bells on their ankles above fringed moccasins. Butch once saw performances like that at the Indian Ceremonial over in Wisconsin Dells, the tourists snapping pictures of them with their Sure Shot cameras, their kids mesmerized by the show. Powwows are mainly shows for the tourists, anyway, Butch figures, those city types who come up from Chicago expecting central Wisconsin towns like Clearwater, or nearby Baraboo, to be wilderness territory with pioneers and wigwams.

The man in the shirt and tie introduces himself as Randall Bell; he's the newly elected chief of the tribe. So far, the city hasn't really had much contact with him; Butch's only communication with him up to now has been a couple of phone calls.

"So this is the place?" Bell says, squinting at the half-constructed field. A crow, springing on its legs near the dirt of the infield, searches for worms or insects.

"Yep," says Butch. "Here she is."

Bell turns to the older man and introduces him. "Donald Youngbear's our tribal medicine man." Youngbear shakes their hands, murmuring an unintelligible greeting that sounds like "Yuh." His gray bushy eyebrows arch, and his slightly sagging eyes have folds of skin around them, like windows shades slightly pulled down.

"Medicine man, eh?" Rollie stares at the beadwork pendant on his chest; he's seen them at souvenir shops in the Black Hills when he takes his two-week vacation and stays at a campground outside Spearfish. Donald Youngbear squares his shoulders toward the field, and his head doesn't move, though his brown eyes move side to side.

"I've done a real good investigation," Rollie says, trying to sound professional and thorough. "I pretty much covered the area with a fine-tooth comb, tried to gather clues. But there really weren't any to speak of." His lips twist to one side. "I'll tell you right now, there's not much out here."

"We sent some stuff for DNA tests down at the U," Butch says, trying to give a little more credibility to the investigation. What he doesn't mention is that the archeologist in charge of testing was required to study the site by the state, as was NAGPRA, the Native American repatriation group.

Bell squints at the field through the parallel rows of half-finished bleachers. "Mind if we have a look around?"

"Be our guest." Butch swings his arm toward the field like it's his backyard.

The two men walk onto the field, along the markers set up by the archeologist—grids of string attached to metal sticks. Beyond them, at the edge of the outfield, the crow spots something, then bobs its head quickly, snatching up a worm or insect with its sharp beak. Donald Youngbear bends low, staring silently at the dirt, then the grass line, then the dirt again. His necklace sways like a pendulum. He lowers himself to one knee, rubs his chin, closes his eyes a few seconds. He opens his eyes, digs at the soil with his fingertips, scoops up a handful of dirt. He slowly closes and opens his hand on the soil.

"Say," Rollie calls from behind, "I don't think you should disturb the dirt there."

"It's okay," Butch shushes Rollie. "Let 'em poke around a little. Then it'll be done."

Youngbear pours the dirt back, stands, returns to Bell's side, still holding his dust-caked palm in front of himself.

"Not much to see, I guess." Rollie offers, strolling over.

Neither of the two Native American men says anything.

"Not exactly an episode from CSI, eh?" Rollie adds, uncomfortable at their silence.

Butch scratches his head and fills in from his perspective. "You know, all the archeologist found so far are a few old bones. Been here hundreds of years, I s'pose. Most of 'em are fragments."

"Fragments?" interjects Bell.

"Yeah. There was nothing to write home about, really."

Bell's thick lips frown, weighing his face down. "All our ancestors who have passed on are of tribal concern."

"So what do you do about them, then?" Butch asks, looking at Youngbear.

A strand of his hair, loosened from his ponytail by the wind, cuts a gray diagonal line across Youngbear's face as he stares solemnly at some point on the horizon. His cheekbones are high, his body is frail, arms thin. He hunches a little at the shoulders. Butch wonders if he's sixty-five, seventy, or even eighty. It's hard to tell, with the furrows in his forehead and the creases in his face. His head doesn't move, but his brown eyes keep shifting back and forth in synch with the crow as it pivots its head left, then right, and finally calls out with a *caw caw caw.*

"The medicine man can't talk of the dead," Bell says. "He can't speak of them at all."

"Why's that?" inquires Rollie.

"Because he believes it might disturb them in the afterlife."

Rollie tips his head back with a knowing look. "Oh. Oh yeah."

Youngbear strolls past the bales of wire and into the open field beyond, gestures with a nod of his head for Bell to follow. The two of them pace the land, then converse in low voices a few minutes.

"What's going on *now*?" Rollie asks impatiently.

"Don't know," Butch whispers, though the two men are too far away to hear him. "With these reservation people, you never really know *what's* going on. I mean, they don't really *say*."

Rollie lowers his voice, too, following Butch's lead. "Kinda odd birds, aren't they?"

As Rollie and Butch stand there, the only sound is the occasional gust of wind that flutters the yellow *Police Line* ribbon strung around the perimeter. A few gray clouds scuttle on the eastern horizon, and Butch wonders if it'll rain tonight.

Finally the two Indian men return. "Our medicine man believes this is a burial ground. That it's sacred ground."

"What's that mean?" Rollie inquires.

"It means he's felt the presence of the souls here," Bell explains. "We'll need to stop back again."

"Yeah, well," Butch says, finally giving voice to his agenda, "we kind of wanted to get this investigation thing moving along. We're planning to build a county road on the back acres over there," he says, pointing west. "And we want to finish up this field so we can get our Lakers on it. Season starts in June, you know." He gives the two a nod. "You boys baseball fans?"

Both of them shake their heads no.

"You know, the Lakers," Butch says proudly, ignoring their disinterest, "They're going to be good this year. Real good. My nephew plays for them. I played with them back in the old days, even. Won a few championships back then."

"Youngbear believes," Bell says, veering the conversation back to the subject at hand, "that this site is connected to the Man Mound site, west of Clearwater. He plans to come back here and hold a prayer ceremony for the dead souls. He'd like to bring some tribal elders along."

"Oh, sure. Sure," Butch agrees.

In the parking lot, Rollie seems agitated. "So, what do you think about that prayer ceremony stuff?" he asks. "We don't have to let them on the field, do we?" He raises his voice. "I mean, they're not really part of the investigation or anything."

"Relax, Rollie. No big deal." Butch tries to settle him down. He's had more experience with the reservation people than Rollie has. "You don't want to buck the reservation. Not these days. You know, politically correct, and all that. Let them do what they've got to do. It's just harmless hocus-pocus anyway."

"I don't want anyone botching things up is all," Rollie says, trying to get in the final word on the matter.

"Just let them do their little thing, and then it's done." Butch chews pensively on the inside of his lip a few seconds. "Then we move on." He strolls out toward the pitcher's mound, and Rollie follows. "It's a shame. I still don't get why they think all this property is their personal sacred ground."

169

Butch kicks at the soil near the pitcher's mound, and a small puff rises. "Sacred dust, eh, Rollie?"

Rollie nods in agreement.

"It's all settled," Butch says. "We let them do their prayers, then it's play ball. Right?"

"Right."

After Rollie drives off, Butch, pausing near the long fender of his silver Concorde, notices that bird, still bobbing out there, its iridescent head pivoting left and right, its eye black as obsidian. *That a blackbird?* he wonders, *or is it a grackle?* He could never tell those two apart. *What the hell does it see out there? Something in the grass, maybe. They can see things too small for the human eye.* For an instant, a memory washes over Butch, and his face goes hard, as though someone just covered it with a thin layer of quick-drying cement. He picks up a stone from the gravel parking lot, rolls it over and over with his fingers, feeling its smoothness, the way it fits just right in the palm of his hand.

Butch turns and faces the bird. With a sudden motion of his stocky arm, he tosses the stone, which tumbles through the still air, then thumps on the ground several yards from the bird. Startled, the bird rises, its wings expanding, hooking the sky with their black curves. It circles, banking, then lands on the dirt beyond third base. Butch reaches down, picks up another stone, and this time he rears back, throws hard, a motion that makes his arm ache. As the stone kicks up a puff of brown dust a few feet from it, the bird flinches, its feathers splaying, but doesn't fly this time. "Stupid bird," Butch mutters. He rears back with another stone. He throws. He rears back; he throws again.

CHAPTER

24

Luke swings his bat in the batting cage, hits the ball squarely, and watches it fly the ninety feet to the other side of the nylon net. This ninety-foot-by-ten-foot cage defines his limits this morning—this yellow mesh net outlines his life. He tosses another ball into the air, swings, cracks a grounder that only has a chance to bounce once before it spins to a harmless stop at the back of the net.

He cracks baseball after baseball until sweat trickles from his forehead, its rivulets meandering and burning his eyes. He pauses, wipes his face with the sleeve of his hooded sweatshirt. A fly ball is not a fly ball in this cage, he knows—it's just a baseball that rises ten feet in the air, hisses against the ceiling of the net, then rolls softly into a corner. He hits line drive after line drive, each one cutting the air inside the batting cage at ninety miles an hour until it reaches the far side of the net and stops suddenly, with a kind of cushioned sigh. His lower back begins to burn, but he knows he has to get in shape in a week, his thirty-seven-year-old body aching each time he pushes it to the limit. He knows that at tryouts, he'll have to compete with muscular twenty-year-olds—some of them back from playing ball at the junior college—who might glance at him at the end of the bench and mutter to their buddies, "Hey, who's the *old school* guy?"

He swings again, hits what should be a long, high drive, watches it drag the top of the net around itself and get caught there. He hit that ball just right. It would have flown a long way, he knew; it would have been something to watch, he thinks, if it wasn't for the damn net that enclosed it.

He thinks about how, weeks ago, he would have returned home to tell Louise about how well he was hitting today, the bat centered right on the ball. But impasse between them continues; these past weeks, their silence grows, separating them like a thick glacier. The longer it lasts, the more difficult it is for him to try to contact her. He knows it's his pride, his rock-stuck-in-a-field Tanner stubbornness that's making him act this way, even though, sometimes, he aches to speak to her.

Luke hits the last few baseballs. Jogging to retrieve them, he picks up the balls one by one, cradles them in the bottom half of his sweat-shirt and returns them to his duffle. Then he notices the one that got caught, still dangling from the far end of the net. The ball is trapped in the knotted nylon like a round leather fish. Luke stands there, paralyzed; for some reason, it makes him feel like he can't move.

THE NEXT DAY, when a baseball rises from home plate, he can finally move his legs again. He pushes off, sprinting to his left, knowing just how far he has to run. Reaching out with his glove, his tendons stretched and screaming, he snags the ball. Then, as though it's a crucial game situation, he stops quickly, cleats biting into the turf, turns, and throws the ball—a frozen rope—straight to the second baseman. If a fast runner was tagging and trying for second, he would have been out by ten feet. On the next hit, Luke turns and digs for a line drive that's hit toward the rust-colored snow fence in the outfield. As it hisses above his head, he leaps high into the air, and the ball snaps in the web of his worn Rawlings glove.

"Woohoo!" somebody calls from the infield as Luke tosses the ball back.

That afternoon of tryouts on the high school field, Luke is flawless. He dashes in to catch the looping Texas leaguers, sprints back to get under the high deep ones, ranges to his left or right to track down fly balls. He goes for the short pop-ups he shouldn't try for and somehow gets there in time for the scuffed leather sphere to drop into his oiled leather mitt. His glove becomes one with the skin of his hand—not just a piece of leather he's slipped on, but a natural appendage, something that seems to have been growing there for years. All afternoon during batting practice, he believes he can fly out there. *Fly.* Not just run and jump, but *fly,* a synchronized motion of muscle and tendon and bone, a perfect harmony of body and spirit. He's at one with this game that, right now, is so much more than a game.

With each catch, he becomes more adrenalized, more anxious for the next one. Soon he's so confident he thinks he could catch anything that's hit to center. *I'll never drop another one. Not ever,* he tells himself as he places his hands on his knees and crouches, ready to uncoil, hearing himself pant, but not feeling fatigued.

On the next pitch, the batter hits a high fly, and Luke sprints to his left. It's a long run, but keeping his eye on the tiny pinhead of leather dropping from the sky, he knows he can get there. As he stretches out to catch it, he collides hard with something. The wind is knocked from his lungs, and suddenly he's tumbling head over heels on the grass and coming to rest, motionless on the ordinary earth as the baseball lands nearby with a dull thud.

He rolls over and sees Josh Sobieski—the mayor's nephew—sprawled on the ground next to him. Sobieski sits up, clutching his ribs. "You goddamn dufus!" Sobieski shouts. "Watch where you're freakin' going!"

Coach Ron Saltos—a sixty-something former Lakers shortstop who now sells used cars—trots out to check his players. His nylon jacket fills with air, making him look pudgier than he is. "Holy buckets," he says as he reaches them. "You fellas okay?"

"I guess," Luke replies, the air returning to his lungs.

Shaking his wrist, Josh lifts himself to his feet and shoots a hostile glance at Luke. "Goddamn showoff. Such a freakin' ball hog."

"Easy, easy," Saltos says, holding his hand up to Sobieski.

"Sorry." Luke squeezes out the word.

Josh doesn't acknowledge the apology, just brushes the grass from his sweat pants and saunters over to his buddies in left field.

"Maybe you should cool off a little," Coach Saltos says as Luke climbs to his feet, catching his breath, the sweat darkening his T-shirt. "You know, take a break. Grab a Gatorade." He uses a coaxing tone, as if he's trying to get Luke to test-drive a used Pontiac over at Clearwater Motors.

"Naw. I can field a few more."

"Relax, kid. You made the team hours ago." Saltos shifts the Skoal in his cheek, squeezes his rubbery face into a grin.

A surprised, relieved smile crosses Luke's face.

"You play a decent center," Saltos continues. "I'm real impressed. In fact, you look like your dad out there."

"My dad?" Luke knows Saltos was on the Lakers during the few years his father played.

"Yep. I had to blink my eyes, just to make sure it wasn't Dwight out there. Hell, I miss that stubborn old guy."

Luke gives him a wistful nod. "Same here." He turns and jogs toward the infield as Saltos limps behind.

Luke sees Sobieski mocking him as his friends chuckle. Sobieski's one of the new breed of ballplayers that Luke dislikes—guys that are all muscle who reigned as hot shot jock kings in high school. Bulked up on weights and their own inflated egos, they work out on Nautilus, turn their ball caps backwards, and are proud of the diamond stud in their ears. They habitually check the blue screens of their flip-up cell phones expecting calls from their girlfriends. Worse yet, they're quick to put down their teammates behind their backs. According to Lance, who played with these guys the past years, Sobieski gets moody and sullen when he doesn't get enough playing time. Sometimes he throws his bat hard behind the bench when he pops out. Sobieski and his buddies used to drink until three in the morning, show up for practice hungover, slide on their jerseys— creased and stinking of sweat—and still play well.

As Luke approaches, Lance calls to him. "Hey, Tanner! Good show out there."

"Wasn't a show," Luke says modestly, slipping off his glove.

"So," Lance says, raising his eyebrows. "What's the latest? You out on parole, or what?"

Luke just shakes his head.

"What the hell was that all about?" Lance prods.

"Yeah, what's the story?" asks Joey Tartuga, a utility infielder and bartender at the Wildlife. "I hear you got busted by the sheriff."

"Go figure. Busted for going on my own property." Luke tips his head back against the rough plywood of the dugout.

"Heard you got a goddamn fine for that," Joey says. "For crossing Rollie and Butch's line."

"Aw, those guys are shitheads," Lance says, yanking at the strap on his orange and black shin guard and fastening it around his thick calf. "Luke's got every right to go out there."

"So, that pretty girlfriend of yours had to bail you out?" Joey kids.

"That's the rumor," Luke says flatly.

Lance lowers his voice. "So, buddy, what's goin' on with you two, anyway?" he pries.

Luke rummages in his duffle bag, takes out a bottled water. He's not up for discussing this topic, even with his old friend.

"I heard the sheriff turned up bones on the field," Joey persists.

Lance pulls out a piece of Double Bubble and peels off the wrapper. "Yeah. I guess NAGPRA's involved now."

"What's that?" Joey asks.

"Native American investigators. Sent out by the feds." Lance pushes the gum into his mouth with his index finger. "Guess the mayor's not too keen on that."

"Yeah. 'Cause he doesn't want the damn Indians mixed up in this," Josh Sobieski barges into the conversation. Luke shoots a look in Josh's direction. Josh, his yellow-lens wraparound glasses propped on the brim of his cap, wears a puka shell necklace around his neck and bounces a new baseball off a rolled-up tarp. "He wants to keep the investigation local. Those Indians want to drag their feet on everything."

Lance chaws on his gum. "Too bad, Sobieski. It's federal law." He blows a translucent pink bubble, which pops with a smack.

"The whole thing's bogus," snarls Josh. He gives Luke a stare. "Some idiot should have just thrown that bone back in the weeds."

Luke feels defensive but holds back his words. He returns the stare.

"You know what else?" Josh adds, snaring the baseball with his bare hand as it bounces. "Some idiots don't have the sense to hang up their spikes when they're washed up." He turns to his pals, and the three of them snicker.

The comment angers Luke; he doesn't really want to stoop to a reply, but he can't help muttering, "Some kids just don't know when to shut the hell up."

Josh spits sunflower seeds onto the ground behind the tarp. "Ooooh," he scoffs, "I'm really scared."

Sensing the tension, Coach Saltos approaches the bench with a fungo bat and a white plastic bucket filled with baseballs. "Okay fellas," he says, puffing his cheeks out. "Enough jawing. Let's take some infield." The infielders jog out, and Lance dons his black catcher's mask and his fat Johnny Bench catcher's mitt, then steps behind home plate as Coach Saltos slaps a few ground balls to third and short. The players go through their drills, the ball cutting geometric shapes in the air as each fielder gobbles up a grounder and throws to first. Then the first baseman pivots, fires the ball to Lance, who flips the ball back to Saltos, and the cycle begins again.

AFTER PRACTICE, Luke is the last person to leave the field. He'll meet up with Lance later for a couple of beers at the Wildlife.

On his way back, Luke pauses at the new ball field. Standing near the half-built bleachers behind home plate, he stares out at the construction.

Is this place cursed, or is it blessed? Luke muses. He wonders if uncovering this burial ground could cause bad fortune, like when you disturb an ancient mummy's tomb. He's heard about such things, about some archeologists who invaded King Tut's Egyptian tomb, then met with sudden and untimely deaths. Maybe he's part of the curse, too, since he discovered the first bone on the infield. But then, maybe the bone will bring good luck, be a talisman for him. He hopes it'll give him that extra step or two he needs, that extra spring of muscle, that long stretch of his arm as he dives for a falling fly ball.

Luke envisions the finished field: The slender grass blades waving the sky closer. The warning track—made of hard-packed sand—to let the outfielders know they're approaching the fence. A yellow foul pole rising at the corner of the left-field fence, telling if a long drive is fair or not. A scoreboard, maybe—not an electric one that hums, plugged into huge gray cables, but one where a town kid sits on a platform, dropping the zeros or ones or twos into the boxes after each inning. Lights, eventually. Lights on the top of ninety-foot poles so there could be night games. And, of course, a flagpole in center: a long, thin flagpole, like a fishing rod reaching to catch the afternoon sun, its new flag fluttering.

CHAPTER 15

Louise eases her El Camino into the reserved stall at the casino. With a shudder, she hugs herself and tosses up the hood of her parka for protection from the abrupt rain shower as she hurries across the parking lot. Lately her world stretches only from Madison to the casino and back. Lately her world is nothing more than an asphalt snake flattened for forty miles.

As she enters the casino, which is now open twenty-four hours, she tries to focus on her morning tasks—unlocking the cash box, then sorting the rolls of nickels and quarters, always so bright or so tarnished as they lie in the plastic cups. But her first order of business is to check on a *service needed* machine in aisle 16. Those nickel Island Treasure machines always seem to mess up. She grabs her keys and strolls through the aisles, many of them empty this early in the morning before the buses and tours begin to pour in. At the slot machine, she sees a man—in his seventies, or older, sitting on a vinyl chair, his mouth half-crooked in a frown. "Damn thing jammed up on me," he says, pointing to the two images of 7 and 7 and a third of a lemon. She clicks off the yellow service light on top and opens the front panel with her key. She stares inside at the computer workings, spots two nickels stuck together in the coin slot.

"Here's the problem," she says as she tries to separate the coins, which almost seem welded together.

The old man looks up at her. "My problem is not winning," he scoffs.

She has an impulse to say, *Your problem is coming here in the first place,* but she bites her tongue.

She hands the man two nickels, then closes and locks the front of the machine.

"So what do you think?" the man asks. The collar of his beige shirt is soiled. "Should I try this machine one more time, or is she going to clam up on me again?"

"It's your money. Do what you want," she says, and regrets that she's sounding a bit short-fused as a result of her dark mood this morning.

"But now it's your luck, too," the man counters, "because you touched the nickels."

"I wouldn't count on my luck," she warns, and turns to walk back up the aisle of blinking video machines, their cheesy animated islands, rainbows with pots of gold, and monkeys swinging from vines. As she reaches the end of the aisle, she sees the man pull the handle of the slot, hears the giddy sound of the circus music as the reels spin. He glues his watery eyes to the three icons as he loses again. "Damn," he says, slapping his palm on the counter, upending the ashtray.

Back at the cashier's counter, she scans the Clearwater morning paper, reads the front page headline article—claiming that a human skull was found at the new ball field site, and an archeologist has been called in from Madison. Mayor Butch Sobieski is quoted as saying he hopes the investigation could be completed soon so the ballpark and the adjacent road could be finished. It's technically city land, he adds, and thus the investigation is of concern to city hall. The article goes on to say that the skull—now kept in a lab—was identified as that of a Native American woman, about twenty-five years old, and it dates back approximately six hundred years.

She wonders if Luke discovered the skull while he was working on the field. For an instant she pictures him, clicking against it with his rake as he pushes aside the dirt, picking it up, holding it close to his face, and staring into its eye sockets.

It's been a couple of weeks since she's heard from Luke, since he left a message on her sister's answering machine. It sounded, oddly enough, like a casual message, asking her to call him back, as if nothing had happened between them. Yet she could still sense a kind of sandpapery tenseness beneath Luke's voice.

Without thinking, she had reached over and pressed the red button on the machine. The hollow mechanical voice emerged from the plastic speaker: "Message four deleted."

She thought of the way Luke always seemed lost for words, somehow unable to bring up the right things to say to her. Sometimes he seemed wrapped so tightly, just like those rolls of green sod he delivered.

On her way back from work, Louise thinks about the skull they found. She sees herself picking it up, trying to read the cracks and crevices of the cranium. She imagines flesh covering it as it transforms into the face of a Native American woman. Six hundred years ago, she thinks, the Clearwater Valley was completely covered with trees. Pit fires, wisps of smoke rising from dwellings of birch bark and stick. This small woman might have stood near Clearwater Lake, staring out over its calm water. She might have bent to her knees and filled a birch bark container, taken it back to the village, and set it down next to the fire where her husband and perhaps a child might be waiting. She wonders if this simple woman marveled at the blue brightness of lake water, smelled the aromatic scent of the curling wood smoke, felt a tingle during a kiss before sleep. She imagines the woman's bones brought to life not just by flesh and sinew and muscle, but by something else, something even more important.

Louise flutters her eyes, focuses on the blinking white lines of the highway. *How far have I evolved from this woman?* she wonders. *How often do I marvel at the sky, the taste of a berry? Lately, each day is filled with structure, repetition, counting coins. Clearing jams in machines. What about passion? If I don't have that, am I any better off than some dusty skeletons encased in glass?*

Louise idles her El Camino a block from Luke's house. She considers just talking to him, face to face, telling him that she's planning on applying to grad school, then maybe moving somewhere for a master's program, the way she'd always dreamed. She figures that she at least owes him that much. She thinks she might have seen him last week, standing alone in the outfield of the practice field as she took the shortcut through town, and she had an impulse to pull the car over, but she didn't. Now that she's actually right here, on his street, she can't get herself to step out. She sits there for a long time on this warm evening, feeling the vibration of the engine, feeling the heat rising through the floorboards. She clicks the chrome air conditioner button off and on again, although she knows it doesn't really work.

She stares at the big porch where the two of them used to sit on the wicker sofa on warm, humid evenings like this one. They'd whisper to each other, their words easy and natural as the nighthawks that floated over with curved black silhouettes like parentheses in the sky.

She closes her eyes a few seconds, imagines herself bursting through Luke's front door. Maybe he'd look up at her from the oak table and give her a startled smile, his lips slightly open as if he's about to release the words she wants to hear. Maybe she'd show him the color photos she'd just taken—the eight by tens she has in a folder on the front seat—and he'd hold one in his hands and stare at it a few seconds, pondering it, then he'd look her in the eyes, a grin lighting his face, and say, "That's great. Louise. Really great." She always needed his eye, his vision; he always seemed to see the world the way she did, the way it was meant to be seen. But then again, she thinks, Luke might just toss her an indifferent scowl—shrouded in silence.

With that thought, Louise feels short of breath; the layers of heat squeeze her rib cage, and her heart beats like a bird's wing fluttering against an opaque window. She presses hard on the accelerator and is almost surprised that the tires aren't melted to the pavement, that they screech a little as they catch. She drives past Luke's bungalow, not turning her head. She drives out of town, and it takes all her strength not to look in the rearview mirror to see if those headlights following her are Luke's pickup.

A few miles outside town, in the twilight, Louise notices the huge plumes of water spraying from the irrigation pipes beside the road. Impulsively, she veers to the shoulder, slams the car door, and faces the newly planted fields.

In a moment, she's slipping off her sandals and running across the fertile, wet ground, running without a thought about why she's running, just running. She slips on the slick earth and falls to her knees, and mud splatters her white blouse, her navy pants. She climbs to her feet and keeps running.

Soon she pauses at the spot in the field where the spray of water—rotating clockwise in the distance, will reach her. She tips her head back, stretches her arms to her sides and closes her eyes. At first, a fine, exhilarating mist caresses her, cools her, and the sensation takes her far away. Her bare feet sink into an expanse of fine white sand on a Mexican beach. She's at the base of a rainbow-threaded waterfall in Hawaii. When she opens her eyes, she frowns, seeing she's standing near a dented irrigation pipe on the flat ordinary fields of Clearwater, Wisconsin.

Damn that Luke, a voice in her mind shouts. *I hate him. I love him.* She's not sure, but she thinks she might be shouting the words out loud.

When the spray finally reaches her, it's much colder and heavier than she ever expected. She braces herself, trying to keep her balance. As the water pummels her, her eyes start to burn, and she thinks it's from the water's stinging force, not from the tears she's beginning to cry.

CHAPTER 16

Tonight, Butch Sobieski can't sleep. He tosses in bed, the scenes from over thirty years ago replaying through his mind.

"I GUNNED 'EM DOWN," Jim Whitebird bragged one night after a game. "Damn, I was good!" He stood, one foot on the end of the bench after the rest of the team had left. Butch and two of his buddies sat at the opposite end of the bench; the field lights were out, and the clubhouse was closed. Chief Bender was the nickname the guys on the team gave Whitebird, after that Native American pitcher who made it to the Baseball Hall of Fame. Butch knew Whitebird had disdain for the other players, not to mention a ninety-mile-an-hour fastball. Slim and lanky, Whitebird always pitched

Butch inside during batting practice, jamming him, making Butch look bad as he kept hitting the ball weakly to short or third. "This team would be nothin' without me," Whitebird said between big gulps from his can of Bud. "This team would be last place."

"At least I'm not a goddamn ringer," Butch scoffed. It burned Butch to see this Indian guy, who sometimes came to games with booze on his breath, talking in such a smart-assed way. Butch noticed that most Indians around Clearwater shut up when you talked to them. But not Whitebird; it was like his mouth was full of firecrackers and he was always shooting it off. Everybody knew that Whitebird was coaxed off the reservation to play ball by the Lakers coach, who actually promised to pay him $25 a game—under the table—when he pitched. Otherwise, Whitebird rarely came to Clearwater; he was content to stay on the reservation, doing some minor auto repairs and odd jobs.

"Hey," Whitebird countered, "You take what you can get. Too bad you're not getting any."

"You're so full of shit," Butch said, spitting on the dugout floor.

Whitebird had caused quite a stir in the leagues those years; he was even scouted by a few minor league teams. The townspeople usually supported him because he was such a good pitcher, but his greatest fans were from the reservation, a growing group that attended every game.

Butch knew *he* would have been the Lakers starting pitcher every Sunday, if it weren't for Whitebird. As it was, he had to settle for relief pitcher. But what really bugged the hell out of him was that the coach always put Whitebird right into the lineup when he waltzed in late for the games, often without warm-ups. One time the *Clearwater American* did a feature story on Whitebird, lauding his talents. "One Indian on the team is one too many," Butch sometimes griped to his pals behind Whitebird's back.

Back then, Butch was the new deputy sheriff of Clearwater. He liked the job, especially the respect and friendly nods he got in the town of Clearwater, because people all over town knew the Sobieskis. Proud, upstanding Sobieskis worked in the lumberyard and on farms; his father was co-owner of the local Savings and Loan and city council president. Sobieskis were the backbone of this town.

That evening, Whitebird waited on the bench to catch a ride back to the reservation with his wife, Lilly, who was a slim Indian woman with long legs and a reddish-brown skin tone. She wore tight skirts to the ball games, unlike the other Indian women, who came in sweatshirts and pedal pushers or black stirrup pants. Butch often thought that if she wasn't Indian, he might even find himself attracted to her.

"Hey Bender. Your old lady coming, or did she jilt you?" Butch called. Usually Butch and his buddies had this time to drink a couple beers and jaw among themselves, and it irritated him that Whitebird was still hanging around.

Whitebird purposely ignored him, bouncing a baseball off his forearm and catching it.

"She's back at reservation," Butch said, imitating a Tonto-like Indian voice. "Getting laid by best friend." He tipped his head back and laughed, and his friends joined in.

Butch's memory isn't clear about who instigated the challenge. All he remembers is that after he downed a few more beers, there they were, standing in a face-off, Butch with his bat at home plate, Whitebird with a pile of baseballs near the pitching mound.

"Give me your best fastball, goddamn it!" Butch shouted, while his two buddies cheered him on, calling, "Hit him, Butch! C'mon. Hit the shit out of him!"

Standing in the glow of the headlights from two pickups in the parking lot, his hat pulled low on his forehead, the brim bent sharply along its edges, his muscles flexed beneath his short-sleeved Lakers T-shirt, Whitebird stared Butch down. Then, with a strange, slow motion, he wound up for the pitch. He always had that lazy motion before he threw the ball, lifting the glove and ball toward his chin as if he were studying it for a second or two, reaching way back with his arm and pausing there, then lurching forward with a sidearm throw. The only thing that wasn't lazy about his delivery was when the ball jumped from his fingers toward the plate like a pale streak of light.

Butch swung and missed, hearing the *zing* as the baseball struck the screen of the backstop behind him. Whitebird shouted a loud sound, like a war whoop. "Wheeahh! Strike one on Mister Deputy!"

Butch felt a burning sensation, sure as if you'd taken a cigarette and touched it to the back of his neck. "That pitch wasn't over the plate," Butch blurted defensively. "Not even close."

Whitebird stuffed a ball in his thick-fingered mitt, wound up, drew his arm back, then brought it quickly forward. This time Butch timed his swing right; with a sharp, echoing *crack*, the ball rocketed toward left field. It towered there a few seconds, then finally came down, a barely visible white blur falling beyond the 350 sign.

"Wheeahh!" Butch mocked.

Whitebird just stood on the mound for a few seconds—motionless and expressionless.

"C'mon," Butch yelled, his adrenaline stoked by the solid hit and his pals cheering him on, "Gimme another one."

Whitebird nodded at Butch, tipping his cap brim with his fingers in an odd way, as though he were a gentleman ballplayer from the 1860s. Crouching in his stance, Butch watched Whitebird wind up, like he was doing an elaborate dance under water. Then he swung downward with his arm. But what he threw wasn't round, and it wasn't aimed at the plate. The silvery object tumbled end over end rapidly, and it was speeding straight at Butch's head. He began to duck from its path, but there was no way he could get out of the way. The full can of beer grazed him on the side of his temple. Butch fell on his back in the dirt, hearing the can of beer smack into the backstop and hiss as it sprung a leak. Butch seethed; anger radiated through his whole body as he heard Whitebird's laughter, a sharp laugh with jagged edges.

Butch pulled himself from the ground. "Screw you!" Butch drew his bat back and threw it hard toward Whitebird, who didn't move or even flinch, just waited there casually as the bat cartwheeled end over end toward him. Finally, at the last instant, he dodged the bat as it bounced past him. Butch wiped the blood trickling down his temple, then charged Whitebird, who stood there defiantly on the mound.

His buddies dashed out to Butch, grabbed him just a few feet from the mound, and pulled him, protesting, back to his car. "C'mon Butch. That's enough. Let's get another goddamn drink."

A few weeks after the incident, Butch got a call just after two A.M. in the dispatch office about a commotion behind the Water-in Hole. He drove in the city's unmarked police car along the grassy field a couple blocks from the bar. There he saw a couple guys in the middle of the field—two men he didn't recognize—who were standing over a third man on the ground, taking swings at him. He clicked on his radio, and called in to Linda, in case he might need backup: "We got three men involved in a fight here. I'll check it out." The headlights flashed across them for a couple of seconds as Butch pulled his car to a stop by the curb, and at that moment he realized the man on the ground was Jim Whitebird. He recognized his blue flannel shirt, his longish black hair beneath that odd-shaped brim of his ball cap. For an instant, Whitebird, mouth open in agony, stared up at the head-lights with a pleading look as one man held him down and the other beat him. Butch clicked the lights off, and in the stillness of the night, he rolled down the window and heard the sickening sound of slap-ping flesh as the men swung and hit Whitebird again and again. And there was no sound from Whitebird, no groans or cries for help.

Butch knew he should step out of the car and do something. He was, after all, a county deputy, sworn to uphold the law. He knew he should throw on the flashing red lights of the cruiser. He knew he should hustle across the field, flashlight in hand, and break it up. Deep down, he knew that was the right thing to do. Instead—re-membering that beer can tumbling toward his head, and hearing Whitebird's mocking laughter and sneering face—Butch just sat there a few seconds, staring at the squad car's darkened dashboard. Then he reached over, clicked the ignition on, backed up and drove off slowly, under the canopy of the elm-draped neighborhoods. *Let the boys have their little fight,* he told himself.

Back at the station—a small addition alongside city hall—Linda, the dispatcher, Sheriff Burt Worthy's wife, looked up from her ro-mance novel and asked him what was going on.

"Nothing," Butch replied, pulling a bag of Sugar Babies from his front flap pocket. "Fight broke up just as I got there, and everybody took off."

"Damn those bars," Linda said. "If they were smart, they'd have last call at midnight. Ought to cut the drunks off."

She nodded toward the police log on the main desk. "I already recorded your call. You logging in, or what?"

He shrugged, tossed some Sugar Babies into his mouth. "I guess," he said as he chewed. He listed the time and wrote in the log: "Two men observed . . ." Then he crossed out the words and wrote:

"No activity observed in field after complaint was called in," and a tinge of guilt rippled through him. With a quick motion, he closed the log, snapping the leather cover shut. He held the yellow bag of candy out to Linda. "Want some?"

The next day, as Butch was making his rounds, he heard the rumors about Whitebird's disappearance. People noticed him leaving the Water-in Hole around two A.M., and that was the last they saw of him. "Heard he mouthed off during a pool game," Butch overheard a grizzled farmer say when he stopped for a beer at Elmer's the next night. "Some good ol' boys followed him down the street and beat the livin' shit out of him." The man turned to Butch. "You know anything about that, Butch?"

"Hey, fellas," he replied, holding up his bottle of Cold Spring in protest. "I'm off duty, okay?" He paused, feeling that echo of guilt in his chest.

Rumors—with their tributaries and rivulets—made their way through town. Some said Whitebird, after being beaten up and threatened, left the reservation and the county for good. The men who did it, people claimed, were drifters from Chicago or Detroit. Others said Whitebird was playing ball in the minor leagues somewhere in the South. But one rumor that spread through town bothered Butch the most—it was the story that Whitebird was beaten to death out there on Tanner's field.

The day after the incident, the sheriff's office phone started ringing with calls from worried, flat-voiced people asking questions—Whitebird's mother, his uncle, his wife. And the following afternoon, Lilly, Whitebird's wife, pulled into the parking lot in her dented DeSoto. Butch watched her, crossing the lot on those long legs in tight black stretch pants. He recalled how some of the guys on the team had commented on those sexy legs, her nice ass, and how they wouldn't mind messing around with her some night.

She sat in front of Butch's desk, swallowing hard. Her face was solemn, partially hidden behind the long, shiny black hair, and the skin of her cheeks looked smooth as a polished reddish-brown agate. As he studied her, Butch was surprised to see that this woman—who he always thought was Whitebird's age, about twenty-two or twenty-three—looked to be all of seventeen, if you pushed it.

"What do you know about it?" she asked tentatively, her eyes still lowered. He knew, for a fact—and she probably did too—that when it came to reservation people involved in an incident, the Clearwater police force took a less-than-active role.

"He ever talk about leaving the reservation?" Butch shifted the focus, aiming a question back at her.

She gave a half shrug with one shoulder and stared at her lap. "Once in a while." There was something fragile in her voice. Then she added, "I mean, all the time. It was his dream to get signed. You know, by the minors."

"Well, there you go," Butch tapped the corner of an empty envelope on the desk. "You know, sometimes, people just take off and don't come back."

Then she lifted her eyes to him, brushed back her dark, shiny hair that covered half her face. It was the first time she'd really looked at him, and he was surprised by her eyes, their chocolate brown color, their intensity, as if they could look right into him. "But I heard he was out on that field. I heard something went on out there." Her voice was stronger now, with a little anger beneath it, a strand of leather tying itself into knots.

Butch gave her a condescending squint. "Where the heck did you hear that?"

"Some guys from the reservation. They told me . . ."

"Oh," Butch interrupted with a forced chuckle. "You know how reliable *that* talk is."

"So," she continued, "I heard you were on duty. Did you see anything?"

He didn't like the way she was asking these questions—he felt as if he were a tin can she was trying to pry open. He shifted a little in his chair, flexed the muscle of his pitching arm, rubbed it with his index finger, then glanced at the calendar on the wall—on it, a picture of the smiling city council holding shovels—a groundbreaking ceremony for the new Clearwater firehouse. "Well, we got a call from the bar owner that night," he finally said with a factual tone. He cleared his throat to let the next words slide out. "'Course, by the time I got there, the field was empty. I sure didn't see a thing." He shuffled some parking tickets on the side of his desk.

Tears made glistening half-moons on the rims of Lilly's eyes. As she leaned over and reached for a Kleenex, Butch noticed, for the first time, the loose blouse she wore, and how it bulged out a little around her stomach. It became obvious to him that she was pregnant. A part of him felt sorry for her, getting knocked up by an older guy.

Jailbait, he thought. *I don't know what they call it on the reservation, but that's what we call it in Clearwater.*

"Somebody must have seen something," she insisted. She dabbed at her eyes. "Jim's a good guy. He acts tough sometimes, and sometimes he drinks too much. But all in all," she said clearly, strongly, "he's a good husband." Her hands touched her stomach softly. "I love him. Please," she pleaded, "you have to find him."

"We can fill out a missing person's report. That's what we do in a case like this, when somebody runs away or something. People disappear all the time, you know."

She just stared so intensely at Butch that it almost hurt. "I know he didn't just run away," Lilly said. She reached into her leather saddle-bag purse. "Because I drove out to look and found this. It was near the ditch."

Butch recognized the wrinkled Lakers cap, its angular bend on the brim, the way Whitebird always molded it. He saw the sweat marks on the brim, whitish, like tree rings. He turned the cap over and over a few times in his hand, hoping that the dark smear on the side of the cap wasn't a blood smear, but just a grass stain.

"He never went anywhere without his cap," Lilly told him.

"Could be anybody's cap," Butch offered, keeping his voice steady, flattening any sign of emotion.

Opening a file drawer behind him, Butch pulled out a missing person's report, slid it into a black Royal typewriter. He asked a litany of questions required by the form and typed in the answers: height, weight, color hair, color eyes, clothing, last seen . . . "I'll do this report, but the reservation, you know, has to pick things up. From their end, I mean." He bumped against a nervous pause; he wanted to end the conversation, to wrap things up. He checked his watch; it was almost time for his lunch break. "So I guess that's it."

"That's it?" Her voice was wavering and tense. "That's it?" she repeated, this time with more resignation.

Butch ushered her to the door, then peered at her out the office window. She stood with her head bowed as she leaned against the fender of the car. She seemed to be staring into the empty hat in her hand, her index finger gently tracing the inside of the cap, where the sweat made concentric, salty rings. Then, with tears rolling down her face, she clenched her fist and pushed it into the hat, as if she could push right through the cloth. Butch swallowed the guilt, like rusty nails in his throat. He watched Lilly wipe the tears from her cheeks with her sleeve, fold the empty cap and slide it back into her purse, then drive away.

He pulled the missing persons report from the typewriter, the carriage making a metallic sound as it spun. He scanned the details on the sheet: *6'1. 175 pounds. Black Hair. Brown Eyes. Wearing blue flannel shirt and jeans. Last seen . . .* He stopped reading right there, as an image of Whitebird's anguished face appeared. Just as quickly, Butch closed his eyes and pushed the face away. He had things to do, he told himself, order to keep. He had that call about Mrs. Zantow's car, stalled in the middle of Third Street. He had to check the back of the junior high, where some kids broke windows overnight. He had a busy afternoon ahead, and he had to get started right away. No time for a missing Indian—he was just some black haired, brown-eyed guy who could have been a million other guys. Let it rest. Butch leaned toward the corner of his desk, lifted the stack of junk mail and disheveled papers, and slid the report beneath the pile. Rolling his swivel chair to the open file cabinet, he gave the gray metal drawer a quick push, watched it glide smoothly on its rollers until it latched with a slap.

TONIGHT BUTCH CLICKS on the lamp and throws off his tangled sheets. He stares at the wall of his bedroom, the photo of the league championship team, a photo that made the front page of the *Clearwater American*. He sees the gray oval of his face in the front row, tossing the camera a cheesy smile. Whitebird is noticeably absent; in the team photos from the previous years, he always stood in the back row, spine arched, head cocked arrogantly to one side. Behind the photo, cracks in the plaster wall branch off, spreading to smaller and smaller cracks, like a map of a river. It's already three A.M. *Got to get some sleep,* Butch tells himself. *Bury the memories. Bury them back there, where they belong. People disappear all the time.* He leans back slowly, his head touching the pillow, sinking deeper, deeper into its softness. Into forgetfulness. *Gone.*

CHAPTER

17

When Luke and Virginia arrive at the field on Sunday morning, the tribal elders are already huddled together near the storage shed. The morning is cool, damp, and overcast, the low clouds capping the horizon with a gray lid. Sitting in the truck, Luke sips the weak but bitter Rainbow coffee from a thermos. He wonders why he let Virginia talk him into coming here to the prayer ceremony. "I can tell right now I'm not going to be very good at this," Luke says.

Virginia turns toward him from the passenger side. "Nobody said you had to be good." She tugs at the sleeve of her gray wool jacket with a galloping pony design on it. "You just have to be open minded, that's all."

"You kidding? Me, open minded?"

When Virginia gets out, he reluctantly follows, and, pulling the hood of his sweatshirt over his head, he lingers by the truck. He notices a squad car parked on the street beyond the field. It's Sheriff Rollie, his squad's parking lights aimed ahead, the engine idling, as if he's ready to take off for the next emergency.

Ray Youngbear strolls up and shakes Luke's hand. Ray looks different from the last time Luke talked to him; instead of a formal blue sport coat and black tie, he's dressed in a faded tan western shirt and jeans, and he wears an Indian necklace decorated with green and black beadwork.

Ray nods toward Rollie's car. "I see they've got a cop out here to make sure there's no Indian uprising."

Luke chuckles. "Maybe you should invite him over. And the mayor, too. I imagine they'd get a lot out of this."

"Yeah. I heard about their little meeting with my dad the other day. You got some nice people in this town. But those two, well . . ." Ray rubs the side of his temple. "How should I put this? Let's just say they're a bit out of touch with our culture."

"You mean *racists*?" Luke twists his lips to one side.

A knowing smile ripples across Ray's face.

"So, what's this prayer ceremony all about?" Luke questions, pulling the hood down from his head.

"Can't talk about it." Ray shrugs. "It's sacred." He glances at the tribal elders, silhouetted by the horizon, which is beginning to brighten with a narrow band of pale pink. "At first they were a little upset that I invited you. My father believes only tribal people should be involved. He's a traditionalist, being shaman and all. A real spiritual guy."

"I'm sure he is."

"Yep, his favorite story is about the time he watched the burning of a church somewhere in Iowa. It seems it was built on a sacred Native American burial ground."

"Why'd they burn it?

"Well," Ray continues, his voice low and melodic, "the tribe won the court suit, so the local fire department was asked to set fire to the church one night. Somebody snapped a whole roll of film while that church just burned down. Funny thing—only one picture turned out. Those flames were a perfect image of a warrior riding a horse. My father claims he actually *saw* that warrior rise up for a few seconds while he watched."

"Wow. So, did you get to see the picture?"

"Sure did. My father kept it on his desk."

"What'd it look like?"

"Fire," Ray says with a knowing wink. "That's all I can say. Fire."

Later, Virginia and Luke watch from the edge of the parking lot as the contingent strolls onto the area where bones—some of them clustered into bundles—were discovered. A layer of fog—undulating in the light breeze—hangs over the bare earth. Luke half-expects a pale ghost to rise from the soil in the center of their circle, do a loop like in *Ghostbusters,* and then evaporate into the March morning sky.

Burial ground or baseball field? Luke finds himself thinking. *Which is it?* He considers what his father would say about a prayer ceremony on a baseball field. He'd probably scoff and say "Smoke and mirrors. That's all. Just smoke and mirrors."

The elder Youngbear seems to ponder a distant object, narrowing his eyes beneath his high tanned forehead. He says a few prayers in the traditional Potawatomi language. The harsh yet musical *g* and *sh* and *k* sounds rise from his lips and carry to the parking lot. He makes graceful, circling gestures with his arms toward the earth, then toward the sky. Beyond them, on the far side of the field, the translucent cloud of exhaust from Rollie's squad car curls upward and fades.

Afterwards, Virginia leans against the fender of Luke's truck. "Well, what did you think?" Luke can tell by Virginia's expression that she's inspired by being present at her first prayer ceremony. She told Luke she's read about these and discussed them in the classes she teaches at the U, but, new at her position as state archeologist, she's never been present at one.

Luke just gives her a blank look. He doesn't have an answer for her. He knows he should have gotten more out of this ceremony, but he can't get to that part of himself, as if it's buried beneath layers of gravel.

Virginia slams the truck door shut with a hollow *clunk* and keeps her eyes fixed on the windshield. Seeing her irritation, Luke finally says, "Okay. What was I *supposed* to feel?"

"Well, maybe something about the people who've passed before us," she offers with an unexpected passion, her high cheekbones half in shadow from the lowered visor. "Something about what we've lost when a whole culture disappears."

He takes a sip from his coffee, his eyelids half-closed, then slides the key into the ignition, keeping his thoughts to himself. The engine turns over a couple of times with a harsh, metallic sound before it starts.

That evening, Luke walks among the rows of pines beyond the half-finished outfield fence. He feels a little guilty for the way he acted after the prayer ceremony. And he knows that Louise, like Virginia, would tell him to get in touch with his emotions.

Lately Luke has his doubts about religion, about what happens to a person after the flesh is gone. He grew up a traditional Catholic and, as a boy, even learned a few Latin prayers from his father. At age ten, he was an altar boy, wearing a black cassock and white smock at six thirty A.M. Mass, his head bowed reverently beneath the life-size plaster statues of the saints that always seemed to be watching you with their piercing glass eyes. In grade school, he studied his catechism lessons each day, believing every word: The water turned to wine. Lazarus rose from the dead. The angels rolled the huge stone away from the front of the tomb.

But now it seems like all his questions are becoming more and more complex, and, like chasing quick-moving iridescent butterflies, the more he thinks about things, the farther away the answers seem to flutter.

He tries to focus on the immediate things—like the row of eighty-foot-tall Norway pines that, in the last light, rise like green fire. They're what every hitter should have for a backdrop when the pitcher throws the ball from the mound. No distractions, no fans' soda cans reflecting the sun, no pale houses confusing your vision— just this lush wall of green, helping you see, clearly, that white baseball as it leaves the pitcher's fingertips and spins toward you.

He wonders how these trees must have looked when his father played, thirty years ago. Maybe they were half the size, or maybe they stood fifty feet high. He wonders how the azure sky beyond them looked, or if the small, ragged clouds hooked onto their branches the way they're doing right now. His father taught Luke the world through words of advice, puzzles that young Luke was left to figure out in his later years. "Don't forget where you're standing," his dad would say. "But don't be afraid to move, either." Other times, his father shared one of his favorite sayings, musing, "The ol' world sometimes wears a disguise. Be careful of what you think you see."

How much of the world did his father see when he spent eight hours a day on a creeper gliding across gray concrete? Most days, Luke thinks, all his father got to look at was the underside of a John Deere harvester, its oil pan stained dark, like a sky about to rain. No wonder he died young, Luke thinks. As Dwight worked year after year to keep himself and his son and his business afloat, his debts got deeper and deeper, until all his days were surrounded with gray. The sky his father always thought was endless blue was actually made of dented aluminum.

What happens when you die? Luke wonders. *When you exhale your last breath, are you simply gone from this world?*

Luke strolls, watching the fireflies above the grass in left field: they ignite, then go dark, then ignite again, but in a different place. As the fireflies float among the pine boughs, Luke thinks how the roots of these trees are deep and ancient, yet their new green needles always stir the sky. His foot bumps against something. He stoops to see what it is.

Reaching beneath a layer of dried brown pine needles, he pulls out a worn baseball. It must have been here a long while, he figures, because some of its red stitching has been eaten away by the seasons, the gradual gnawing of heat and rain and snow. He studies its face, its cracks and crevasses. He stares at the 216 stitches curving upward on one side of the ball, downward at the bottom. *Like the earth*, Luke thinks, rotating the ball in his hand. *Always perfectly balanced between a smile and a frown.*

CHAPTER 18

The Water-in Hole is almost full on a Saturday night, and the jukebox with orange neon tubes pumps out country songs by artists the locals keep playing over and over: Merle Haggard, Johnny Paycheck, Travis Tritt. In addition to the regulars—old Cyrus and Walter, anchoring their red vinyl stools at the bar—there's a group of men from the reservation sitting at a wooden table in the corner. Above the lit shelf of liquor bottles and a commemorative liquor decanter in the image of Elvis, the blue and white stream on the lit Hamms beer sign flows endlessly over a rocky riverbed. Luke and Lance split a pitcher of beer, and all night they've been laughing about the old days in high school and the Lakers' chances in the Central Wisconsin Amateur League.

Lance takes a gulp from his mug, pulls out a Marlboro, and lights up, adding to the smoky haze. Luke nods at the cigarette and says,

"You in training for the season, or what?"

"Always in training." Lance lets out a muffled laugh as he takes a drag and tugs at the neck of his jersey that's stretched across his barrel chest, a chest just right for a catcher who needs to be a big target behind the plate.

Two women saunter past their booth carrying bottles of Bud Light. One of them, Diane, who went to high school with Luke, gives him a friendly smile.

"How's it goin', Luke?" she says flirtatiously, flipping her red hair back and putting one hand on her hip.

"It's going." Luke gives her a fleeting smile.

"You guys don't want company, do you?" Diane asks. As some patrons walk by in the shoulder-to-shoulder bar, she bumps her slim thigh against his knee.

He can tell by Lance's drunken expression that he's about to nod yes, but Luke quickly replies, "Naw, we're leaving soon," though they plan to stay a while.

"What? And miss all the fun?" Diane kids.

"Yeah," Luke replies. "We're pretty darn boring, I guess."

"Okay, then. See you around." Before she continues through the crowd, she seems to wink at him. Or is it something caught in her eye? Luke wonders.

"So, Lukey." Lance interrogates, leaning over the table stained with beer rings. "What's up with you and Louise lately?"

"Dunno," Luke dodges the question, shifting his eyes to the eight-point buck mounted on the wall.

"You two didn't really break up, did you?"

Luke's in no mood to discuss his breakup tonight. "Who knows what's true," he mumbles.

"Hey, man," Lance blurts. "I know what's true. You two should just get back together."

"Huh?" Luke is a little caught off guard by Lance's candid advice.

"Yeah. Just find her and take her in your arms and make out with her. Get it over with, for chrissakes. I can tell you're goddamn crazy about her. So why don't you just *go after* her?"

Hours later, at midnight, fueled by the night's whiskey and beer, the small bar becomes more raucous; Cyrus and Walter, their voices raised to shouts, exaggerate their gestures and slap each other on the backs as they solve the world's problems: global warming, the latest Mid-East crisis, when the crops should be planted around Clear-water. Josh Sobieski and his two buddies order shots of Jack Dan-iels, raise them in the air, and clink them together before downing them. Two lovebirds in their twenties, their hands clutching bottles of Point Beer as they wrap their arms around each other, make out near the rest rooms in back marked *Bulls* for the men and *Cows* for the women. The jukebox blares Waylon Jennings and "I Got Home at the Wrong Five O'Clock," a snappy lament that provokes half the crowd to join in and sing. A cardboard Captain Morgan, his saber raised, salutes the scene in approval.

Luke stands to order another beer at the bar and nods at Ray Youngbear, sitting with a table of Native American men who work at the casino. Luke watches Gerald—a Native American man who comes here regularly—make his way through the crowd to the far end of the bar. In his forties, Gerald wears his stringy long hair in a pony tail topped by a Yankees ball cap. His face is ruddy and pock-marked.

Gerald makes the mistake of trying to order right next to Josh and his boys, who anchor the corner, elbows on the bar. From the other side of the bar, Luke can see that Josh and his friends are loaded. They've been at the bar all night, talking too loudly and throwing their hands into the air. As Gerald waits, a ten-dollar bill in his hand, he says, "Three bottles of Bud" to Elmer. When Elmer steps over, Josh muscles in, waving his arm in front of Gerald's face. "Three more shots here, Elmer!" he calls, and as he does, Elmer nods and turns to pour the drinks. Gerald gives Josh a look and says under his breath, "Hey, I was next here."

Josh pokes his buddy with his elbow and responds sarcastically, "No shit? I think *we* were here *first*."

Gerald ignores him and waits for Elmer to slide the three shots toward the boys before ordering again. "Hey, bottles of Bud here!"

"We need a chaser," Josh interrupts. He leans onto the bar so his shoulder edges Gerald out. "Three taps." Elmer, the stout bartender in his fifties with a moustache, obliges. He doesn't make eye contact with Gerald, but turns to the diamond-shaped draft beer handles and pours three Cold Spring drafts, each with a half inch of white foam that curls over the rim.

"C'mon," Gerald says. "Damn it all. C'mon."

"C'mon what?" Josh sneers. "Where we going, Jerry? Hold your horses."

One of Josh's friends, Darryl Hutchinson, slaps his palm on the bar and laughs as if it's a really good joke. "Good one, Josh. Hold your horses. Good one!"

"Stupid one," Gerald says under his breath. "Damn stupid."

"What'd you say?" Josh barks, but Gerald doesn't respond, just keeps his eyes fixed on the back bar, the three shelves of liquor lit by an orange glow from beneath. Elvis freezes, his sequined cape in mid-swirl, a black microphone poised close to his face. "I said *what'd* you say?" Josh demands.

Gerald ignores him, and Elmer finally clunks three bottles of Bud onto the bar. After Gerald pays and tips Elmer, he turns, squeezing between Josh and a tall bar stool. As he does, his elbow—

accidentally or not, it's not clear—bumps Josh's glass of beer, and half the beer sloshes over his wrist and to the floor.

"You dumb shit," Josh snarls.

"Hey, Chief" Darryl chimes in. "You spilled his freakin' beer."

"I b'lieve I was bumped," Gerald says, trying to back away, but Josh and his two friends stand and surround him, standing too close, muscles tensed.

"Guess you're gonna have to buy me another one," Josh demands with a swagger.

"He should buy us *all* a round," Darryl agrees. "He's got plenty of cash from up at the casino."

"No way," Gerald says with a shake of his head. "No way I'm buying for you guys."

With that, the three men begin to push at Gerald's chest and shoulders. Seeing that Gerald is on the verge of trouble, Ray and the other man jump up from their table and hurry through the crowd.

Ray tries to grab Gerald away from the three, and when he does, Josh's two friends turn toward him. Huddled together, grabbing each other's shirts, the six men shove each other, gliding backward and forward in unison like players in a rugby scrum. When Alan Jackson's "He's Gone Country" blares from the jukebox, their shuffling almost resembles a strange group dance. Luke takes a couple of steps toward the altercation, but then stops. He knows he should do something to bail Ray and the guys out, but isn't certain what.

In an instant, Elmer lifts the hinged section of the bar, and, quick for a short and stout man, he's yanking at their shoulders. "All right, boys. Knock it off. None of this shit in my bar." When the men back away from each other, Elmer points at the trio of Native Americans. "You fellas had way too much tonight. You're outta here!" he says, swinging his arm toward the front door beneath a Miller sign where a girl reclines on a lit moon. "You finish those damn beers, then get out."

"Aw, hell," Gerald says. He chugs half his beer, slams it on the bar, and reluctantly moseys through the crowd, followed by Ray and the other man.

Elmer turns to Josh with a chiding look. "And you guys cool off. Hear me?"

"Whatever you say, El," Josh slurs. "Now how 'bout another chaser? Some screw-off spilled mine." The three of them break into a laugh as the Native American men push through the door and spill onto the sidewalk.

Rollie, staked out near the bars, sits in his squad car in the alley on the south end of the town square. He sees the Chevy Silverado truck—black and jacked up with the chassis raised high above its big wheels—back from its parking stall and lurch into the lane. He thinks he recognizes the vehicle, and as he gets a glimpse of the reservation plate and the bumper sticker that says *Native and Proud*, he's sure it's Gerald's truck.

Rollie guns his cruiser, the dark blue Ford Crown Victoria pouring it on as it gains on the truck, which has peeled out and is already a block away. *Goddamn them,* Rollie thinks. *They think they can speed right through town. This isn't the reservation. We've got rules.* Rollie sees the red taillights veer toward the middle of Eighth Street, then swerve back, then drift toward the center again. Rollie gains on the truck, tracing a straight line right up to its bumper. He hits the dash switch, activating the red lights that flash out of his grille and reflect off the shiny finish of the Silverado's tailgate.

The truck brakes, wobbles when its tires bump against the curb, then finally coasts to a stop. Rollie releases his seat belt and steps out.

At that moment, Gerald roars out, the double-wide tires firing gravel that pings against the front of Rollie's cruiser like a sudden hailstorm. Rollie hops back in, floors it, and the big 440 engine bolts the car forward like a dragster gunning off from the starting line. The force of the take-off presses Rollie's body into the cushioned upholstery. There's a ding in the center of the windshield from a piece of gravel, and the chipped star begins to branch out, spidering across the glass and into Rollie's line of vision.

Rollie knows their souped-up Silverado won't be able to outrun his Crown Victoria as they take on the abandoned straightaway leading to County 66, but still, it's a challenge. As he catches up to it, siren blaring, red lights jabbing the night, the tiny crack in his windshield spreads wider and wider, sending out tendrils like a county map.

Rollie roars right up to the bumper of the truck, which is already doing about eighty. He thinks he sees one of them flipping him the finger, and as the two passengers turn to look at him, he imagines them laughing.

At that moment, something fills Rollie. Like the cracks on the windshield, but darker, the anger branches to Rollie's entire body, spreading quickly through his fingers and toes and into his brain.

The truck slows slightly and starts pulling over.

Rollie's unclear about what happens next. He pulls his foot off the gas, but then it's as though there's a weight, a five-pound stone pressing on his right foot, and he presses the pedal again. The cruiser roars and lunges forward into the truck, slamming right into the sneering chrome bumper. The impact jolts through Rollie's palms, and it feels like both of his wrists are sprained. The truck swerves and begins to do a slow, almost graceful spin in front of Rollie's vehicle. The oversized truck tires hit a patch of gravel on the opposite side of the road and kick up a beige curtain of dust. Rollie hears the low-pitched crunch of sheet metal hitting a solid object as the truck strikes an electrical pole beyond the ditch. The truck flips, landing on its hood, glass splashing in the air like beads of water after someone does a cannonball in a pool.

Rollie pulls his squad to a sliding halt at the edge of the road. Feeling a little numb, he pulls himself from the cruiser and just stands there a few seconds. The sound of the horn blaring steadily from the overturned vehicle drills into his skull. Like eyes that won't close, the truck's lights still shine, their yellow cone-shapes reaching into a cornfield.

Approaching the wreck, he sees the driver's body has been tossed a few feet from the car; the man lies motionless on his back, as if he's frozen, both legs bent awkwardly to the side beneath him as though he's in the middle of a run.

Ray Youngbear, dazed, drags himself from the front seat. Blood from cuts on his forehead branches across his face as he limps across the ditch toward Rollie. "You ran us off the road!" Ray shouts. "You bastard!"

Rollie lunges toward Ray, giving him a hard shove, and Ray falls backward on the asphalt next to the yellow line. "Stay down on the ground!" Rollie orders, pulling his gun from its holster as if he's captured an escaped convict. "And keep your damn hands where I can see them!" Standing over Ray, Rollie makes a call with his walkie-talkie. "We got an accident on 66, south of town," Rollie says, trying to sound businesslike, to keep his voice from shaking. "We got injuries."

Within moments, Rollie sees a tiny flashing red light that grows larger as the rescue vehicle, following 66, traces the straight line between town and the accident scene. It's Arnie, his deputy. As the vehicle approaches, the pulsing light makes Rollie's thin face flush red, then go pale, then flush red again. He's already rehearsed exactly what he'll say, and he won't waver from that story. *Came upon an accident scene. The inebriated suspects must have lost control of the vehicle and then hit the utility pole.* He can't think of an explanation for the cracks in his windshield, but he'll come up with one. *Then one of the men got out and assaulted me. I'm telling you, Arnie, as soon as they're out of the hospital, we're locking 'em up. You goddamn straight. We're locking every one of 'em up.*

CHAPTER

19

The dried jawbone can't weigh more than a few ounces, yet it takes all Luke's strength just to lift it. *This is not what I wanted to find on a beautiful new ball field,* he thinks. He holds it tighter, squeezing it, as if trying to feel its pulse, to sense its meaning. He waits for it to speak to him, to say something he needs to hear. But no words are spoken. Silent, worn molars erupt from its base; the empty sockets fill with tiny sandstorms of dust.

Rearing back, he throws the bone hard, as if he could toss it halfway around the earth. He sees it tumble, end over end, its pale yellow color startling the midnight blue sky. The bone spins toward the thin line of the horizon and almost disappears, but then it begins to curve like a boomerang. It turns slowly in an arc and flies right back to his hand again. When it slaps the center of his palm, it cuts right into his skin.

Luke wakes from the dream, sits up in bed with a gasp, his palm still stinging.

After climbing the pull-down stairway to the attic, Luke searches for the box that holds his family keepsakes. He finds the varnished two-by-four-foot cedar chest that's been in his family for generations, storing everything from scraps of kindling to stiff baseball gloves and cleats with the toes curled upward. For a time it stored his father's gold-leaf cigar holder and cigar boxes, but, in recent years, since Luke acquired it from his father's estate, it's been used to house sentimental items. He stares at the knots in the wooden lid, following their reddish-brown spirals around and around, as if they could lead him to the past, to some clues to the land ownership.

As he lifts the lid, the scent of mothballs mixed with aromatic tobacco rises up. He finds, next to a couple of pocket watches in the corner, his father's baseball jersey, number 21, sealed in a plastic bag. Luke's hand glides across the flannel fabric, his pinkie finger poking through a couple of moth holes on the sleeve.

He pulls out an envelope marked with his father's cryptic handwriting that says, "Photos." Luke comes across the sharp-edged tintype photograph of a woman he often studied curiously when he was a boy. The formal portrait shows the woman posed in front of thick velvet curtains tied with cords and tassels. She appears to be in her early twenties, her black, shiny hair tied behind her head. She is dressed in a long skirt and a lacy white blouse. As a boy, Luke liked the striking beaded necklace she wore, and he wondered about the dark face, high cheekbones, that intense glare. There was something about her expression—was it fear or perhaps anger?

Luke had asked about the woman, and his dad gave the photograph a quick frown, then said, "Just some old friend of the family. That's all I know." Now, as Luke studies the back of the photo, he notices initials scratched into the tin: *T.E. Who was she?* he wonders.

He continues to dig through the box and comes upon the photo of his great great grandfather—a man dressed in a dark suit with a silk necktie—posing proudly in front of a painted backdrop of an 1880s park where women stroll with parasols. For most of his life, this man was a farmer who worked the fields around Clearwater harvesting grain and wheat and, according to Luke's dad—for a couple of years during the droughts—nothing at all. Luke often thought how hard that life must have been—finding your own water, clearing trees from the valley, gouging a plow into the soil behind a horse, then holing up in a crude log home during the bitter Wisconsin winters. As a boy, Luke pictured his great great grandfather hunched over a stone fireplace, staring at the glowing coals. But this man in the photo doesn't seem hunched or burdened at all—in fact, he stands, his back arched confidently, his arm propped on a velvet chair. He poses in front of that painted backdrop as if he knows he is the only real thing in the photo and is proud of it, as if he knows that some day, a young boy named Luke Tanner might be spanning a hundred years by staring into his eyes.

Luke turns the photo over; on the back, scratched in someone's handwriting, it says, *Grandpa Frederick.*

For over an hour, Luke sifts through photos and letters, hoping to find some information he needs. Just when he's about to give up, he notices the shape of a small black square inside a yellowed envelope. He pulls out the photograph—one he doesn't remember seeing before—and is amazed to discover an image of his great great grandfather, his arm intertwined with that mystery woman from the other picture. It appears to be a photo of some important occasion, since the two are dressed in formal clothes. Her face is stern and puckered, an older version of that young woman who looked so out of place in her 1800s dress and high-topped boots. Her raven black hair—with streaks of white, as if someone delicately painted it with a fine-tipped brush—is tied back in a braid. Her eyes seem sadder, her expression more vulnerable. Her neck is still adorned with that beaded necklace—tucked inside the collar of her dress—that he recognizes from the other photo. He flips the photo over, and it says, *Frederick Tanner, wife, Two Eagles (Ojibwe).*

Wife? Luke thinks. *Wife?* He feels his adrenaline rise as the realization sinks in: *That mysterious woman is my great great grandmother.*

Suddenly his past seems to open up like a huge chasm, and he feels as though he's falling into it, tumbling head over heels through dark air. Clutching the photograph in his hand, he runs to the bathroom mirror and looks closely at his reflection. He stands there, staring into his face, a face he thought he knew so well. Emotions surface inside him and swirl like dust devils. He imagines other faces beneath his. His father's. His mother's. His father's father. His mother's mother. Face after face appears, extending into infinity. His fingers trace his features as he slowly runs his hand over eyebrows, nose, cheeks, like a blind man trying to read Braille.

Luke drives from stop sign to stop sign, his truck like a pinball bouncing back and forth. Though it's just after midnight, no one in Clearwater is on the streets except for him; it's as though the town has tipped sideways and all the people have dropped off the edge. He pulls up to a stop sign on Oak, cracks open a can of Miller, and takes a few swallows.

His brain races with thoughts. He's always considered Native Americans as people different from him. Who were they? He knew them only as a fringe group, barely tolerated by the town fathers, living on the reservation. He feared the kids from the reservation when he was young, especially when fights broke out after school. He knows little about their culture. What he does know is that tonight he feels exhilarated, yet confused, emotions tangling inside him like fish line hopelessly knotted on a bale. Tonight he's aware of the rich, red blood running through his arteries, blood that makes his heart crescendo inside his chest.

Then he wonders: Why did his father always seem so prejudiced? Why, at times, was he disparaging about the Native American people? Was he trying to deny his heritage, or separating himself from the nearby reservation? Perhaps it was a business decision, knowing how narrow-minded the townspeople could be. Luke will never know for sure what self-doubts, what emotions were in conflict beneath the steely surface of his father.

He idles at the downtown stoplight. The opaque eyes of the buildings watch him, as if waiting for him to decide: stay where you are, tires fusing to the pavement, or move forward. *Everything looks different,* he thinks, *and yet it's all the same.* He finishes his beer as he waits at the intersection. *Which way now? Left? Right? Nowhere?*

When the light changes, Luke takes off across town, passing the broken-down houses of Clearwater's south side. He passes through this neighborhood each day on his way to work, taking note of the residents—in front of one house, an overweight man, his pale belly showing above faded purple Zubaz, fixes a Falcon on a dirt driveway. Next door, another man—heavy and wearing a black Harley T-shirt and a faded red handkerchief over his greasy strands of hair—sits with his wife or girlfriend on white plastic lawn chairs in the front yard, drinking twelve-packs of Milwaukee's Best. They seem proud of their lawn ornaments, especially the paint-chipped deer, frozen in mid-stride. One house has a wooden wishing well decorating the front yard, but Luke knows there's no deep shaft of water to make a wish—only a cloudy plastic base where, on a windy day, the scuttling wrappers and sparrow feathers circle one another.

As he drives south of town, Luke thinks about the articles Virginia found in the archives yesterday. She handed him a stack of photocopies, saying, "Here. I think you should read these."

One article talked about the legend of an Indian chief who, the elders said, was buried on his horse beneath a mound on the edge of Clearwater Lake. The mound was left more or less intact, despite some of the housing construction that erupted along the lake road. Today, the mound appears like a knoll along the flat shoreline, a sudden hill for kids to run up and down. Luke thought how appropriate to be buried on your horse—the chief, placed in death the way he was proudly carried in life. He still led the way for his tribe, one arm high in the air, riding into eternity.

He was surprised to learn, in the next article, that the neighborhoods of Clearwater were built on almost a hundred Indian mounds. According to an 1860s map of the county, an Indian village sprawled along the river, surrounded by effigy mounds shaped in the images of bear and deer and Thunderbirds and even humans. The early settlers had plowed over the mounds, flattening them for crop planting. The houses from Water Street to Eighth Avenue are built right on the ancient mounds, and Luke gasped as he discovered that even his own father's house—the house where Luke grew up—was built on a mound.

"All that history, so close to you," Virginia told him. "Right under your feet. And you didn't even know it."

Right under my feet, he thinks as he slows and pulls into the Potawatomi casino parking lot. He jogs toward the tinted double doors, dodging the slowly backing cars. Inside, he's surprised by how many people are at the game tables this late on a Thursday night. He sits at the bar and drinks a tall draft beer; he watches the gamblers line up at the cashiers' windows, cash and credit cards clutched in their hands. Finishing his beer, he strolls down the aisle, and notices an elderly woman, cane propped next to her, one hand on the Island Treasure slot machine, one hand poking a cigarette into the pucker of her mouth.

The woman shifts her sagging eyes from her machine to Luke. "Gonna win tonight!" her gravelly voice spouts, and he doesn't know if she's referring to him or to herself. *One win*, he thinks, *one or two hundred dollars, and then what? Then you limp through the parking lot with your cane, get back on the shuttle bus, go home, and die. Is that it?* Some part of himself is caught up in the moment and wants to believe her words, while another part doesn't give a damn what happens tonight.

He pulls up a stool in front of the first open machine, slides two twenty-dollar bills into the slot, and the credits ring up. He plays nine lines at a time, watches the symbols blur, then stop: Bar, Jackpot, Lemon. He pulls the slot again and again, and the symbols freeze in random order, none of them matching. After several more pulls without a payout, most of his money is already gone. *Move, dammit!* a voice in his head says. Then another voice says *No, stay. Stay.* He heard somewhere—was it from Louise?—that if you stick with a losing machine long enough, it'll swing over to winning. Or was it the other way around? He's not sure; all that matters right now is that he's playing the game, egged on by the intoxicating circus music as the machine beeps out its little tune. It's an ego thing, almost: as he keeps losing, he becomes even more determined to win. *Man against the goddamn machine*, he thinks. He orders another beer from an attendant. He tells himself he can't possibly keep losing. He tells himself he's got to win eventually, and he just keeps betting the maximum, pushing the Spin button one time, cranking the handle the next, getting a few small paybacks when a cherry appears. His desperation weighs him down with each pull, and he can't get up from the hard vinyl stool.

"Aw, hell!" he spits when he realizes he's already out of money. He feeds another bill into the hungry metal mouth, pulls the handle that makes a *Ca-chunk* sound. Hears the bubbling computerized sounds as the symbols appear, all of them losers. "Son of a bitchin' machine," he mutters.

He considers his options: *Move. Stay.* He bets the max again, pulls hard on the handle. *Ca-chunk. Ca-chunk.* The sound of a shovel striking a rock beneath hard soil. He looks away from the screen, and when the Jackpot symbols appear in front of him and the machine sings out with its bright, steady bell, he's caught off guard. Then it sinks in: the triple jackpot on the screen is worth a thousand dollars. An absurd red light—like a tiny squad car light—blinks atop the machine, calling the attendant.

A Native American woman strolls over nonchalantly with a key, confirms his winnings, begins to write a check. "No," Luke says. "I want cash."

She shrugs at the request but then leads him to a cage in the back. The window is empty, the attendant gone on a break. She lifts a pager to her lips. The door swings open on the back wall, and Louise steps out; she gives him a startled look.

For an instant, Luke thinks of turning away, but doesn't. She seems to hesitate, as if she's going to return to the back room. Luke composes himself and considers telling her about his tangle of emotions: about his past, his Native American heritage, about how lost he feels. He knows she's the only person who could help him sort his way through this maze that has sprung up around him. He thinks about his words, spilling and spilling onto the counter in front of her like so many coins. He stares into her face, tries to interpret what she's thinking, but feeling unsure, he says nothing. Why can't he ever seem to read what's etched beneath the surface of her face? he wonders.

"Yes?" she finally says, her back straightening as if she's lifting something.

"I, I won," Luke blurts out. He doesn't know why he says it—money has never impressed Louise. But he repeats the words again, like he's a drowning man, grasping at the surface, and those words are his only rope. "I won."

"So I see," she says. She peers at the payout sheet. He can tell she's holding back by the way she seems to be biting the inside of one cheek. Maybe her words are bottled up, too, he thinks, and she wants to pour them out like a waterfall. He's hoping she will. But when she looks up at him, all she says is, "How would you like it?"

He wants to say, *We've got to talk, Louise. We've just got to. About me, about you, about everything.* Instead, he says, "Bills. Large bills."

"Fine."

Her perfunctory statement sounds like any cashier dealing with any customer, and he realizes they're both playing a stubborn game. She treats him as if he's a stranger, and he hates that. He feels a flush of heat and sweat as he waits for her to say something else, anything. A word. *Move. Stay.* Just a sound would be enough. *She'll say it now,* he thinks as he waits, the seconds dropping between them. *Now. Right now.*

All she does is reach into the cash drawer, pull out a stack of bills. With her slender, porcelain fingers shaking, she snaps the crisp notes—one by one—onto the countertop, counting them aloud as she does. After counting the bills a second time, she slides them beneath the bars, then pauses a moment and looks up at him as if she wants to say more, something besides, *So I see* and *Fine.*

But she doesn't. Luke steps aside, and the customer behind him—a man in his thirties, dressed in a tan sport coat and slacks—leans toward Louise.

"Hi again," the man says confidently. "I'm back from Chicago."

She smiles at him and says, "Well, welcome back."

"You brought me luck last time I was here," he says with a chuckle as he slides a credit card toward her. "Remember? I couldn't lose at that poker table."

"Sure. I remember," she says, her tone sounding almost flirtatious.

Luke, lingering between the rows of progressive slots, hates the way she self-consciously flips her hair—in a long blonde braid—off one shoulder, hates the way she leans toward the man, her elbows propped, slim fingers cradling her face—the way she used to lean toward Luke when they were first dating. Her laughter—no matter how light it seems—punches Luke's stomach, makes his insides ache with a radiating pain.

At that moment, Luke, standing there still holding his cash, can't help but feel his luck is running out.

Luke stops his pickup in the deep weeds on the side of the country road. As he steps over a barbed-wire fence and into the dried cornfield, the moon sends slivered shadows through the stalks that scrape against one another in the breeze and scratch Luke's legs, as if trying to slow him down. He feels a sharp pain as the serrated edge of one leaf cuts his hand. He glances at his hand, but sees no cut—only feels the steady sting on the soft heel of his palm.

He reaches the middle of the field, takes a deep breath, letting the winnings and the losings fall away from him, letting the land controversy and Louise's indifferent face drop away from him. Letting his childhood drop away, letting the image of his father's dying face drop away. Letting the town of Clearwater, that once was *his town*, drop away. Something's changed these past weeks, and he hates it that it's not the same. He closes his eyes a moment; his heavy past and his heavier future drop away from him like handfuls of dust. Then he opens his eyes; like a newborn, he sees the moonlight for the first time and feels purified by it, feels his body, his bones wiped clean and polished by the soft, cleansing light amid the darkness.

As a breeze picks up, he takes his wallet from his pocket, pulls out a few ten-dollar bills, lifts them in the air, lets them drift from his fingertips. Then he pulls out a few more, lets them go. He watches as the bills are caught by the wind, watches them twirl through the air until they're indistinguishable from the sharp, thin, leaves of the corn.

CHAPTER 30

"You look like hell," Ray Youngbear says the next morning from his hospital bed. After his nearly sleepless night, Luke's T-shirt is rumpled, his hair like a bird's nest, his eyes puffy and bloodshot.

"I could say the same about you," Luke replies. He frowns at the blue bruise shaped like a storm cloud on Ray's forehead, the bandages on his shoulder and rib cage. "Jesus." Luke shakes his head. "I'm sorry this happened."

"Not as sorry as *I* am," Ray says. His voice sounds like rough gravel. "Christ, you know Gerald died in the rollover." Ray shifts to his side with a kind of careful, slow-motion movement that people in hospitals seem to use. "I'm going to be out of work for a while. Collecting sick leave."

"So how long are you in here?"

"Couple more days. Gives me time to sleep, eat, watch TV. Maybe work on some drawings." He gestures toward some pen and ink sketches on a manila portfolio. Luke glances at the top page, sees the bold outline of a mandala or a prayer wheel. Or is it a car tire? Ray grimaces as he props on an elbow, takes a drink from the plastic glass of red liquid on the stainless steel table. "Louise stopped in here earlier."

"She did?" Luke says. His eyes flinch a little with the mention of her.

"Yeah. She was really upset when she heard about our little *accident.*"

"What else did she say?" Luke asks, fishing for something she might have said about him.

"Not much. She just went on about Rollie, and the town. You know how she feels."

"Oh, yeah." Luke's voice falls. He wonders if he's included in that feeling.

"So level with me, Luke," Ray says, sensing there's something else on Luke's mind. "Why are you here?"

Luke stares at the windowpane, the film of dust coating it from the outside; the early morning sun burns his bloodshot eyes as if he were peeling onions. "Don't know. I'm just looking for some answers."

"Answers?"

"Yeah. I thought the shaman's son had all the answers." Luke gives Ray a hopeful smile and puts one hand on the stainless steel tray lined with get-well cards, cheery pastel meadows and flowers on their covers. "You know—like you told me once. Everyone has to figure out their part in the whole."

"I said that, did I?"

"Yeah. You did. Remember?"

"Well, forget about parts of the whole. Forget about all that shit. I don't have any answers."

"What do you mean?"

"I mean . . . ," he says, wincing at the pain as he sits up and faces Luke, "I just feel angry right now. That's what. I feel so goddamn angry." He takes a quick breath. "And that bothers me." He lowers his hand to the tray, knocking over a couple of the cards. "Maybe it's not right, but all I've been doing lately is thinking about getting back at that goddamn sheriff."

"So what the hell happened out there?"

"I'd tell you the whole story," Ray says, his voice calming as he shifts his eyes to the faded blue sheets, "but what good will it do?" A nurse, birdlike in her white clothing, floats past the open doorway. Ray tips his head back and gazes at the plaster wall, coated with thick, glossy shellac. "It's just your sheriff, doing his duty."

"Don't call him *my* sheriff," Luke scoffs. "I despise that guy as much as you do." Luke strolls to the window, peers through the eggshell blinds that sag in the middle. He turns back to Ray and says, his words like strings pulled taut between two fingers, "I just feel like I should *do* something, Ray."

"So? Do something, then."

"But I don't know where to start. What the hell can I do?"

"More than likely, nothing. This'll go down as just another incident where the sheriff screws the Indians, and the mayor backs him up. Hell, I've seen it happen before. Your town paper already described it as a 'one-vehicle accident.'"

"I saw that."

"The tribe wants me to press charges. But it'll come down to my word against Rollie's." Ray lets out a raw cough. "And guess which one of us a white judge from Clearwater is gonna believe?"

224

CHAPTER

31

Inside the courthouse, the county board sits at a long table with a beige Formica top, reminiscent of a school lunchroom. The bases of the four table microphones are littered with papers, Styrofoam cups, and napkins with interlocking brown coffee circles. Butch, dressed in a conservative gray suit, anchors the middle of the row of county commissioners.

Luke swallows hard as he notices the single microphone placed in front of the table—the spot where he'll have to make his case. Not used to speaking in public, Luke repeatedly goes over his statement in his head as sweat dampens the underarms of his shirt. He faltered during speech class in high school, and he's not certain if he's got the confidence to stand up at the microphone and speak, or if what he has to say is convincing enough. He just has to do it, he tells himself.

Just tell the truth, Louise used to say to him. And she was right, he thinks—maybe one simple, honest word will lead to the next. And then the next. At a time like this, Luke wishes she were sitting here next to him, encouraging him.

Although the chairs are padded with faded taupe leatherette, they're still hard, and the one to Luke's right is slashed with a little stuffing poking through the cut. As the hearing begins, Virginia gives him a supportive nod from the gallery. She's presented at several hearings, and, prior to today's meeting, she versed him about what the county commissioners are likely to ask and how he might respond. "It's a room full of bureaucrats. They'll probably try to stonewall you. That's been my experience."

"So how am I supposed to stand up for myself?" Luke asked.

She loosened the button on her blue suit jacket. "I think you'll do just fine," she finally replied.

Luke pulls a note with a prepared statement from the pocket of his khaki pants, the paper softened from being folded and refolded. He studies the hand-printed notes he worked on late last night. The words seem to make sense one moment, then blur and turn to hieroglyphs the next.

After an hour of discussing road repair, Butch tips his chin toward the mic, clears his throat authoritatively. "Next is this land thing," he says, his undercutting tone making the subject sound almost unimportant.

City Attorney Bob Sewell stands. Luke watches the commissioners—all men, all in their fifties and sixties—nod complacently as Sewell's law-school terminology echoes off the empty second-floor gallery in the back of the room. Terms like "parcel identification number" and "limited market value" and "equalization" spill from his lips. It occurs to Luke that some of these men might have known his father, might have even liked him. But right now, the land question is more important than friendship. As Sewell speaks, his words remind Luke of beads of mercury, gliding elusively over a plate of glass. "The county ruled, over a hundred years ago, that American Indians could not own land. So, gentlemen," Sewell, the word-magician, concludes with a flourish of his hand, "The twenty acres adjacent to the ball field are actually city land. The person who claims he owns it, by virtue of being an heir, actually does not. Based on these findings, and given that funds have been appropriated, we'd like to begin work on the I-94 access road as soon as possible." He smiles, a silver filling showing on one of his teeth. The men nod, not because they're really agreeing, not because Sewell's words have swayed them, but because, after all these years, they're simply used to going along with the status quo, the steadily flowing river of the city's needs.

One man with a thin face, George Drummond, lifts his head above water to ask Sewell a question. "How's this affect the reservation's latest land claims?" he asks with a skeptical tone, "I mean, with this Native American protest thing lately, we've got to be a little more sensitive about these issues . . ." Luke has a sudden hope that not all of them have taken Sewell's comments as Scripture.

"It's not related, George," Sewell says, interrupting him. "It's entirely separate. The person who's making claims about this land is not a registered tribal member or anything."

"Oh, all right, then." The man's doubts seem assuaged, and he sinks back into silence.

The microphone makes a low-pitched thump as Luke adjusts it to reach his chin. He glances up. Butch lowers a stare on him like a heavy chunk of ice, and a couple of the town fathers tip their faces toward him with ashen, disapproving looks. He feels as if he's going to forget his entire speech and end up stammering. Luke knows

Butch and Sewell have probably spoken to the commissioners beforehand, influencing them. "I appreciate the opportunity to speak on this issue," Luke says, his voice polite but tight. To him, his voice sounds emotionless, flattened, which is the exact opposite of how he feels about the issue. How can he find the courage to stand up against this town he's been loyal to all his life, a town he loved, a town that always seemed to love him back?

He clears his throat and delivers his statement about the land rights, about Butch's interference, and about the city's role. Some of the board members gaze blankly at him with pasty, indifferent faces—one swirls his coffee, another shuffles paper, and one more begins to tap his pencil on the tabletop. George Drummond seems to nod at him sympathetically, but Luke's not certain. As Luke continues speaking, he notices Butch, in the center of the table, with a grimace on his face as he pretends to focus on a bothersome hangnail.

Luke concludes by explaining that the Indian treaties, created by the federal government, existed before the city of Clearwater was even established. Fortunately, Virginia has helped him research these legalities, and that has given his argument credibility.

Butch leans toward his microphone to make a rebuttal, to do his best to stir up some silt and hopefully make the issue more opaque. "Gentlemen," Butch says with practiced politeness, elevating his voice with a lofty, superior tone. "City and county boundaries were established over a hundred years ago. I'm sure there are documents in the county that support this. I hope Mr. Tanner doesn't intend to disregard them." He tosses a condescending look at Luke.

Luke wonders if this is a prelude of what to expect at the court case in which he'll testify on behalf of Ray, which he's agreed to do.

Composing himself, Luke makes his final point. "That land is part of an ancient burial ground," Luke injects words with passion and conviction. "It's sacred land. The city has no right to disturb it. Besides the burial issue, I plan to file a claim with the city, showing proof of family ownership of the land parcel."

Butch's jaw tightens like he's chewing on ball bearings with his molars. "You have no claim, Tanner. Where do you come up with such crap?" He looks over at the board members, then adds, "Pardon my language."

The discussion between Butch and Luke escalates steadily into an impasse that narrows to just a few words:

"Sacred ground," Luke says.

"Public interest," Butch counters.

The words seem to take on shapes. Butch's words form into a granite wall, and Luke's words become a large bird—a falcon or an eagle—flying full speed toward that wall.

"Public interest."

"Sacred ground." Luke repeats the words, chanting them like a mantra; he believes the words more than he ever did before. He understands now that the land where his ancestors lived is more important than he is, and that it will outlast him, outlast Butch, outlast all the wood and bricks and mortar of city hall. "Sacred ground!" The words come from far down inside Luke, emerging from a place he didn't know he owned—a deep pool, a powerful reservoir of strength. He knows now that he can stand up to these people. He's only one man, but they can't stop his words from exposing the truth, can't stop the words from beating their wings.

When Virginia finds him in the hallway, Luke's face is still red, flushed, and his nerves still frayed.

She gives him an approving smile. "You stood up to them."

"I don't know *what* I did," he says, shaking his head.

"You said what you needed to. You made your point. But something tells me you might be in for a long fight."

Butch exits the chamber doorway and makes his way down the hall. As he sidles past, he gives Luke a patronizing smile and a pat on the shoulder. "Your dad would have just let all this go, you know," Butch says. "He was a smart man, your dad."

"My dad *would have* wanted me to do this," Luke replies with a cutting stare.

Pretending that he doesn't hear Luke's reply, Butch continues down the hall, jovially greets some commission members, then disappears behind the opaque glass door of the city hall lounge.

CHAPTER
32

After a home-style breakfast of eggs, pancakes, and hash browns at the Rainbow this morning, Luke feels full, and yet a part of him still feels empty. He aims his truck down Center, cuts over on Oak, and follows it up the hillside, where he finds himself in front of the Clearwater Memorial Gardens Cemetery. He clicks off the engine. Through the curved windshield with the tiny nicks that catch the sunlight, he can see the west end of the cemetery, where his father is buried. The thing about a lost father, Luke thinks, is that once he's gone you don't ever know exactly where he is.

In his rational mind, Luke knows he's been buried here, adjacent to the row of tall pines, for almost twenty years, but at the same time he knows he could be somewhere else.

He could be inside the engine of Luke's rust-dotted blue truck in the morning, its pistons misfiring as he cranks the key. The engine clears its throat a few times, then chugs and chugs and finally shudders to a start, a pale globe of exhaust appearing behind it and rising up above the power lines.

He could be in the arrowhead collection—those beige and tan stone points so carefully chipped and sculpted five or six hundred years ago—that Luke keeps framed on the wall. It was once *his* arrowhead collection. He could be there, somewhere just beneath the surface of the stone as Luke turns a spear point over and over in his hand, feeling the symmetrical frozen ripples, like a small flint pond.

He could be inside the baseball in the flatbed of Luke's truck, a ball Luke found in the tall weeds behind the high school practice field the other day. Beneath the scuffed leather skin and red stitches, he could be the yards of yarn that's wound around and around itself. He could be tangled somewhere within those circles, like stories that begin at the same place they end. He could be in the core itself—hidden inside that porous cushioned cork center of the baseball, the elastic heart that makes it jump so quickly from the wooden knots of a baseball bat or stop with a sudden *pop* in the web of Luke's outstretched glove.

He could be the wind, the wind that seems to have no beginning or end, sighing through the needles of the pine trees at dawn.

Luke remembers what the priest told the mourners at his father's funeral. He said his father had gone to a better place, a heavenly place, filled with peace and tranquility. But Luke—then just a teenager—could never really get himself to believe that. As Luke rode back from the funeral, his uncle's Lincoln rolling over the acorns that sputtered beneath the tires, he thought there had to be more than those vague and general words, those rote prayers, the scripted benediction. There *had* to.

He could be the needle in Luke's compass—the half red, half white magnetized piece of metal that bobs and sways as if it's being pushed by an invisible breeze. When Luke walks with it in his palm, the nose of the needle wavers left and right, searching for true north. It points the way, letting Luke know how much ground he needs to cover.

He could be that first blade of bluegrass in early spring that sprouts from a seed no bird has plucked from the soil. Luke takes care not to mow over that one blade that grows so thin and tall among the others, a blade that somehow avoids the soles of shoes and the worn wheels of kids' bicycles and makes its way upward, as if it could puncture the blue dome of the sky and turn it green.

Standing at the grave site, Luke looks down at the headstone that says *Dwight Aaron Tanner*, and, beside the words, the tiny angels frozen in gray granite. He fills a plastic jug from a nearby spigot, waters the yellow faces of the chrysanthemums in the plastic vase. In his mind, he asks his father questions, like why he never told Luke they were both part Native American. Questions Luke can't resolve. He closes his eyes, he lets a prayer rise through him. Not a rehearsed prayer, not a memorized one that was drilled into his head in grade school, just a few quiet words.

The damn thing about him, Luke thinks, is that a lost father could be anywhere, but when it comes down to it, he's nowhere to be found. When a father's gone, all you can do is guess about him and try to figure out the meaning of his cryptic words. When a father's gone, he's the wave on a lake, and the horizon, and the billowing cloud forming on that horizon and the small campfire the rain put out when Luke camped with him as a boy—a fire Luke still feels sometimes, flickering and fluttering and trying to restart itself inside his chest.

CHAPTER
}}

From the window of his second-story office, Butch sees five men pile
out of a car. While three of the men linger by the vehicle, two of
them head toward city hall. One wears a suit jacket, and the other is
in shirtsleeves and jeans. It bothers Butch as they stride right across
the bed of petunias beneath the undulating shadow of the American
flag. The men pass the newspaper rack where the headlines of the
Clearwater American glare at them:

Investigation of Sheriff's Office Continues

After Police Chase Fatality

AIM to Meet with Reservation Officials

The stockier man accidentally bumps the newspaper rack as he
passes, Butch notices, or does he give it a nudge? Either way, the wire
rack tips over, a couple of papers splaying on the sidewalk.

234

They reach the mayor's assistant, and Phyllis looks up from her computer and feigns surprise. By then Butch is back in his padded swivel chair, pretending to study an appropriation for the new flower boxes that will hang from wires on the lamp posts around the town square. *A little beautifying never hurts,* Butch tells himself, and he scribbles the word *Approved* at the bottom of the proposal and signs his name as the men enter his office.

"There's talk of police brutality up on the rez," Bobby Morris, one of the AIM leaders, says to Butch. His voice is raspy, a sound like two pieces of sandstone being rubbed together. "People are pretty worked up." Morris is in his early thirties, lean, with muscular forearms showing beneath the rolled-up sleeves of his charcoal gray knit shirt.

Rollie, sitting in on the meeting, says, "If you're talking about the accident . . . I was just tailing a DWI." His face goes flat as a pond with no wind. "I was just doing my job—that's all."

Redness surfaces beneath Morris's tanned cheekbones. "So you're saying they just *imagined* being run off the road?"

"That's correct."

Morris seethes. "That's bullshit, and you know it."

"Bullshit?" Butch interrupts. "These guys break the law, and you've got the sheriff's office under the spotlight? For cripes sakes . . ."

When he trails off, there's a long pause. The chubby Native American man with long braids sitting next to Morris studies the photos of former mayors on the wall, his eyes shifting from one to the other and then back again. He doesn't say a word, Butch notices, not a single word.

Morris finally speaks. "The version I heard," he says slowly, suppressing his anger, "is that the sheriff *forced* their truck off the road and into the pole. They were slowing down at the time." He turns his head to Rollie. "Then you goddamn rammed into them."

Rollie shifts in the upholstered chair, trying to hide his agitation. "Maybe you better get the facts straight," Rollie counters. "The suspects were driving drunk."

City Attorney Bob Sewell, standing in the corner, shushes Rollie. "Listen, Mr. Morris," he interjects. He clears his throat, his Adam's apple sliding up and down. "This Mr. Youngbear was intoxicated, as were the rest of the people in that vehicle. He could have claimed *anything*. The thing of it is, we don't know what's true right now, and what's not." Tugging at the button of his suit jacket, he gives Morris what looks like an innocent shrug.

Morris turns to the man next to him. "This is ridiculous," he scoffs. "We can't talk to these jokers. They're covering their good ol' sheriff's ass, is what they're doing."

"Now listen fellas," Butch pipes in, trying to ease the tension. "We're just a little town, for criminy sakes." He forces a chuckle, leans his elbows on the desk next to the commemorative pens with the word *Clearwater* emblazoned in gold across them. "We don't get all that much lawbreaking here. He gestures to Rollie. "Rollie here, he wouldn't hurt a fly. I mean, shit—if you pardon my French—this man has been sheriff here for almost twenty years. He's got a clean record. I can assure you of that."

"That's not what our people are saying about him," Morris counters. "And, for the record, they've got a few things to say about you, too, Sobieski." Morris opens, then closes his fists. "So let's get to it," he says. "We've drawing up a list of demands."

Butch holds up his palm like a crossing guard who just noticed an oncoming vehicle. "Demands? Let's not stir up a hornets' nest here, Mr. Morris." He shifts in his swivel chair, a forced smile on his lips.

"Let's be reasonable, and we'll get this all taken care of. What do you say?"

Morris pauses, purses his lips as if he's about to spit, then says to his companion, "I say we're outta here." The two of them stand abruptly. The chubby man shoves the chair behind him, and it tips backward, balancing for a second on two spindly legs.

Later, the Native American men arrive at Rite Away Auto. Johnny slides out on his creeper from under a Chevy. He wears a tight black AC/DC T-shirt and a gold and red NASCAR cap with a checkered flag pattern on the brim.

"You boys need repair, or what?" Johnny asks, nodding at their '90s Bonneville.

"Nope," says Morris. "We're just here to look at a truck."

"Truck?" Johnny says, knowing what they're referring to but playing dumb. He wipes his hands on a pink rag, stained with grease.

"Yeah. A black Chevy Silverado. From the rollover on 66 last week."

"Oh, *that* one," Johnny rubs his bicep. "She was totaled. Got a few parts from it, but not much."

"Parts?"

"Sure. Spark plugs, rearview mirror, couple speakers from the radio." He motions nonchalantly with his chin to the garage, where the hulk of a dark gray engine hangs on a set of chains in the shadow, like a side of beef in a slaughterhouse. "That there's the engine."

"So where's the body, then?" Morris glances at the garage door, the opaque glass panes coated with what looks like a layer of carbon.

"Body? It's long gone. Put her in the crusher." He points his thumb to the left.

In the salvage yard beside the garage, the four men see a two-by-three-foot-high rectangle of flattened metal, the crumpled folds of the fenders and hood, a few thin strips of chrome sticking out from it like antennae from an insect's head. The scent in the air is bitter, a pungent odor of rubber seals and fresh antifreeze.

"Yep. The recycling plant from Madison picks up on Tuesdays," Johnny affirms.

"When did you crush it?"

Johnny tips his NASCAR cap back and wrinkles his nose. "Dunno. Couple days ago, I s'pose."

Morris gives his men a skeptical look. He touches the compressed metal, and, though it's in the shadow of the building, it feels still warm from friction.

Johnny gives them a smile, his big horse-like teeth showing. "So," he nods at their slightly rusting car parked beside the pumps, "you boys got anything you want to turn in for salvage?"

THE NEXT DAY, around four o'clock, Butch reaches into his box of Swisher Sweets. "Lighter," Butch calls into the intercom, and Phyllis appears at the door, bringing his favorite lighter, which she keeps in her locked drawer because otherwise he'd be too tempted to smoke all day; city hall is, technically, a nonsmoking facility, but Butch allows himself this one luxury.

Flicking his ivory-coated lighter, he watches the orange flame drawn horizontally as he inhales. He tastes the satisfying sweetness of the sugar-cured cigar. He smoked his first Swisher Sweet as a kid, winning it at the county fair by throwing baseballs at record albums hanging from strings. "Sure you're old enough for that?" the carney asked him, and he was quick to respond, "You bet." Butch sets the lighter next to the glass snow-globe on his desk—there's a miniature city hall inside it, and if you shake the globe, the snow fills the air around the building like confetti. *Pretty*, he thinks. When he tips his head back, watching the tendrils of smoke rise to the ceiling, where they flatten and curl on themselves, he hears the first voices.

In the beginning it's a faint, high-pitched cry, like a couple construction workers calling out directions for a backing lumber truck. But there's no construction job going on in downtown Clearwater. He parts the drapes, peers out his second-story office window as the first of them march around the corner and head toward the town square. The men strutting in front—whom Butch recognizes as Bobby Morris and his AIM thugs—are followed by other men. They're carrying signs and yelling. More and more marchers—a few women, even—round the corner and flood onto the street.

Butch yanks the cigar from his mouth. "For cripes sakes," he snarls. "Phyllis! Get me Rollie's cell phone!"

Butch watches the crowd spill across the front lawn of city hall and all the way to the tarnished green Civil War statue. The crowd looks to be mostly Native American, Butch confirms, but there are some white faces, too. He sees a man step to the front of the crowd, lift a bullhorn, and begin to speak. He can tell, from his voice, that it's that damn Morris. Butch knew he couldn't trust that guy. "Tell security to lock all the doors," Butch commands Phyllis.

"We want justice!" Morris yells into the bullhorn, his amplified voice echoing off the buildings of the town square.

As Morris makes accusation after accusation about cover-ups and brutality and land rights, cheers rise from the crowd. He pauses and hands the bullhorn to another AIM leader—the chubby one with the long braid. The man's low, guttural voice churns up a chant from the crowd: "Stop police brutality!"

Butch glares out the window at the protesters. *Assholes*, he thinks. Then he barks the word loud into the glass: "Assholes!"

"Think we better call for backup from Portage or Sauk City?" Phyllis offers from the doorway, out of breath and hardly able to push the words out, her fingers pressed to the side of her thick neck like she's checking her pulse.

"Naw," Butch says without turning away from the window. "Rollie and the guys will be here soon. Let's not get everybody mixed up in this. Give it a little time. Maybe it'll just blow over." He tries to stay calm, but his insides are churning like a cement mixer. Butch watches a few more trucks pull into the parking stalls, and more people jump out and join the protest. "Where are they getting these idiots?" he asks aloud.

In a few minutes, the crowd seems to move as one, rippling, swaying like thick smoke blowing off a tire fire. They inch closer and closer to the front doors of city hall. Butch, gnawing on the cigar's tip, sees a white van pull up in the street beyond the town square. The side panel of the van reads *WISC TV—Your Eyewitness News.* "Aw, for crying out loud," Butch whines. He checks his watch. "Where the hell's Rollie?"

Butch scowls at the handwritten protest signs: *Mayor Supports Brutality,* one of them reads. *Impeach Sobieski,* another one reads, and still others say *Justice Now!* For an instant Butch recalls what Nixon once said about clearing those protesting bums off the White House lawn.

"Think I should go out there?" he says to the window. "Think I should?"

"No," Phyllis says with a protective, motherly voice. "You stay *right here*, Butch. Just let Rollie handle this."

Hearing the shouts of the crowd, Rollie feels a little nervous as he slides on his riot helmet with the Plexiglas visor. He's never had to pull riot gear out of the back closet of the sheriff's office. He grabs some canisters of tear gas, hooks them to his belt, and steps from his cruiser.

Near the city hall steps, the speeches continue, the rhetoric getting angrier and angrier. Rollie, making his presence known, hangs at the back of the crowd with his bullhorn, not confronting anybody, the way they taught him in police academy.

Rollie assesses the crowd: most of the rowdies are young males in their twenties, he sees—obviously reservation boys looking to raise some hell—and there's a sprinkling of white civil rights types and college students. The cameramen from the TV news station—big black cameras on their shoulders—zero in on the AIM leaders, who shout and shake their fists. Then the cameras pan to the crowd, the mob yelling, some of them waving protest signs. Rollie looks to his left, spots deputy Arnie and the two assistant deputies, decked out in riot gear, taking their posts at opposite sides of the town square. All three stand at ease, arms behind their backs, tear gas and clubs strapped to their belts, the way they've been taught. Rollie does likewise.

Rollie squeezes the handle of the bullhorn, waiting for a pause in the lashing rhetoric of the AIM leaders. He's watched scenes like this dozens of times in the movies he's collected over the years, like *Dog Day Afternoon,* and he'd always wondered what it would be like to be in the middle of one. At the same time, it's frightening for him to watch this happening right here on the town square; it's like the crowd is a powerful creature, surging and moving at will. When Morris insults Butch and the sheriff's office again and again, Rollie figures it's about time to move in.

"All right!" he shouts into the bullhorn, trying to sound calm but still authoritative, "Listen up, people!"

Nobody turns to look.

He feels foolish as he glances at the on/off switch on the bull-horn, flips the switch to *on*. "Listen up, people!" he barks again, his voice amplified this time. A few men at the back of the crowd turn. "This is an illegal assembly. You have gathered without a city permit."

"Bullshit!" one burly man scoffs. "You asshole!"

Rollie repeats the words, then adds, "You will disperse immediately or face arrest."

"Just try it, goddamn it!" calls one young Indian man in a faded denim shirt with the sleeves cut off. Morris aims his megaphone toward Rollie and shouts back: "What are you gonna do, sheriff? Run us off the road?" With that, the voices of the crowd erupt.

A block away, Josh Sobieski and a few other men from town saunter toward the protestors. When he reaches the edge of the crowd, Josh tears a sign from the hands of one man. In an instant, three Native American men turn toward Josh, and suddenly, there's an explosion of shouts, fists, cries. Cardboard signs smack against heads and backs. Fists thud and slap against chests and jaws. Cameramen duck away, then zoom in on the fighting.

Rollie moves quickly toward the brawl. Even with the sound of the melee, he can hear the sound of his pulse, like a horse's hooves galloping inside his black helmet. When he reaches a Native American man who is taking a swing at Josh's friend Darryl on the ground, Rollie slides his black club in front of the Indian man's chest and yanks him away.

A tall, muscular Native American man shoves at Rollie. "Pig!" the man shouts. Pulling out a tear gas canister, Rollie rips out the pin, tosses it between the man's legs. Rollie backs away, breathes through his gas mask as the white gas billows from the canister, and the man—his eyes scrunched closed, choking as if his lungs are filled with cinders—waves his arms in the air and stumbles the other way.

The crowd seems to surge toward Rollie and then back away. They're like an ocean wave, and they're in his control. After a few minutes, the crowd disperses. There's still a little scuffling and shouting, as people scatter, some men running toward their pickups and driving off, some jogging into the neighborhoods as tear gas canisters sizzle, sending up billowing white clouds. Morris, the last to stay, has his arms pinned behind his back by the deputies.

Then Rollie notices Luke standing on the perimeter of the square. He can't believe what he's seeing: Luke's holding a sign that reads *Land Justice Now!*

Rollie marches over, glaring at him. "What the hell are *you* doing?"

Luke just stands there, not answering.

Rollie pulls out a pair of cuffs and raises them toward Luke.

"Go ahead," Luke goads, holding out his wrists. "Take me in again."

What's this?" Rollie squints one eye, and his lips curl over themselves as he puzzles at Luke's response. "You think you're with AIM now? Think you're some kind of Martin Luther King, or what?" He shakes his head. "You're making it way too easy for me."

Luke is silent, still holding out his wrists.

Rollie pauses, thinking maybe he's being baited. "You know what? I'm not going to do it."

"Why's that?"

"'Cause it looks *bad* for our town, that's why." Rollie wags his head as Luke stares at him defiantly. "I mean, what the hell's *wrong* with you, Luke? Since when are you one of *them*?"

Inside city hall, Butch stands, agonizing as he watches the riot settle down from the security of his office. *Nobody's going to do this to my town,* Butch thinks. *Nobody. I won't let them.* Just then a lone protestor saunters to the middle of the square. Butch sees the man rear back with an object, sees his arm swing down. The image of Whitebird throwing the beer can right at Butch's head that night years ago fills his mind. Now, like then, Butch barely has time to react. He hears the shattering sound as the brick explodes through the window pane, the glass flying across the room. Butch feels a sharp pain on the side of his head. Fallen to his hands and knees, Butch looks up, half expecting to hear Whitebird's mocking laughter.

Then next thing Butch knows, he's hurrying down the marble stairs, Phyllis trailing and pleading with him to stop. But he won't stop. He can't. As he rushes past the gold-leaf-framed oil portraits of former mayors and councilmen, they don't look at him, their gaze forever frozen on some distant horizon.

When he bursts through the front doors, Butch's vision compresses to a tunnel, a narrow, burning tunnel, and at the end of it is that one fat-faced Indian, the chubby AIM guy, Morris's smug sidekick, that bastard who just threw the brick. Butch runs through the tunnel and right up to the man. Shouts blur around Butch as he takes a roundhouse swing and punches the man hard in the face. The chubby man falls backward and crumples to the ground.

It's then that Butch turns and sees a black camera pointed toward him. As the camera moves closer, he sees a face reflected in the dark glass of the lens. It's an angry, convex face with puffy, squinting eyes, and small, fish-like lips. A threatening face, one he doesn't recognize, though somehow it looks familiar. With a quick swing of his arm, he knocks the camera hard; it twists and falls to the ground, taking the face with it.

244

CHAPTER 34

After changing from his navy suit to street clothes and a blue wind breaker, Butch slips on a pair of sunglasses and exits through the back door of the courthouse. Duane the janitor unlocks the door, then quickly secures it behind Butch. Glancing left, then right, Butch notices Rollie and Arnie cruising the blocks in their squad cars, making sure there's no more trouble. Butch refused to talk to the media after the protest this afternoon, though the TV crews hung around the town square for hours. He instructed Phyllis to tell people that he left city hall, that he's not in town this evening and is unavailable for comment.

Butch watches the city crew picking up the signs and litter from the tipped-over trash barrels, and he winces as he surveys the damage—saplings snapped near the Civil War statue, overturned park benches blocking the sidewalks. There's plenty for the crew to take care of, to get this scenic town square back to where it was before all this craziness took place. And if any city crew can do it, the Clearwater crew can. They already boarded the broken window on the second floor; they'll have a new window in there by tomorrow morning, all sealed and caulked. And once Duane gets up there and polishes it with some Windex 'til that glass shines, no one will know the difference.

As he makes his way down the street, Butch feels his temple throb. Phyllis touched up the cut from the broken glass with some ointment and gave him a Band-Aid. He's decided not to tell anybody about the wound; the town should know that their mayor is strong, that he came out of this whole stupid attack unscathed.

An hour ago, Butch briefed Sewell in his office—the door closed, locked—then sent him to make a statement to the media people. "A misunderstanding," Butch told him. "Make sure you say this is just, you know—just a misunderstanding between the town and the tribe."

"Okay, okay. What about Ray Youngbear's claims? I mean . . ."

Butch sat behind his desk, staring at the creases in the pink palm of his hand like they were a road map. Then he shifted his eyes to the photo of city hall being built in the old days, brick by brick, granite slab by granite slab.

"What about them? He was drunk. He got bounced around pretty bad in the accident. Had a head concussion, for Christ's sakes. Who cares what he claims? He's full of shit."

Sewell sighed. "Now, Butch, you don't expect me to say all *that.*"

"No, no, no," Butch replied. "Not that, exactly." His eyes traced the broken window, the jagged edges, the circular whorls in the layer of plywood covering it. He leaned toward Sewell. "I expect you to level with them. You know, set them straight. Tell them it was just a one-car accident."

"I hear Tanner might testify as a character witness. The guy's been talking to all kinds of people, you know. Including their tribe's lawyers."

"We'll find ways to discredit Tanner. Criminy, he's an Indian sympathizer. A white man storming city hall with that bunch. He'd make up any damn lie to make the city look bad."

Butch lifted a stack of envelopes on his desk, tossed them in an uneven pile. "Look at these," he scoffed. "I guess Tanner's started some damn petition. And a letter-writing campaign about the road."

"How many did you get?"

"Aw, maybe a hundred. Or a couple hundred. Most of them are tribal people, anyway. So that doesn't count for much."

"Are there *any* townspeople writing in?"

"Well, yeah." Butch chewed on the word. "There's some traitors."

As Sewell pondered this, his features seemed to bunch up in the center. "Any thoughts about concealing the evidence?"

"Huh?"

"About the Silverado being crushed at Rite Away. You know—before anybody could get a look at it."

"Aw shoot. Tell them that's the way they do things at Rite Away. It's policy to crush the junked vehicles and ship 'em to Madison for recycling. We're environmentally conscious around here."

"Right." Sewell tugged at his lapel. "Of course."

Now, as Butch steps over the bent protest signs on the sidewalk, red paper leaflets scatter everywhere in the breeze. As one tumbles toward him, Butch, without breaking stride, crumples it under his shoe.

He comes to a large van that takes up four parking stalls at the corner of the square. On its sides, the black painted letters read:

Channel 27 Newscam

Your Eyewitness News Satellite Uplink

The damn thing is as big as a motor home, Butch thinks. He frowns at the satellite tower on top of the trailer, like a flagpole with a black wire spiraling upward around it. At its top, a yellow strobe light flashes every few seconds. A guy—who looks like he's in his twenties, just out of college—eats a sandwich at the base of the three aluminum-grate steps that lead into the trailer. "Quite a day here, eh?" the kid says. Butch doesn't reply, but can't help pausing and peering curiously into the open doorway of the trailer.

"Wanna have a look?" the kid says, excitement making his high voice crack.

Butch climbs the first two steps. Inside the trailer, a whole wall is covered with black and gray video decks and monitor screens that a man and a woman are fooling with. Butch feels his body shake as the protest erupts again on the tiny color screens, some of them with audio, some on mute. On one screen, the protesters are battling Rollie and Arnie. On another, there's an interview with Morris, the damn AIM leader, words flying from his lips. On another, Luke Tanner speaks about land rights. Then there's a cut to the chanting crowd. The whole mess looks bad on the clips.

Butch is stunned when, on another monitor, he sees footage of himself, taking a swing at that chubby AIM man. Then Butch sees himself pivot and take a swing at the camera. As the camera falls, he sees the quick swirl of trees, then a blue smear of sky, and then, for a few long seconds, a close-up of grass. The video clip repeats in a loop—trees, sky, grass. Trees, sky, grass. Butch feels as though an electric current is running through him, and as much as he wants to, he can't step back from the trailer, and he can't stop looking, either.

Inside the trailer, two technicians in matching navy blue WISC news shirts scurry between tape decks and monitors, checking settings. "Never mind those two," the young guy says. "They're a little preoccupied right now. They're setting up to send a feed back to Madison." He beams at Butch with his I-just-got-my-mass-communications-degree smile. "Pretty fascinating, isn't it?"

Butch finally manages to break from his paralysis and back down the stairs. "So," the kid calls as Butch hurries across the street, "you gonna watch at ten?"

PART

}

CHAPTER

35

Strolling through downtown Clearwater in the predawn, Butch is thankful to see the TV crews and their trailers have left. The tense scowl melts from his face as he scans the downtown. It soothes him, the way the brick buildings march shoulder to shoulder around the town square, the way the glowing four-sided courthouse clock faces north, south, east, and west. No matter how dark or cloudy the night, Butch thinks, that big yellow moon is always there, watching over the town. Though the Rainbow Café's neon sign is dim, Butch knows that in a couple hours, Ruth will open the back door and start balancing a tray of porcelain cups; Hans will rub his gray-shadowed eyes, then pull out a cast iron pot to begin making his soup of the day. Butch knows that within a couple hours, townspeople will emerge from their homes, farmers from their fields, and businessmen from their stores to stop at the Rainbow to get what they need: a good hearty breakfast and a cup of coffee. It'll help the people focus on their tasks, their jobs that keep things running. *Progress,* Butch thinks. *Progress and steadiness. Like clockwork. That's what's important here.*

And the place *was* running smoothly, Butch thinks, until the Native Americans started this war. Now they want more land for their casinos, he thinks, and building permits, and fishing rights. *They want the shirts off our goddamn backs,* Butch thinks.

As he follows the sidewalk to Center, he reaches the crosswalk. Butch opens his thermos mug of brandy-laced coffee, pours some in the cup, and takes a gulp to steady himself. He swallows hard, his Adam's apple grazing his starched white collar. He tugs at his navy tie, too tight, like a garter snake wrapped around his neck. Pausing at the red light, he tries not to think of the snowdrift of envelopes piling up on his desk, the letters—drummed up by Tanner—protesting the building of the road. He tries not to think of that certified letter Bob Sewell received yesterday, stating that the tribe will press charges of assault and battery against Butch. And the phone call from Bob Sewell telling him that the WISC cameraman plans to file charges, too.

Even though there are no cars at this time of the morning, Butch waits patiently for the cross signal. Like any law-abiding citizen, he waits for the light to blink from red to yellow to green, and as he does, he can hear the hum of the switches inside the metal power box. He listens hard, and he can actually hear the lights themselves make a faint *click click* sound as they blink on, then off.

Before work, Luke opens the door, surprised to see Butch, arms stiff at his sides, standing on his front porch. Butch looks a little disheveled; his shirt tail is pulled out from the side of his trousers beneath his suit jacket, and his sandy hair swirls atop his head like a puff of silt. His body emanates sweat and Old Spice cologne. He gives Luke what seems like a congenial nod, and musters a smile, as if he and Luke are old friends. "I know we've never seen eye to eye on things," he begins. "But I thought I'd drop by. You know, to talk."

"I don't think we have much to say."

"Let's just chat a minute. You know, man to man." Butch stuffs his hands into the pockets of his suit pants in a mock gesture of humility. "I mean, we're both reasonable people."

Luke steps aside to let Butch in. "Nice place here." He admires an antique lamp with a Tiffany shade and the floral wallpaper in the dining room. "Look at that lamp. And that wallpaper's Louise's touch, I bet."

Luke crosses his arms, impatient with Butch's string of mundane pleasantries. "I don't think you came here to talk about lamps. And I've only got a few minutes before work."

Butch leans against the wainscoting. "Well, I came to let you know that I did check into those records," he says, his voice sliding toward a more official tone. "Bob Sewell and I—well, we did some looking into that land issue."

Luke doesn't respond.

"Listen, Luke," Butch says, "I can see how you started believing you owned that land. Frankly, I don't blame you for misunderstanding. Not one bit. And believe me, I know just how you feel. But the point is. . . ." He forces a yellow-toothed half-smile. "I mean, the city's point is . . ."

"Is what?" Luke asks defiantly.

"Here's the thing." Butch steps a little closer, like a used car salesman trying to sell a vehicle that's been on the lot for months. "What it all boils down to is that land's kind of a no-man's land. Heh heh

heh," he chuckles nervously as though this were funny. "It's like a de-militarized zone or something, you might say." He runs his finger along the edge of the Tiffany lampshade. "So I'm here to settle this, once and for all."

"So you're here to make a deal?" Luke says incredulously.

"It's just an arrangement, so to speak. We'll pay you a little extra for the west section of land. I mean, even though the city *al-ready* owns it, technically, we'll still give you something for it, a pretty decent price, really, so we can go ahead with our road plans. That is . . . ," he pauses, "if you'll agree to drop the lawsuit." A patron-izing look spreads across his sweaty face. "I think that's more than generous, don't you?"

Luke glares at him. "I think that's bullshit."

"Listen to the way you're talking," Butch says, straightening in-dignantly. "I came in here for a civilized conversation, is all. And just listen to you."

"You came in here to try to shut me up."

"Listen, Luke," Butch says, his tone becoming harsh, his neck turning a mottled red. "You started this whole damn mess in the first place. And look what it snowballed into."

"I didn't *start* anything."

"You know," Butch says slowly, tipping his face toward the ceil-ing, "things were going great until you found that goddamn bone. In fact, things were perfect around here. Then you and your high-and-mighty archeologist friend from the university started stirring things up. I mean, talking to the press, riling up the people on the reserva-tion, and . . . Do you have any idea what you've done here?"

Luke gives him an indifferent look.

"You've torn this town in two, that's what you've done."

"Look, Sobieski. I didn't *do* anything to this town." Luke says, staying calm and confident. "Your town never was perfect. Maybe *you* thought it was, but when it comes down to it, it's just a dumpy little town in the middle of Wisconsin. That's what it is." The words almost surprise Luke as they roll from his lips.

"Don't you run down my town like that."

"I talked to Ray Youngbear," Luke says, shifting the subject. "I know you and Rollie are just covering each other's tails. And people in town are starting to realize it. Nobody trusts you any more, Butch."

Butch's face suddenly droops like it's made of melting plastic. "That's a lie," he says. "You and your Indian pals are a bunch of liars."

"Face it, Butch. Maybe you and your pals are the liars."

Butch angrily points his stubby finger into Luke's chest. "Who do you think you are?" he says, his voice raised. Then he sends a salvo Luke's way. "I know who you are. You're a half-breed, that's who you are."

Luke realizes then that Butch has been scouring his family records. "Get the hell out of my house," Luke shouts. As he says the words, Luke realizes that his own voice—strained but clear—sounds a lot like his father's voice.

Butch collects himself, straightening his suit jacket, tucking in his shirt, and hiking up his pants. "Well, just think about it, Tanner," he says, his voice calming to a businesslike tone. "The land offer stands." Then he turns casually, as if he's leaving a city council meeting for a lunch at the Rainbow.

Butch enters the Rainbow without making eye contact with anybody, sits on a stool at the far end of the counter. He sees the issue of the *Wisconsin State Journal* folded in half on the counter. The sidebar headline reads:

Clearwater Riot Investigation Continues
Mayor Involved in Melee

Butch flips the paper over. The Rainbow has the usual mid-morning crowd, but today the conversation isn't spiced with jokes, and it doesn't revolve around which crop just got planted, or the chances of rain, like it usually does. Today, as Butch sits alone, the talk is all about the recent incidents in the town, and it maddens him to hear it. Beneath the stockyard report on the radio, Butch picks up hushed conversations from the farmers at the back tables.

Ruth brings his usual cup of coffee, and Butch pours the cream from a small stainless pitcher with a jittery hand.

"Well, that was really something," Ruth offers, "and right on our own town square."

"Yep," Butch says curtly, in no mood to discuss it.

But Ruth persists. "I do sort of see what they're upset about, though," she offers. "And what Luke Tanner's talking about."

"Huh?" Butch glares at her. "Since when are you on Tanner's side?"

She shrugs her small, bony shoulder beneath the thin white blouse. "Well, I'm not altogether on his side. But I see his point about the land." She takes a towel from her waist, swirls it to mop up some coffee rings left by previous customers. "And I'm not the only one. I guess not everybody's on city hall's side on this one, Butch." She dabs at the side of her graying hair with her palm. "Just so you know."

"So, they going to prosecute 'em?" Walter asks, sliding onto a stool next to Butch. "You know. Those creeps who started the whole thing?"

The cream in Butch's coffee cup churns in a spiral, like an aerial view of a hurricane you see on the weather channel. "Sure are." He takes a sip, and the coffee's a little too hot, and it scalds his tongue. "I've got an appointment to talk to the feds this afternoon."

Walter tips his Hybrid feed cap back on his head. "So we'll take care of those AIM assholes?"

"Yeah." Butch glances at the calendar on the back wall that's been there since 1979; on it a farmer holds a bushel of faded corn next to a green John Deere tractor. "And Tanner," Butch adds gruffly.

"Luke Tanner? You kidding. He's a local. You don't think he's in on this?"

"There's a lot you don't know about Tanner," Butch says offhandedly. "And for that matter, his family."

Walter, who has big teeth for such a small man, takes a bite of his cinnamon sticky bun. "Say Butch," Walter says, changing the subject, "I hear you were a big TV star the other day. That's what the fellas said."

"So what if I was." Butch feels the humiliation as he leans back a few seconds, his stare fixed on the back wall where a bass is caught mid-jump, its eyes opaque gray marbles, its mouth open wide.

Walter leans toward him, a moustache of white icing above his upper lip. He takes another bite of the roll. When Butch doesn't say any more, Walter says, "I mean, I'm on your side on this whole thing. But Cyrus and the boys are starting to wonder what the hell got into you after that protest. And we're starting to wonder what we're going to do about everything."

His right eye twitching, Butch hates it that Walter seems to be seeing right inside him, that this stupid little man is seeing right through to Butch's own insecurities. "Same thing we always do when shit happens," Butch says, trying to come up with an answer. "Nothing. I mean, it'll all go away, eventually. Then we'll move forward. Everything goes away, eventually." He doesn't realize it, but by the time he finishes his last sentence, he's raising his voice to an angry pitch.

He turns to leave and knocks his cup off the counter. The cup breaks, and the tan tongue of liquid spreads, spilling over the black and white tile floor. The china pieces skitter. Butch stoops to pick them up, and Ruth calls out, "That's all right, Butch—I'll get it." The group of farmers stop talking and glance over at him.

Butch marches down the sidewalk in front of the Soap Box Launderette, past the women in the picture window folding white sheets. They lift their heads toward him, but he keeps his eyes focused straight ahead. Then he hears a voice behind him.

"Butch."

"Just let me alone." Butch keeps striding, arms swinging at his sides. "Just *never mind* the goddamn coffee," Butch barks.

"Butch!" Rollie calls again, jogging up to him and grabbing him by the arm. "Where you been? I've been trying to track you down all morning. They found something else out there at the field."

The drained, pallid expression on Rollie's face makes Butch stop. He spins toward Rollie.

"What the devil did they find *now*?"

"I guess that archeologist woman found some more bones. But they didn't match. They weren't from that old Indian village. She says they're *recent* ones."

"Recent?" Butch swallows like there's a chestnut blocking his windpipe.

"The archeologist had 'em tested." Rollie rubs his sleeve with the embroidered red and gold CPD patch. He raises himself up and down on his tiptoes, seeming almost excited by this news. "Filed a report, I guess."

"Somebody's lying."

"I don't know, Butch. Radiocarbon dating doesn't lie. DNA lab tests don't lie. Besides, she turned up some pieces of clothing and some buttons with the bones," he adds. He pauses, adjusts the vinyl bill of his patrolman's cap. "Guess it's a murder case now. A whole new investigation."

Butch just stands there expressionless a few seconds, his eyes closed, his face calm, as if he's suddenly fallen into a deep sleep.

"You know," Rollie is saying, "we ought to update our lab facilities. Get some new equipment. You listening, Butch? Butch?"

Just before five o'clock, on his way home from city hall, Butch notices two figures standing on the sidewalk in front of his house. *More reporters,* he thinks angrily. *I won't say another word to them. I'm not talking to anybody, not until I consult with Sewell.*

He hesitates, wondering if he should just keep walking right past his house, just barge right past them without talking. As he approaches, he realizes that it's two women—an older woman and a younger one. The older one has high cheekbones and long black hair that's streaked with gray. Dressed in a western-style denim blouse and jeans, she doesn't look like a reporter. The other woman—who might be in her late thirties—stands behind, her arms crossed.

"Mister Sobieski," the older woman calls in a voice that sounds smooth.

"I have no comment," he snaps.

"Mister Sobieski." Her voice is more insistent.

He points at them threateningly. "I'm not talking to reporters. Get the hell off my sidewalk!"

"I'm not a reporter," she counters. As he approaches, her stare bores into him, and he pauses. Those eyes—chocolate brown and intense—look strangely familiar to him, but he's not sure where he's seen them before.

"Then who *are* you?" he demands.

"I'm sure you don't remember me, but I know *you.*"

"Leave me alone," he says, and he tries to brush past her.

She steps in front of him, blocking his path.

Those eyes, he thinks, *those eyes. And that face.* It's like a ghost he's seen before, inhabiting a deep, buried corner of his dreams, and now it's rising up, right in front of him, terrifying him. *Who the hell is she?*

"I spoke with Luke Tanner, and he said I should talk to you. So my daughter and I . . ." She nods to the woman standing behind her, and the woman gives Butch a bitter look. "We're . . ." She falters a moment, and then her voice gains strength. "My daughter and I are here to talk about Jim."

"Huh?" Butch's word is a balloon that bursts.

"I'm Lilly Whitebird. Jim Whitebird's wife."

Her words stun Butch as surely as a cold, hard object hitting him right between the eyes. She moves toward him, too close, and he begins to recognize the face of the young Native American girl he talked to years ago in the dispatch office.

"It's taken thirty years of wondering," she says, "But I never did get an answer, so I'm going to ask you again. This time I want the truth. You were there that night. So what do you *really know* about what happened to my husband?"

Butch opens his mouth slightly but isn't sure whether he utters another word. At five o'clock, a few blocks away on the square, the town clock's steel hammer pounds against thick brass. With each resonant gong, Butch feels a sensation like a china coffee cup is shattering into sharp shards inside his chest.

262

CHAPTER 36

He tosses a baseball in front of his face. He loves the way the clean, white ball rotates slowly in front of him. Then he whips the bat around, startling the air, and the ball vanishes in a split second. Luke watches its flight as the ball draws a symmetrical arc in the sky, that beauty of rise and fall. It thumps on the earth more than three hundred feet away. He hits a few more, jogs out to pick up the baseballs, gathers them like leather eggs in the front of his T-shirt. His frustrations diminish with each swing as he takes his stress out on a small leather sphere, a tiny planet that he hits hard, sending it far away. Out on this field, there are no arguments, no wars, no sickness or dying. Time stops with each resonant crack of the bat. There's no lying or deception, just two basic truths you can hold in the palm of your hand—a leather baseball, a wooden bat. Just two basic truths, doing their dance of connection. With each well-timed swing, Luke senses a graceful, yet powerful oneness with his physical being. The boy he once was and the man he is now become one.

BEFORE DAWN THE next day, the horizon glows slightly in the east, a few faint stars still pricking holes in the dark dome of the sky. Standing in the paved lot of Man Mound Park, Luke waits in the cool morning for the repatriation ceremony. On the drive out here with Virginia, he thought about his father's burial, years ago, and now he feels something welling up inside him—some emotions he doesn't fully understand churn around and around. He sticks his hands into the pockets of his jean jacket as he anticipates the repatriation ceremony. *Will I feel something?* he wonders. *Will there be a vibration as the souls enter the earth, a hum? An electric sensation traveling through my feet and up my legs? Or will I feel nothing at all?*

Like a bubble of molten lava, the sun erupts on the horizon, and the ceremony begins. On a small roped-off area near the Man Mound, the elders stand in a circle. The ancient bones recovered from the burial site on the ball field are wrapped in handmade red, white, black, and yellow quilts. While one man crouches and beats a leather drum between his knees, Donald Youngbear, the tribal shaman, leans his gaunt body over the remains and chants, with his tenor voice, some prayers in the Potawatomi language. After the brief chant, a Native American boy in his early teens does a short, soft-stepping dance. Then there's a pause as all the participants, including a tribal matriarch, eat the food they've brought. Each of the elders smokes some tobacco. Wisps of their smoke intertwine, then spiral upward, reaching the tree branches, where they're quickly carried away by the wind. *Something.* The word plays through Luke's head as he takes in the scene. *Or nothing.*

The ceremony concludes as Youngbear lifts soil in his palm and covers the bones. The other elders let handfuls of dirt sift through their fingers to the shallow graves. As he watches, Luke can't help but be haunted by the memory of his father's funeral. He sees himself solemnly following the priest from the hearse to the cemetery plot. From a distance, young Luke noticed how unnatural the mounds of dirt looked next to the grave—the way they were rounded and covered with green plastic turf. At the graveside, the priest recited a benediction, shook holy water onto the casket, then blessed it, swinging a brass censer back and forth, tracing the shape of a cross. Luke recalls the scent of the incense, the sweet, aromatic cedar mixed with the pungent, freshly dug earth. He remembers the casket descending into the grave, lowered slowly by cloth belts that creaked as they unrolled. When Luke heard the sound, he wanted more than anything to cry out for his father, for himself, to cry out at the unfairness of the universe. Instead, he was silent. He controlled his emotions, held them inside, because he thought that's the way his father would have wanted it. "Hold on," his father told him a month before he died. "You're a Tanner, remember. And Tanners are strong. Just hold on." Luke didn't shed a tear that morning of the funeral; he didn't cry for the next days or weeks, either.

The night after the funeral, he picked up the bronze Model-T bank his father gave him and held it in his fist. But no matter how hard he squeezed, the bank held its shape, its walls too thick.

Now, watching the elders replace the thick sod carefully with their hands, Luke, still trying to be strong, pushes back his tears. He pushes everything back.

As Donald Youngbear and the elders linger by their cars, talking, Virginia—her face glowing pink in the early sun—sits in the pickup, jotting a few notes. Luke stands alone at the edge of the lawn, pondering the ceremony he's just witnessed. *There's got to be something beyond us,* he thinks. *But what? God? The Great Spirit? Maybe the power comes from beneath our feet. Maybe,* he muses, *the earth has a soul.* He studies the grass in the park, thinks of the tiny pale roots, inching downward—pictures those roots growing longer, reaching, spiraling and branching, going deeper and deeper, twining toward the center of the earth. *Maybe the soul has roots,* he thinks, *roots that go down deep. Deeper than any of us ever imagined. Maybe the soul passes its wisdom up through our feet, making us better than we ever thought we could be. But only if we let it. Only if we open ourselves to it.*

Luke focuses on the silhouettes of the tree trunks, parallel black lines holding back the deep red explosion of sky. *And what about my own soul?* he wonders as a shiver coils through him.

Before he realizes it, he's leaning into a run. He can barely feel his legs moving beneath him as he sprints toward the far end of the park, his heart pumping faster and faster. He runs frantically, as if a wild animal is chasing him, as if *he's* the wild animal, running for his life. Dashing across the incline of the Man Mound, Luke reaches the reburial site, stops, and bends toward the freshly laid sod.

Dad! he wants to shout out. *Dad!* he wants to scream, and he thinks maybe he does cry out in anguish as he kneels and clutches a square of sod to his chest. A moment later, hands are grabbing him, pulling him up.

"Stop!" they're saying, though their voices sound like they're miles away. "What are you doing? This is sacred ground!"

"I know," Luke shouts back at them. "I *know*!"

On the way back, Virginia is sullen, after asking Luke what he was doing out there and getting only silence as a reply. Luke just steadies the wheel, his eyes fixed on the asphalt sliding beneath the car like a slice of night sky. He wishes Louise were sitting next to him in the truck, so he could tell her about everything that's happened the past few weeks. He wishes he could tell her that he's finally found something inside himself that he never knew existed. But what makes him think she'd listen to him now? At the Clearwater city limits sign, the asphalt county highway turns to rough concrete with raised tar strips, and Luke feels the jolting rise up through the tires and floorboards.

Back in Clearwater, Luke veers into a parking stall near city hall.

For a few seconds, neither of them talk, and then Luke finally says, "I apologize if I insulted anyone out there."

"Apology accepted," Virginia replies, though she still looks a little upset.

Then she mentions that she's made a copy of all the documents for Luke. She pulls them from her backpack and hands them to him.

"So, are you headed back to Madison?" he asks.

"I am," she says. "With the latest developments, I guess the feds are taking over now." She steps out of the truck and lingers with him on the sidewalk.

"I appreciate all the help you've given me," Luke says sincerely.

"Well," she replies, "I did what I could here. The rest is up to you. So," she inquires, "what's next for you?"

He thinks of replying: *Just the court suit, a field to finish, the baseball season. Just figuring out where I stand with Louise. Just the rest of my life.* Instead he just mutters, "I'm not sure. How about you?"

"Well, I've got another site to investigate, first thing tomorrow. The state never lets me rest."

"I know the feeling."

Her face slightly blushing, Virginia reaches out awkwardly for a handshake. "It was good to meet you, Luke," she says. "I'll keep thinking about that field of yours." Then she adds, "And what's under it."

"That makes two of us."

CHAPTER 37

In the silence between his knocks on the door, Luke hears the muffled tapping of the moths against the thick glass of the opaque porch light. As he waits, adrenaline rushing through his body, he feels like one of those moths: fluttering nervously with tattered wings at the frosted glass as though he could break through to the light.

The seconds seem to stretch thin and long, like wires pulled taut, extending for miles, years. Luke had heard, via the grapevine, that Louise was staying in Clearwater at Andrea's house for the weekend. Hoping she'll be here, he raps again. Still no answer. He wonders if he should go back to his truck and just floor it down the empty, tree-draped street, speed past the city limits sign, where he'd drop off the edge of the earth. Just as he's about to turn around, Luke hears the lock click, sees the doorknob rotate slightly.

The sliver of light widens a couple of inches, and he sees Louise, dressed in a teal blue silk nightshirt and lounging boxers. Luke blinks at her through the white afterimage that appears from staring too long at the porch light. Her blonde hair is highlighted by a few strands of reddish gold, as if she wove it with fire. Her cheeks seem to steal all the light from the porch as she just stares incredulously at him without speaking.

"Thought you might want to go for a walk," he blurts. He realizes his words might sound too simple. Nervousness ripples through him as if he's sixteen again and on a first date, and he shrugs, stuffs his hands into his jeans pockets, but they don't quite fit, the palms hanging out. What he really wants to do is reach out and embrace her, but he can't do that, not right now.

"A walk?" she asks. He doesn't like the uncertain tone of her voice, like a door about to close. "It's nearly midnight."

"So?" he responds. The azure depths of her eyes tip him off balance. He knows he should say more, but he doesn't.

Louise straightens, the bones of her shoulders shifting beneath the silk top, and her face flushes. "I don't know, Luke. I really, just . . ." she stammers.

"Louise." Luke fears the conversation is about to slam into a wall and end right there. "Please. A few minutes. That's all I ask."

She gives him a resigned half-smile. Through the narrow opening in the door, he sees her slip into a back room, then reappear, dressed in jeans and a black leotard top. She moves fluidly as she approaches the door, and he's forgotten how much he loves that movement—that ease, that oneness with herself.

"Is this okay?" she says wryly. "Or are you taking me someplace formal?"

Relieved to hear a sense of humor in her voice, he's pretty sure he smiles. "I hear the Legion has a dress code, but I bet they'll make an exception."

He leads her down the middle of the street where the low full moon coats the rooftops of the neighborhood with shimmering silver light. "Okay," he says, in a light-hearted voice. "Scenic walking tour of Clearwater, coming up."

"Is there such a thing?" she retorts, though somehow she doesn't seem all that serious.

"I don't know," he says. "Is there?" He lets the question hang in the warm air.

She glances down at a plastic grocery bag he's carrying, and when she asks him about it, he just gives a furtive reply: "It's a surprise."

When they approach the water tower at the edge of town, Luke jogs ahead. Leaping over the small black wrought-iron fence, he waves at her to follow.

"We're not actually going to climb up there, are we?"

"Yeah, we are."

"What about your fear of heights?" she asks, referring to his phobia about high places.

He doesn't reply, just holds out his hand and takes hers. "Come on."

She sees from the determined look on his face that he really plans to make the climb. It's not the Luke she's known these past years—the cautious, feet-on-the-ground Luke—and she likes that.

Trying not to look down, Luke begins his climb focusing, one by one, on the aluminum rungs of the ladder, rungs that feel cool beneath his fingers as he pulls himself upward. The wind tugs at him, and he turns his head to see Louise, following right behind him. The plastic bag—its handle looped on his wrist—swings, clanking against the riveted aluminum panels of the tower.

Luke recalls the night when they were first dating and Louise had asked to climb the water tower. "What are we waiting for?" Louise had coaxed, one foot poised on the first step of the ladder.

"How about if we just go to the lake instead," Luke offered. Luke hadn't yet told her about his fear of heights, and thought he might seem weak if he got halfway up, froze, and had to clamber back down.

At the lake Louise had told him about the time in high school when she and her friends climbed the tower with a carton of eggs and a few cans of Pabst in a backpack. Louise had dropped the eggs, one by one, watching them splat like vague yellow stars on the ground below. She told Luke how, on a rebellious impulse, she had purposely aimed a few eggs at the steadily passing cars, hoping to shake up things.

Tonight, he has no real plan, and he's not certain what he'll say to her when they reach the platform. All he knows is he wants to climb to the top with her. He doesn't just want to—he *has* to.

He sees the grated platform that circles the base of the imposing silver tank, its panels fastened by rusted rivets that make him wonder why it never sprung a leak. Above him looms the word *CLEAR-WATER*. He never knew the letters were so huge and thick, and right now he feels as though they might slide from the aluminum and onto his shoulders, weighing him down, burying him in an avalanche of heavy black paint.

When Luke is a few steps from the top, a swirling wind picks up, rippling his blue short-sleeved T-shirt. Feeling as though anchors are strapped to each ankle, he pauses, gripping the rungs tightly as the ladder seems to waver beneath his grasp. Yet he releases one hand, turns toward Louise, and helps her up.

Finally standing on the platform, but not ready to look down, Luke faces the tank and notices the names spray-painted or scratched into the surface—decades-old names and dates, lovers who have come and gone. *Gina and Tommy Forever, Class of '88,* their names surrounded by a heart. *Therese and Al, Class of '92.* In bold black letters, *Margie and Jonesy, Class of 99.* Luke figures they've probably broken up, gone to college, left town for good. It's the way of the world. Then he sees, crudely scratched into the surface, the words *Denny + Louise,* and he feels the quick sting of jealousy.

"Aren't you going to look?" Louise asks, leaning over the railing.

Luke cautiously turns and looks out at the town: Far below, the asphalt streets, narrow as arrows, crumble to gravel as they point toward the city limits. Porch lights and street lights blink like jewels. Farther off, the ball field looks so compact that Luke hardly recognizes its symmetrical outfield fence, its diamond-shaped infield enclosing the perfect circle of the pitcher's mound. Farther out, beyond the bluffs, the horizon draws a flat line. It's exhilarating to be up here with Louise, and he'd like to put this feeling into words: the rush of the climb, the thrill—and relief—of having her standing next to him as they gaze at the landscape.

Louise's blonde hair dances upward, spiraling around her face, then falls to her shoulders again. He studies her eyes, wondering, for an instant, if he can see the town and its lights reflected in them.

"Clearwater doesn't look the same anymore," Luke offers.

"What makes you say that?"

"Maybe it's that I've just never seen it from this angle."

She notices the pearls of streetlights, strung in symmetrical grids. "The lights make it look almost pretty, I suppose." Leaning her slim waist against the railing and changing the subject, she says, "I hear you stood up to the mayor and the council."

"I guess you could say that," he chuckles.

"That took guts."

"I just said what I had to say," he responds modestly. "That's all."

Louise takes a few steps on the platform, and Luke follows.

She pauses. "I'm planning to get my own place at the end of the summer," she says.

"Oh," he responds. It's neither a question nor a statement.

"I've enrolled in grad school," she continues. "Never too old, I guess." She forces a smile.

The realization of what she's saying is like a stone striking Luke in the chest, but he tries to keep his composure. "Good," he utters, though the word chokes in his throat. The sight of the distant ground below suddenly makes him dizzy, and he has to close his eyes a moment. "Good," he says again, hating the word. Luke wishes the land itself would erupt, would buckle and shake, altering its shape for her. Anything to change her view. Anything to change her plan. "So, it's grad school," he says. "And then what?"

"And then, I don't know," she responds.

"So that's it?"

"No, that's not *it*," she says with a soft breath. She shifts her distant gaze and looks him directly in the eyes. "There's more than just school and a job. I think you know that, Luke."

Luke nods; he wonders if she can read the faint nudge of a smile that begins to emerge from his face.

"So what about you?" she asks. "Any plans?"

He brushes his hair from his forehead. "Plans? I've barely sorted out what's happened the last few weeks." He slides one hand in his back pocket. "I guess I don't have all the answers."

"Heard you made the team."

Luke is surprised she knows this. "Yeah, I did. Can you believe it?"

"Sure, I can."

"We're playing Sunday. Our first game, finally." He takes a breath and faces her. "It'd be great if you could be there," he offers tentatively. "I mean," he corrects himself, "more than great. I *really* want you there, Louise."

She doesn't answer. The sole of her sandal scrapes on the grate below her. "So, you'll be playing the whole season?"

"Well, yeah."

"And after that?"

"And after that . . ." he trails off, his sentence pulled away by the breeze. "I guess I'm not sure." Luke wants to say more; it frustrates him that sometimes his words are like holes in the outfield he keeps tripping on. On the horizon, a haze blurs the line between earth and sky. The air is moisture-laden, and Luke thinks he can see a flickering of lightning inside the faraway clouds. When he turns back toward her, their faces are only inches apart.

Her lower lip quivers, a tiny earthquake. "Luke, I don't know what to think about you," she whispers.

"Why *think*?" Luke asks. "Why not just go with what you *feel*?"

"Sometimes it's like I don't feel anything anymore, and I hate that," she says, a tear tracing a line down her cheek.

He wraps his arms around her, something he's been yearning to do since she first opened the door. "Well, *I* feel something," he says intensely. The emotions he's held in for so long erupt from deep down. He doesn't care how it sounds; he just pours the words out: "I *do* know what I'm feeling. What I'm feeling is passion. It rises up in me every time you're standing close. I can feel it right through the ground we stand on. Without passion, I'm nothing." He pauses a few seconds, pulling her closer. "Without you, I'm nothing."

He's not certain if her face is gliding toward him or if he's moving toward her, but their lips touch, pressing against each other for a few seconds. It's a deep, moist kiss, a kiss that could last for years. Then she ducks out from under his arms. He can tell, by her flushing cheeks, that she wants to say something, but she keeps the words contained, like lightning bugs in a jar.

"Luke," she finally says. "About Sunday and the game . . . What I mean is, if I'm not there . . ." She hesitates.

"Then what?"

"Then maybe you should just forget about me."

Unsteady, he squeezes the handrail tightly, a handrail that's worn to a shine from all the water tower climbers who have clutched it before him. He feels dizzy, almost nauseous, and his whole body wavers. He looks at her face, a face that grounds him. *And what if I can't?* he wants to ask her. *What if I won't?* But instead he says nothing.

Just then her foot bumps the plastic bag Luke brought with him. A can of spray paint rolls out; he had planned—as a joke—to write their names on the water tower. The can rolls toward the edge of the platform, and, impulsively, Luke drops to his knees and lunges for it. He can't quite reach it as it slips off the edge of the platform. Luke watches the can tumble in slow motion—rotating end over end through the humid, indifferent evening air. For those agonizing seconds, he feels as if he's falling with it. With a gasp, it explodes on the concrete slab, the paint spreading into a black star.

"Now look what you've done," he says to her.

"Now look what *you've* done," Louise echoes.

CHAPTER 38

Butch Sobieski doesn't know why he stopped here in the middle of the day; he hasn't been in Seven Dolors Catholic Church for almost a year, but now the place pulls at him like a magnet. His quivering hand opens the carved oak doors, and he stares at the huge gray granite blocks of the foundation that have darkened to an ash color. They could use some sandblasting, and for a split second Butch thinks it's the kind of job his city crew could take care of. But Butch knows his visit here is not about that; it's about something else that he needs. He steps inside, bowing his head in humility, the way the nuns always taught him in grade school.

Inside the church, there's no air moving. Butch sees the votive candles on the side of the altar, the flames glowing inside the orange and red glass containers. Butch thinks about how he used to light those candles before Mass, when he was a boy. *I was holy then,* he thinks. *Just an innocent kid.* He thinks about how far away he's fallen from the church lately, only attending Mass on Christmas and Easter. Still, the stained-glass windows of the saints, the candles, and the huge crucifix on the altar somehow ease the tremors inside him. He dips his fingers into the holy water the way he did as a child, crosses himself, then genuflects, the cartilage in his right knee making a dull cracking sound.

As he walks down the aisle, closer to the altar, legs wobbling as if he's balanced on something, Butch notices the flames on the candles begin to waver. *It's me,* he thinks. *I'm what makes the flame flicker.* Standing near the doorway to the baptismal room, he envisions his own baptism, which took place in this very church, the reverent Sobieski family members surrounding him. He hears the priest's voice saying, "Take away thy sins." He thinks about himself as a baby, his tiny red mouth opening wide in a cry of joy, the cool water from the baptismal font pouring over his little forehead. Water that purified his soul, cleansed him.

Butch kneels in a pew. And suddenly he's looking through the distorted glass of his windshield, watching Whitebird get beaten on that night long ago. When Butch drove away that night, the field in his rearview mirror filled with a silence and a blackness. As he drove away, the high-pitched violin note of the crickets stopped; as he drove away, the whole world went quiet. A while later, Butch circled back, drove his police cruiser past the field again and saw two men digging into the thick darkness with a shovel from the groundskeeper's shed.

Just burying an animal out there, Butch rationalized that night as he idled in his unmarked squad with the headlights out, watching their silhouettes from a distance. *Maybe just some deer that got hit by a car.*

Butch knew that he should do something, and he rolled down the squad's window. But when he opened his mouth, he had nothing to say. No words. That empty field was a place with dirt and rocks and roots where things could be buried. It was a place where you could push your past down, down, down, then cover it up and level it over.

Butch lowers his sweating forehead to the pew; he knows today that he needs to be cleansed, to wash his hands of this guilt. He knows the investigators will peel away the clues, layer by layer— they'll look at the police report; they'll talk to someone who saw his squad car, to Linda Worthy, his dispatch assistant from that night who still works in city hall, to Lilly Whitebird. And they'll find out. He knows they'll find out about the other cover-ups, too; it's just a matter of time. Rollie—not the strongest character in the world— will crack eventually and tell them how Butch covered for him that night he ran the truck off the road, how Butch ordered the truck to be crushed at Rite Away before anyone could see the evidence. He opens his eyes, sees that his hands haven't washed clean. They're a purple color from the way the sunlight slants toward him through a stained-glass window; his whole body is bathed in a deep reddish-purple. He rises quickly from the pew and rushes, panting, back down the aisle toward the front doors.

Driving through town, he gazes at the square with its park benches, its newly planted saplings. The place seems so sedate, so quiet, so normal, he thinks; you'd never know all this was going on beneath the surface—you'd never know this place was smoldering from the inside out. He can't look at the second-story window of his office, or the newspaper racks on the street, the smeared black headlines he knows are about him. *I just did what I thought was right,* he tells himself. *I was protecting a town.*

As he turns a corner, the noon whistle, rising with its steady moan, startles him; for the first time, it hurts Butch's ears to hear it, and he has to pull to the curb and reach up and cover them with his palms. The siren rises and reaches a crescendo, and when he opens his mouth, he believes, actually believes that—all these years—the shrill, high-pitched sound of the town siren has been coming from inside him.

He doesn't know where he's driving; all he knows is that he's leaving.

When he passes the Clearwater city limits sign, he feels somehow free. It's an unexpected feeling, really; he presses the control buttons on his console, rolls down the car's power windows. He always loved the power equipment on this car, the way the seat could be adjusted with the touch of a fingertip, the way the windows and locks responded instantly.

Before he left, Butch asked Rollie if he'd watch Dutchess, his dog. He placed Rollie on a two-week leave with pay, just to let things settle down a bit. With the grand jury investigation beginning in a couple weeks, no doubt a lot of unsavory evidence will hit the fan. Butch told Rollie—flat out—that the best thing to do would be to resign. Now he pictures Rollie, standing at the shore of Clearwater Lake, pulling his badge from his chest and throwing it across the water—as he said he would do. Pictures the badge, like some tiny silver UFO, skipping once, twice, three times on its concave side before, glimmering slightly, it sinks to the bottom of the lake, wavering side to side like an oversized lure.

As he takes a long drink from his flask of brandy, it occurs to Butch that there's no luggage in his trunk, and he likes that idea. He's traveling light. Butch Sobieski is traveling light, and it doesn't matter where he's going. No appointments. No press conferences. No calls from the damn hounding media. He pictures that empty trunk, how you could fit a whole country inside it.

He loosens his silk tie, unbuttons the top buttons of his white shirt. He's unfettered now, and as he presses the accelerator, it feels as if his wide sixteen-inch touring tires are suddenly rising a little off the road. It feels as if his silver Concorde, this twenty-five-hundred-pound car, is actually lifting a few inches off the uneven pavement.

He drives the county highways, following the water mirage, far ahead, that always seems to be pulling away from him. The longer he drives, the more Butch begins to believe that he could actually drive all the way across America in his Concorde, and he'd never have to stop to eat or sleep or rest. He'd drive so far from Clearwater that he'd forget what the town looks like. In his daydream, he pulls into a new small town somewhere, hundreds of miles from here, steps out of the car in his navy blue suit with his briefcase, nods at the townspeople who would welcome him. "I'm Butch Sobieski, from Clearwater, Wisconsin," he'd say to the curious people who would gather around him. "You might have heard of it. I'm Butch Sobieski, and I did more for that town than any mayor in history."

Butch taps his fingers on the dash, as the radio—tuned to the local AM radio station—plays some oldies. Then the announcer—the station's scratchy-voiced owner, Ralph Berkins—breaks in to do the local news. He hears the familiar voice fade, the station almost out of range. He strains, leaning toward the speaker, and he hears the words "local investigation continues. . . ." *Is that a burst of static?*

Butch wonders. *Or is he saying my name?* Butch reaches forward angrily, snaps the radio off.

For the next few seconds, all he hears is the incessant clicking sound of his City of Clearwater pens stacked on the dash, the low-pitched drone of the tires—those tires that seem to have made contact with the rough pavement again.

He lifts his foot off the accelerator, veers the car to the shoulder, and lets it roll to a stop. The pens stop clicking. He closes his eyes and slowly lowers his broad forehead to his purple-tipped fingers on the wheel. Something that's buried begins to rise, and his whole body shudders, as if he's laughing, or sobbing. If someone passed him on the roadside, they'd see his bulky shadow, bowed over the steering wheel, and they might think a man, sitting in his car, is praying.

CHAPTER 39

Before dawn, Luke drives his pickup through the empty streets. He had planned to go to the ball field, but instead of turning off Center, he continues straight, following it out of Clearwater until it reaches the intersection of Old Lake Road. The abandoned road is so dark and the predawn so starless, it looks as though the sky itself has lowered to just a few feet above the asphalt.

Luke wishes he could see his father's headlights closing the distance in the rearview mirror, the way they did that night when Luke was sixteen and tried to outrun him on this very road. If he saw those brights flashing now, he wouldn't stomp on the accelerator and floor the pickup on the straightaway. This time, he'd hit the brake, pull over, then feel the gravel crunching beneath his feet as he'd walk toward his father's car. Unlike that night, when he hardly said a word,

Luke would have so much to say to him, so many questions to ask. He'd lean into the open window of the Chrysler, his father staring at him, eyes like ancient polished stones, his usual stoic expression washed with bewilderment.

"I've stopped trying to lose you," Luke would say.

Then his father would surprise Luke with a quick, hard smile. "Don't worry," he'd reply. "You never could."

LUKE STROLLS ACROSS the field toward home plate carrying his Louisville Slugger and duffel. It's just before sunrise, and he knows that from a distance, he might look like some overly anxious rookie arriving way too early for warm-ups. But he's not here for that; something else calls him to this field at dawn on the day of the first Lakers game.

He takes a moment to admire the field that's finally finished, a field he loves so much, this precisely measured, symmetrical field that caused so much chaos. He inhales the humid, earthy scent of the loam, leans over and brushes his fingers through the maze of grass that's been submerged in darkness all night, grass still waiting for the first touch of sunlight. His eyes follow the even chalk lines that angle outward from the infield—they seem to pause for a moment at the outfield fence, then stretch into infinity. Beyond the fence, the field continues, with no road to scar it. Just the field going on into the distance, as Luke always hoped it would.

It's a place he never abandoned or gave up on. How could he? The land has no voice, so sometimes you just have to speak for it. He knows that sometimes you have to stand with your feet firmly planted on the earth and say *Here*.

A bird hidden in the upper branches of a silhouetted pine startles the quiet morning with its urgent, raspy call. *Caw caw caw. Caw caw*

caw. The cries seem to pull the sun's heavy red crescent upward on the horizon, and Luke knows it's time.

Bending to one knee, he pulls something from his duffel. He unwraps it from inside the wrinkled palm of a leather batting glove where he's kept it for months. He holds it for a moment, turning it over and over in his fingertips, trying to memorize its shape, the roughness and smoothness of its texture. How could he have known, that day when he first dragged a rake across this infield, what lay below him? He digs a hole in the soft soil with his fingertips, presses the bone fragment downward, then covers it with dirt. Eventually, he knows, this bone, like the millions of other bones, will crumble to dust and become one with the fertile soil of the field. Luke closes his eyes; he knows nothing about Native American prayers or ceremonies, but, in his mind, he says a few simple words to put the spirit to rest. As he does, he says farewell to his father, too. Maybe that's all that's needed—not Native American words or white man's words—just a few honest human words.

As he rises from his knees, a low layer of fog, undulating as it's pushed by a light breeze, glides toward him across the field. When it reaches him, it silently parts around his body, moistening his face with a kiss, then seals together again as it rolls beyond him across the grass. When it reaches the boughs of the pines, it rises in pale, flame-like shapes and dissipates. As he watches, Luke can't help but think that's the way the soul moves.

A half hour before game time, Luke checks his antique pocket watch, then glances nervously at the bleachers, wondering if he'll see Louise, hoping she'll soon be sitting there, cross-legged in her jeans, giving him an encouraging look. Luke leans from the dugout and scans the sky, which has been threatening all afternoon. He knows that when you're a ballplayer in this town, the chances of rain are always good and bad. A few drops fall on home plate, pock-marking the dirt around it. At first, the rain taps nervously on the aluminum dugout roof, then becomes an incessant beat. It falls harder, dampening the flag on the pole beyond the center field fence.

"So what do you think, Luke?" a voice calls from behind. It's Lance. "We gonna get rained out, or not?"

"Looks like it," interjects Josh Sobieski from the far end of the bench.

"No," Luke replies to Lance, ignoring Josh's skepticism. He tips his face toward the scalloped gray bellies of the clouds. "We'll play."

"What makes you so sure?" Lance asks, chewing on gum as he rolls his eyes upward.

The rain pours hard a few minutes, small rivulets of brown water rushing along the sloped edge of the dugout. Then the gusting wind shoulders the layer of clouds away, and, just as suddenly as it began, the shower stops. A widening crescent of blue opens. A swath of sunlight seems to move in a wave, sweeping over the uneven spots in center field, pushing away the shadows, gliding all the way to the dugout, where it splashes in Luke's upturned face. The tall pines down the left field line ignite, the wet grass of the field burns brighter and greener than he has ever seen it before, but still the scene is incomplete. *Louise is what's missing,* he thinks. Without her, the first moments of the game, which should be so joyous, would be hollow and meaningless. He keeps looking for her, and pushing back the gnawing doubt that maybe she won't show.

The fans—who remained in their cars or huddled beneath the concession stand awning during the shower—emerge, talking and laughing again as they climb the bleachers and brush the beads of water from the enameled planks. Luke scans the crowd for her, but she's not there.

286

In the on-deck circle, Luke slides on his batting gloves and stretches with a leaded bat as a few people from the reservation—not nearly as many as he expected—file in and sit along the first baseline. Then Luke notices the black-haired boy peering in, his fingers curled in the diamonds of the fence. "Hey mister," the boy calls, recognizing him from that day when he had watched Luke hit fly balls. Luke gives the boy a friendly tip of his cap.

MINUTES BEFORE GAME time, the umpire strolls behind home plate and pulls his black mask on, adjusting the cloth straps. The pitcher finishes his warm-up throws. A murmur rolls through the crowd as Luke, the lead-off hitter, picks up his Louisville Slugger. Luke looks over his shoulder again. Through the screen of the backstop, he finally spots her, sitting in the top row of the bleachers: Louise. *She's here*, he thinks. She gives him a look—her face buoyed up by a slight smile, that expression he knows so well. He stands motionless, while time—like a loose piece of paper pressed against the backstop by the wind—moves neither forward nor backward.

He wishes he could climb the bleachers and slide next to her. He'd brush her hair back gently with his gloved hand, touch her face—bright and perfect as a new baseball—with his bare hand. He yearns to pull Louise tightly toward him, and this time he'd hold on. He knows that closeness, closeness is everything.

Right now he realizes how much he needs her as he walks toward the plate, carrying the weight of this whole ball field on his shoulders. And it's not just the tons of sod and wood and aluminum, but the weight of all those things that can never be measured: the wounds and scars of a whole town, the burden of his father's secrets, the ancient, weathered ladder of his heritage, the tenuous weight of his future.

The murmur of the crowd gets louder, climbing steadily in pitch, and when Luke's name crackles through the speakers, the voices erupt into a cheer. Luke barely hears the sound as he closes his eyes. He pictures himself swinging, hitting the ball hard. Though he knows the odds are against it, he imagines the ball climbing high and long into the sky above the left field fence. He still believes he can teach a baseball to fly.

"I said, *Batter up*," the ump barks as the catcher tosses Luke an impatient glance. The words startle Luke. He knows that ballplayers are just dreamers. So he concentrates on what he must do now. The complexity of these past weeks—with the practices and delays, the land disputes, the aching joints and sore arms—leads to this one, simple moment. Luke knows he must focus on the game, a game played with real, natural things: a wooden bat hewn from a hardwood tree, a glove made from cow leather, a horsehide ball white as the full moon on a clear night. A taut green field of grass etched with chalk lines that separate fair from foul, foul from fair.

Luke stands in the batter's box, his cleats digging into the soil, the barrel of the bat circling as if he's stirring the sky. The pitcher winds up, snapping his arm down, and throws the first pitch, the ball leaping from his hand in a blur. To make the connection he longs for, Luke knows he has to time it perfectly, all his muscles waking.

Halfway to the plate, the baseball—ignited by camera flashes—seems to slow, and Luke sees, clearly, its leather and seams rotating red, white. He waits for it to travel the amazing distance toward home. Luke steps into the pitch and takes a level swing, a motion smooth as love. At that instant, a crow, hidden in the upper branches beyond the left field fence, lifts its wings and bursts into the sky.